KING'S HARLOTS SERIES: BOOK 4

RUDE

J.M. WALKER

ISBN: 978-1-989782-58-3

DEDICATION

To Coby Porter.

Warning:
This book deals with some darker subjects.
If you have any triggers at all, please read
with caution but know that there is always
light within the darkness.

xx

ACKNOWLEDGEMENTS

My husband. You make me strive to be a better person. Thank you for your support and encouraging me to never give up.

My reader group has been my rock throughout this whole series. Although this is only book three, I feel like I've spent every waking hour with this crew. I'm already dreading the day this series ends.

JM's Jems, you girls know who you are. Thank you for everything you've done for me and for all of your support. I can't even begin to thank you enough.

Tammi, Joanne, Angie and Jamie. Thank you for ripping Rude apart and helping me put it back together again.

Wendi Lynn with Ready, Set, Edit. Thank you for fixing my words. Love you to pieces, girl! #TeamPig

Rachel Mizer with ShoutLines Designs. Thank you for yet another epic cover!!! You've outdone yourself with this series.

Tammi Plummer. You keep me sane. You are the best PA a girl could ask for. Thank you for all that you do and for keeping me grounded. #MySemiColon

TD Ross: Girl!!! I was dying to give you this book from the very first word I wrote. I'm so happy you enjoyed Coby and thank you for sticking by me and motivating me. Here's to many many more messages!! ;)

Christine Stanley with The Hype PR. My Poopy! Thank you for all that you do. We don't chat as often as I'd like and we live way too far apart, but you never hesitate to help me in anything that I need. Love you!!!

Twinsie Talk Book Reviews: You girls are my sisters. I definitely wouldn't be where I am if it wasn't for you. Love you all!!

To all the bloggers and authors: Thank you for all of your support in my journey thus far. Here's to many many more book releases! And my readers!! Without you, I couldn't do this. I couldn't write these words. I couldn't create worlds for you to get lost in. Thank you. For absolutely everything.

J.M. Walker

xx

CHAPTER ONE

Coby

THE NAKED BODY beside me didn't do shit for my appetite. I was fucking hungry, and this limp bundle was dead weight compared to the beast within who wanted to come out and play. If only I could feed it. Give it the sustenance it craved. The ecstasy that took over all thought processes while you *fuck* into oblivion.

"You ready for more, baby?" the whore asked, looking up at me through heavy-lidded eyes.

I only looked at her. I couldn't be sure what she saw on my face, but either way, I wanted her gone.

RUDE

A moment later, she swallowed hard and rose from the bed. Grabbing her clothes, she shuffled out of the room.

Shower. I needed a fucking shower. I needed to wash the smell of impurity off me.

The woman latched on hard the night before. One look, and the next thing I knew, she was all over me like a pig in shit. Of course, I acted how she wanted me to. If I would have shown her my true self, she would have left before I could get my dick wet. No woman could handle the beast—the part of myself I liked to think was put there out of retribution for my past transgressions. I was a sinner, and I paid the price by craving things I couldn't get from just anyone.

When the front door shut, I took that as my cue and trudged to the bathroom. But not before I was met with the stare down from Dale Michaels. My Navy brother narrowed his eyes, looking between the door and myself.

"Rough night?" he asked, popping back a beer.

It wasn't even noon yet and already he was drinking. Not that I was one to judge. If I drank, living in the shit world we did, I would probably be slamming back a few as well. Instead, in my case, I curbed that craving through other means necessary. Alcohol did shit for my appetite.

"Not rough enough," I answered, pushing open the door leading to my savior. Hot water. And lots of it.

"I don't get you, man." He took another swig, burped and pointed the head of the bottle in my direction. "You fuck woman after woman but you're still grumpy as shit. You think you would be the happiest man alive with how much pussy you're getting."

Pussy. Sure. I got a lot of it, but it wasn't what I wanted. I shrugged, the movement causing a slight crack to shiver down my spine. "It's only sex. And that—" I pointed to the main door at the front of the apartment "—was just pussy. Nothing more." *Act like a lady, and I'll treat you like one. But if you come to me acting like a whore, I won't be nice.*

Dale shook his head. "Still don't get you," he mumbled, drinking the rest of his beer. He frowned once he realized it was empty and made his way into the kitchen.

Heading into the bathroom before he could bombard me with more questions, I stripped and turned on the shower. Craving the burn from the water, I stepped under the hot spray. A groan escaped me, the bite of the scalding liquid making all my nerve endings come alive. It helped the itch, but it wasn't enough. It was never enough.

A hard knock sounded on the door a moment later, interrupting my current enjoyment.

"Angel needs us at the club," Dale said. "Dante's Kings are headed there."

Fucking fuck.

"Be out in a sec." I finished up my shower, dreading it instantly when I turned off the water. If only my emotions were that easy to turn off.

Dante's Kings were annoying. They were like flies, always getting in the way and shitting on anything they touched.

The motorcycle club did everything in their power to put fear into the people they came into contact with. Only dealing with them a couple of times, I never gave them the satisfaction. They didn't scare me. Nothing did. Not yet, anyway. I had seen it all. Dante's Kings were pussies compared to who I had had to deal with in my lifetime.

"Coby," Dale barked. "Let's go."

So damn impatient. I got dressed, making sure my shirt covered my scars. Tattoos wouldn't even cover them, the skin being too sensitive, so I never even bothered. Nightmares from my past threatened to force their way into my mind. Nagging. Poking. Scraping at the walls of my sanity. Things I had done. Things I still did. Being a Navy SEAL sniper was not all puppies and glitter.

Giving myself a shake, I left the small room.

"Ready?" Dale asked, coming down the hallway toward me.

My body vibrated, my knuckles itching with the need to hit something. "Yes."

He smirked. "Got the itch?"

"Yes," I repeated, flexing my hands. The itch hurt at times. It was arthritis. I knew that. But the darkness inside of me liked to convince me it was the need to destroy. Like Godzilla itself, I craved the day I could tear down the evil that put the innocent in harm's way.

"Let's go." Dale demanded, leaning his head from side to side.

I followed him out to his truck, the urgent need to fight growing stronger by the minute. The closer we got to the clubhouse, the more intense the urge became.

The King's Harlots club came into view ten minutes later. Motorcycles lined the parking lot in all different sizes and colors.

"As much as I can't stand Dante's King's, they sure have some nice machinery," Dale whistled. "I need a bike."

"You don't even know how to ride one," I reminded him, the memory of him falling off mine coming to mind.

"You're a tall fucker, and your bike is too big for me."

I chuckled, shaking my head.

Dale raised an eyebrow.

Clearing my throat, I pasted on a straight face.

Laughing.

It wasn't something I did often. Having feelings stripped from me at a young age, becoming a sniper in the military made sense. I didn't care who I shot and killed. Everyone who fell to their death at my feet deserved it.

"You need to laugh more," Dale mumbled, breaking the unnerving silence.

Yeah, yeah. There were a lot of things I needed to do. Laughing was not one of them.

We pulled into the parking lot, and that was when a flutter of something washed over me, hitting me square in the balls. I couldn't explain the new feeling. It was delicious, making my senses come alive.

Stepping out of the truck, my gaze landed on the source of these new feelings. Or rather, recurring feelings that I hadn't acted upon. Yet.

"Hey, guys," Brogan Tapp, the smallest member of King's Harlots but definitely the toughest, sidled up to Dale. "Max is inside."

"Fucking great," he grumbled, shoving his hands in his pockets and made his way inside the club.

"Hi, Coby," she said, her mouth moving over my name like a lover's kiss, but all I could picture was it sliding over my cock instead.

I nodded once, giving her some acknowledgement.

RUDE

She rolled her eyes, making her way back into the club, but not before I heard her mutter, "Asshole," under her breath.

Smirking to myself, I followed her. Was I an asshole? *Yes.* But only because I knew I wouldn't be good for her. She deserved better. So much better. I had demons, dark secrets, and I didn't need to worry about a woman who I knew could make me fall in love with her. These confusing feelings I got already from just being near her didn't sit well with me. My palms twitched, itching with the need to touch her. Just a touch. My fingers begged to move her dark curly hair off the back of her neck. My arms pleaded to wrap around her small, firm body, holding her against me until I got the calm I was looking for.

Brogan could be it. The one who took the impending darkness away.

I shook my head. No. I would live the rest of my life fucking random women to curb my craving before I ever hurt a hair on Brogan's head. And being with me would do just that.

***

(Brogan)

Coby-Fucking-Porter.

The guy was a God.

Dark. Tall. Quiet. So damn quiet. He didn't need to talk for you to know that he was already looking into your soul. I bet he knew all my dirty and dangerous secrets without me even telling him.

When he grunted, instead of saying hi to me, I wanted to drive my fist into his face and yell for him to answer me. To have a conversation with me. To give me something. But no. He had demanded for weeks that I stop hinting. I had a crush on the guy. Everyone knew it. But, why wouldn't I? He was everything that I wasn't.

I found myself wanting to not only crack his walls but destroy them. I was warned, told to stay away from him, leave him alone. *Blah. Blah. Blah.*

With four older brothers, I wasn't one to give up easily.

After everything that had been going on over the past couple of weeks, I would lie low, though, giving Coby the space he felt he needed. Everything in me told me that something had happened. Call it the nurturing side of me, but I wanted to help. I wanted to ease his pain which wasn't like me at all. The only people I felt the need to protect were my brothers and sisters and now Coby's team.

Vice-One had made themselves known a couple of months ago when they started working on the club after someone tried to blow it up.

Angel Rodriguez, being the owner, was adamant on getting it fixed up. Especially after he met Genevieve Gold. Or Jay. Call her by her full name and she would shove her shitkicker up your ass.

Making my way into the club, I headed to the meeting room that was now filled with two bike clubs and the guys from Vice-One. I never let it be known but I didn't like crowds. Especially if people got in my bubble.

Jay sat at the head of the large oak table, talking to Maxine Stanton, the vice-president.

Max nodded every so often, looking around the large room before turning back to our boss.

"Brogan, you okay?" Meeka Cline, my best friend, came up beside me, grumbling under her breath how there was too much testosterone in one room.

"I'm fine." *I would be better if I was alone or hitting something.* My muscles vibrated. A good workout would be needed after this shit.

A loud whistle sounded around the room, silencing the noisy chatter.

"Tell us what's going on," Angel demanded of Brian Gold, Jay's father. He stood beside Jay, keeping his hand on her shoulder. Although he was the president of Dante's Kings and rough around the edges, when it came to his daughter, he was a big teddy bear.

"Charles has contacted us," the older man's deep voice grit out. "One of our men from another chapter ended up in the wrong place at the wrong time. He was sent back to his club piece by piece, the last one being his dick."

My stomach somersaulted, but not for reasons one would think. It reacted that way whenever I wished I could do something myself. To rip off every appendage that belonged to Charles Brian would be the best gift I had ever been given. I was sick and twisted but I owned it.

"Fuck me," Jay breathed. "Who was it?"

"A prospect, but it doesn't matter who," Brian snapped, shaking his head a second later. "Sorry, nugget. It's been a rough morning."

"I understand." She rose to her feet, pacing back and forth. "Anything else?"

"Another club was blown up in Fort Banks," Brian answered, pinching the bridge of his nose.

"Shit." Dale leaned forward. "You think Charles' men did it?"

"Yes," Tyler Bone interjected. "We do." The vice-president of Dante's Kings, cracked his knuckles. "It's only been the one club so far but we wanted to warn you."

Nothing was said as Tyler spoke the truth. He was an ass. Being Jay's ex, he had caused problems for them. But for whatever reason, he was being civil.

"Why do you want to help us?" Jay questioned, her forehead crinkling in the middle.

"Nugget, why wouldn't we want to help?" her father asked. "I know you've had your problems, but we're in this together. These bastards are trying to destroy what's ours. They killed one of our own."

"I get that," she interrupted. "But why are *you* helping us?" she asked Tyler.

Tyler sat back, rubbing his chin. "I don't know. I do suggest taking my help while it's being offered, though."

Jay laughed. "That's more like it." She let out a heavy sigh, turning to Angel. "What do you think?"

"I think you girls shouldn't be alone. Being one of the only female MCs in this area, you have a bigger target on your backs. These sick fucks ..." he growled. "We have to be careful."

Jay nodded. "Thank you for warning us." She waved a hand in front of her face. "You can go now."

I bit back a laugh. God, I loved her. Jay was good at her job, and she didn't take shit from anyone. Not even her father's club. It always amused me when she threw her attitude at them.

"You've become a bitch, Jenny." Tyler stood, rapping his knuckles on the table top. "We're only trying to help."

"Yeah. Sure. Thanks for that." Jay looked to her father. "Thank you."

Her dad only smirked. "Be safe." He kissed her head and followed the rest of his crew out of the room.

"Well, that was fun," Dale muttered, stretching his arms over his head.

"Oh, yeah." Max pasted a fake smile on her face. "The fact that clubs are being blown to shit all over the state is definitely something to look forward to."

Dale only stared at her, his eyes darkening.

"All right, children—" I rose from the chair "—play nice."

Dale scoffed. "That's boring."

Max scowled, leaving the room and slamming the door shut behind her.

Letting out a sigh, I shook myself. "I'm going to go hit something."

Although I would rather fuck this frustration out of me, I had no one that would accommodate that desire. It wasn't like Coby had any interest in appeasing this ache inside of me. The guy couldn't stand me. He wouldn't talk to me. He wouldn't even acknowledge that I existed. This was a fucked-up time, and I found myself wanting him even more. Call me a masochist but the fact he was being an asshole turned me on.

I was so screwed.

CHAPTER TWO

Coby

CLUBS WERE BEING blown up. That was the information we always enjoyed hearing.

While the rest of Vice-One did their own thing, I circled King's Harlots clubhouse, making sure there was nothing out of the ordinary. But everything was fine. Kosher. Fucking perfect.

My bones vibrated.

When Brogan said she needed to hit something, I almost let it slip that I wanted her to hit me. I wasn't a masochist by any means but I enjoyed a good fight. She was strong, a beast for her size and I knew she could take what I had to give her. But I didn't give her anything, did I? I was a dick, an asshole, a sociopath.

She deserved better, but fuck me if I didn't want to spend at least one night with her.

That new revelation shocked even me. I had never wanted to spend the night with a woman. It was always fuck them and leave them. Well, this was perfect timing. I grumbled to myself, my hands clenching into fists at my sides.

Rumors floated around that she had a crush on me. A crush. Like we were in fucking high school. That tiny little thing in the club was distracting. She had been engrained in my skull since the first day I met her.

Her dark eyes smoldered, burning into my skin and leaving a mark all their own.

She was tiny but definitely not frail. Muscles adorned her small frame, revealing the fact she had worked out hard to get where she was.

"I'm Brogan Tapp," she told me, sticking out her hand.

No response left me. The words couldn't form on my tongue. Who was she and what the hell was she doing to me? Although I never liked talking, I could still form a proper sentence. Until then.

"Aren't you going to tell me your name?" she asked, pulling her hand back. "Or are you going to stand there like a moron?"

My dick jumped at the insult. I wanted to talk to her but I wanted to see how angry I could get her as well. I wanted to see her fired up.

"Well, then ..." She turned to walk away. "Good talk."

I remembered back to that first meeting, the image of her tight little ass in those sexy as fuck leather shorts she had been wearing. The curve of her hips, hinting for my fingers to grab ahold of them.

I muttered a curse and headed back into the club. There was nothing to see outside, and I really needed to hit something.

The vast space, lined with booths and the bar at the back, were empty. My brothers were nowhere to be found. Even the rest of King's Harlots had disappeared, doing their own thing, finding whatever vice it was to curb them of the evils of this world.

Grunting pulled me from my thoughts, leading me to the back of the building. A door at the end of the long hallway was open, revealing Brogan dancing from foot to foot. Her fists flew against a large punching bag, her arms straining with muscles.

My mouth watered. Well, that was new.

Shaking the thoughts of what I wanted to do to her out of my head, I made my way into the room.

Brogan never noticed my presence until I stood right in front of her. She raised an eyebrow but kept on hitting the bag.

I always had issues talking to people. I found that spoken words only led to heartache and lies so I kept my thoughts to myself. But with Brogan, a sense of relief washed over me. She poked and teased but never demanded for me to talk. Not yet, at least. She would. They all did at some point in time. It was only a matter of when.

"Are you going to stand there or help me?" Brogan asked between breaths, her chest rising and falling.

Help you. But those two simple words never left my mouth. Holding the bag, I nodded once.

A small smile spread on her lips before she geared up and started hitting the bag again.

Ten minutes later, sweat coated her brow, drops of the no doubt tasty liquid sliding down between her breasts.

Fuck this. I released the bag and took a step toward her. "Hit me."

RUDE

A sparkle of interest shone in her eyes. "Really?"

"A punching bag can only do so much," I explained, moving closer to her. "Hit me."

Brogan shook out her arms and cracked her knuckles. "All right, Porter, I'll do as you say."

The use of my last name sent a shiver down my spine.

Oh, this would be fun.

***

(Brogan)

Coby demanded for me to hit him. Usually people shied away from that but he was a big guy, well over a foot and a half taller than me. He would be a challenge but I would enjoy forcing him to his knees.

Holding up his hands, he waited. "Hit me." The deep demand sent a course of heat warming through my body.

Pulling my right arm back, I pushed it forward as hard as I could.

Coby blocked it, swatting my hand away like a mosquito and repeated my movement.

My eyes widened at the sudden movement, but before he could make contact with my face, I blocked him.

Oh, he played dirty. I enjoyed the fact that he wasn't afraid to hit me just because I was a woman. Call it fucked up, but when I sparred with a man, I wanted to be treated as an equal. Not the lesser sex.

Coby took a step toward me, forcing me back, and continued to swing his hands in my direction.

I blocked him, following his own movements.

The sparring went on for another half an hour until we were both drenched in sweat and breathing heavy.

My muscles burned, aching from the new workout they had been given.

"Thank you," I said, wiping my face with a towel.

"You're welcome." Coby chugged back a bottle of water, sliding down the wall until he was seated on the blue mat beneath him. "I've never met a woman who wasn't afraid to get hit."

My jaw tingled, remembering the punch it had taken only a couple minutes before. "I've never met a man who wasn't afraid to hit a woman."

"It's training. If you swing at me, no matter your sex, I'll swing back," he said matter-of fact.

"Good." I sat beside him, taking the bottle from his hand, and drank the rest of the water. I figured we could at least be friends. He already knew I had a tiny crush on him but I wasn't one of those women who threw herself at a man. I asked him out. He said no. And that was that. But he wasn't stupid. He caught me staring several times. But how could I not? He was Coby-Fucking-Porter. Dark shaggy hair that fell in his eyes. Long enough to grab a hold of but not so long he needed to put it up in a ponytail. And man buns? Gross.

"How long have you been training for?" Coby asked, stretching his upper body over his legs.

"I've always been active. I have four older brothers, so they taught me to fight. But I've been training hard for the past year." My heart gave a start at how comfortable it was talking to Coby. It was like we had been friends for years even though we only knew each other for a couple of months. And even then, I didn't really *know* him.

"Good, that's what brothers are supposed to do. Protect what's theirs."

"Yeah, except they made it hard to date." I laughed.

"I can imagine. They can get kind of nosy."

Somehow, I knew he wasn't just talking about *my* brothers. "How long have you been in Vice-One?"

"Since the beginning. Five years or so."

"And the military?" I asked, turning my body to face him.

"Long enough," he muttered.

"Do you like it?"

His gaze met mine. "Yes."

I searched his face for any hint that he was lying, but who was I kidding? The guy could play poker. He was straight faced, his eyes showing no emotion, and he never looked away when he answered. "Well—" my palms became sweaty unexpectedly "—that's good I guess."

"You guess?"

"You're not talkative. You always look like you're ready to kill someone and when you walked in on me interrogating that guy, you liked it." Jay had asked me to question one of Charles' bastards, and Coby showed up while I had a knife in the guy's leg. I didn't want to see the judgment in Coby's eyes but I remembered looking at him and seeing something I never thought I would see. *Lust.*

"Do you always say what's on your mind?" Coby crossed his arms under his chest.

"Yes." *Maybe that was a bad thing.*

"I like that."

Or not. "Really? My brothers always give me shit for being so honest."

"No." Coby shook his head. "It's nice. There are too many two-faced people in this world. I like knowing up front if you can't stand me."

I laughed. "Well, as quiet as you are ..." I shrugged. "I like you."

"Oh, I know." He winked.

Oh, dear God. That small movement made my insides turn to mush. "Yeah, well, maybe my honesty has bitten me in the ass this time."

"Maybe." Coby pushed to his feet, making his way to the door before looking down at me over his shoulder. His eyes burned into me, heating my skin as if they were touching me themselves. "Maybe not."

And whatever *that* meant I wouldn't know, because he left the gym as soon as those words left his mouth.

Maybe not.

I was only fooling myself because the only thing that Coby wanted from me was friendship, and maybe he didn't even want that.

The way my body reacted to him, coming alive at the mere sound of his deep voice, proved that I couldn't just be friends with him.

Shit.

CHAPTER THREE

Coby

"OH, GOD. YES. Harder. Please. Right there. Give it to me, big boy. Mmmm … you're so huge. Fuck me."

The ceiling was a wonderful place to look at while I lay awake from the incessant fucking in the next room.

Dale had brought home woman after woman, sometimes two or three a night. Something happened between him and Max. She got pregnant. He freaked out. The sounds in the room across from mine were proof enough that he had fallen off the deep end.

I was an asshole, and I owned that title, but even I wouldn't fuck random women like he had if I got someone pregnant. My stomach quivered.

"Please, baby. God. Yes. Oh, Dave. Right—"

"Dave!" Dale yelled, the screaming stopping suddenly.

"Sorry," the woman cried. "Dale. Please don't stop."

"Fuck you, whore." A door slammed shut followed by some mumbled voices.

Shaking my head, I let out a heavy sigh and sat up. The time on my phone read six in the morning. Great. Another early day.

Getting dressed, I had just slipped on my hoodie when the door opened.

"You awake, man?"

"I am," I said, buttoning up my jeans.

"I'm assuming you heard that shit?" Dale shoved a hand through his blonde messy hair.

"Yeah." As much as I didn't like people being in my business, Dale needed to get his head out of his ass. "You need to stop doing this shit. It's unhealthy."

Dale's eyes widened for a split second before he scowled. "Right. And you're going to approach that hot little thing that keeps you up at night?" He smirked when I didn't respond. "I didn't think so."

Fucker knew me well. "I have no idea what you're talking about." But I still wouldn't talk about it with him or anyone for that matter.

"Okay then." Dale turned to walk away before yelling over his shoulder, "Tell that to the sounds I hear coming from your room at night."

Dick.

Dale chuckled, the door closing behind him, swallowing his laughter.

He was right. I did have a hot little thing on my mind that kept me up at night, but before I talked to anyone about it, I needed to approach her first. I just didn't know how. Not that I was shy but it terrified me to share my darkness with anyone. Knowing once I had her it would never stop. The addiction would only grow until I couldn't breathe, and it would destroy us both.

Fuck.

I rapped on Dale's door. "I'm heading to the city. Do you need anything?"

"A case of beer." Dale pulled open the door. "Angel wanted to meet as well. Something about doing some renovations to make the club bigger."

I nodded. "I won't be long."

"Take all the time you need and maybe get laid while you're at it too."

"Ass," I mumbled.

"I heard that," he yelled, slamming his door shut.

I chuckled to myself and made my way out of the apartment building.

My thoughts traveled back to only a couple of days ago. Sparring with Brogan seemed almost normal, like we had been doing it for years. I could predict her moves; she could predict mine. No anticipation. It would have bothered me under different circumstances. Anticipation was key. Knowing what to expect next was boring.

A ding sounded from my phone, interrupting my impending dirty thoughts.

Brogan: What are you doing today?

Me: Depends.

Brogan: On what?

Me: If you're asking me to do something or not.

Brogan: I want to spar with you again.

And I want fuck you.
But that had to wait until I knew she was ready.

Me: I'll be there tonight.

Brogan: Thank you.

Anything for you, little one.
I was so screwed.

****

(Brogan)

It had been a couple of hours since my text chat with Coby. I didn't even want to text him in the first place, expecting him to give me short answers but it was like having a full conversation with him instead. It was nice. *Nice.* God, I was such a girl.

All my life, a guy had never made me feel this way. I wasn't shy, but I also never approached them and asked them out. I had asked Coby-Fucking-Porter out on a date. Who was I, and where was Brogan Tapp?

I sighed, shoving the ear buds in my ears. Turning on the music from my phone as loud as I could handle it, I stretched.

Leaving my room, I walked past Max and Creena at the bar and gave them a wave.

They waved back and continued talking amongst themselves.

RUDE

Once I left the club, the setting sun cast an eerie glow around the old buildings on the main street. The crisp air flowed around me, sending a shiver down my spine.

My body vibrated.

I enjoyed running. I craved it. I needed it.

Turning the music on as high as I could handle it, I shut off everything and just moved. The music motivated me. It drowned out everything around me.

Pounding my feet into the pavement, I jogged at a slow pace until the muscles in my legs jumped and twitched with the movements.

Coby and I had a sparring session later that evening. I found myself wanting to touch him, to fight him. For him to throw me on the mat and fuck me senseless.

That not so unexpected thought caused me to stumble in my run. A laugh escaped me. *Get it together, Brogan.* He was just a man. Nothing more. But God, was he ever a man.

After getting a couple miles in, I ended up in a part of town that was known as the shady part. Greeneville, Ohio may have been small, but we definitely had parts where locals stayed away from.

I knew I should have been paying more attention but a certain darkness clouded my judgement. Coby made it impossible to focus on anything.

A cool draft washed over me, making me lose my breath. I picked up speed, not liking this sense of urgency that had suddenly overcome me.

Out of the corner of my eye, something moved in the shadows of the alley. It was like your typical scary movie. Stupid girl goes for a run at the wrong time of day. No one was around to hear her scream. And the killer got the satisfaction of not getting caught.

I was the stupid girl when I saw the shadow form into a large man. He creeped out of the shadows, followed by two more men coming up behind him.

My heart gave a start, my legs slowing to a complete stop. I could run away but even I wasn't that fast.

Attempting to run by them, I acted casually, pretending I didn't see them when the first man stepped in my path. *Shit.*

His mouth moved but with the music blasting in my ears, all I could hear was the incessant noise and the beating of my heart.

Slowly pulling the buds from my ears, I took several deep breaths. I lived for this. Excitement. Anticipation. I was a fighter. But I couldn't take on three men by myself.

"What are you doing out by yourself at this time, pretty girl?" the first man asked, his gravelly voice grating on my nerves.

And because of people like this, it was hard for women to run peacefully without having creepers bothering them.

"Is there a rule that says I shouldn't be out at this time?" I asked, staring the fucker head on, and crossed my arms under my chest.

"It's not safe." He took a step toward me. "There are a lot of dangerous people in this world."

Yeah, and one of them was standing in front of me. Guys like him usually reacted first instead of thinking things through.

"I run all of the time, and I've never run into any problems."

"Until now," the man sneered, rubbing the dark scruff on his jaw.

I bit back an eye roll. "Are you telling me that you are going to be my problem?"

"Maybe." He looked at the men behind him. "It depends on if you cooperate or not."

"Please. Like I haven't heard that before. What do you guys want? Money? Sex? For me to beg you to leave me alone?" I rolled my eyes that time, clucking my tongue. "Sorry, gentlemen. I don't scare easy." *I ate men like them for dinner.*

"Aww, too bad," the taller of the men said. "I love making a woman scream. But I love even more when they beg for their life."

At that point, I laughed. It was all I could do not to turn around and walk away. These guys weren't serious, were they?

"What the hell is so funny?" The same man narrowed his eyes, clenching his hands into fists at his sides.

"You're a walking cliché. How can I not laugh? If you're trying to scare me, you're doing a shit job." As soon as those words left my mouth, I regretted them instantly.

Rough hands grabbed me from behind, pinning me against a hard body.

A fourth man. Of course.

Shit. I was not on my game tonight and got distracted.

"A little cocky, are we?" the man holding me snarled in my ear.

"Just being honest." I struggled against him, but he was unexpectedly strong. This was why I worked out but with my height, it didn't help me when it came to men much larger than me.

"You see, little girl," the tall man smirked. "We love a challenge. So, feel free to keep fighting. There are four of us and one of you."

A large hand reached into my shirt, kneading my breast.

Bile rose to my throat.

Breathe, Brogan. You got this. You've done this before.

In my position with the King's Harlots, I had to endure several men touching and groping me but it was still hard to deal with.

"She has some nice tits, Johnny," the man touching me said.

The tall man, who I could only assume was Johnny, grinned. "Good."

Before the man could touch me further, I shoved my head back, hitting him square in the nose.

"Fuck, you bitch," he yelled, landing his fist against my jaw.

Stars danced in my vision but it didn't stop me. I kicked him in the gut, forcing him to his knees before I ran out of there.

"Not so fast," Johnny was on me before I could put any distance between them and me.

"Let me go," I screamed, shoving and fighting in his arms.

Johnny threw me to the ground, shoving me face first into the grass. Dirt and debris dug into my cheeks, my fingers gripping the cool ground.

"Not before we have a little fun," Johnny breathed heavy against my neck, his lower body circling against my rear. "Mmm ... I bet you're nice and ti—"

Suddenly, the heavy weight was lifted off me.

Yelling and cursing sounded, followed by several thumps, before there was complete silence.

Rolling over onto my back, I stared up into Coby's dark eyes. A breath escaped me, not expecting him there.

"Coby," I whispered, sitting up.

He reached for my hand, pulling me to my feet before cupping my cheeks. His gaze searched my face while he brushed the knotty strands of hair out of my eyes. "Are you okay?"

I nodded. I had dealt with worse but it wasn't something that you could get used to. "I'm fine," I reassured him when his frown deepened. "I promise."

His thumb brushed over my mouth, igniting a spark of need somewhere deep inside of me. Releasing me, he rubbed the back of his neck. "Do you know who those fuckers were?"

"No." I brushed the grass off my pants, looking around me to see where the men went. "Where did they go?"

"They ran off after I broke one of their noses." Coby's jaw clenched, his mouth set in a firm line. "Let's go."

"You think we would just let you walk away?" a deep voice stopped us in our tracks.

Coby and I looked at each other before turning around and seeing Johnny standing a couple feet away.

"You see—" Johnny took a step toward us. "You broke my friend's nose. That doesn't sit well with me. And you—" his gaze met mine "—owe me a taste."

I swallowed hard. I was good, and Coby was better, but there was no way we would be able to get out of this unless the men wanted us to.

Coby took a step in front of me, shielding me as much as possible from the bastards.

My heart jumped. I opened my mouth to say something when I saw him slowly reach into his jeans pocket.

The men never noticed, keeping their distance.

"What do you say we go back to my place and have some fun?" Johnny asked. "Or I can just drag you into the alley and fuck you there. Either way, I'm game. But the more you fight, the better it is for me."

Fucker. "You'll have to kill me first," I ground out, stepping around Coby. "I've ate men like you for breakfast."

The guys laughed.

"And what did you do? Paint their nails and do their hair?" the man closest to me asked.

"You know what's funny? The fact that you guys are teaming up on a woman who is half your size. Does it make you feel superior? Does it make you feel like a true man?" What could I say? Word vomit flowed from my lips when I was pissed and backed into a corner.

"You won't hurt her," Coby finally said. He had been so quiet, I almost forgot he was beside me. Or that's what I tried convincing myself. Truth was, I could always feel him no matter if he talked or not.

"We won't?" Johnny crossed his arms under his chest. "And how can you be so sure? You broke my friend's nose."

"You like to remind me of that." Coby feigned a yawn. "Fucker had it coming."

I stepped in front of Coby. Not to protect him but to protect the men. Although they would have it coming, I didn't believe in murdering random assholes.

I would rather them rot in jail first. Now the bastards who kept taking these girls, was a whole different story.

"You see …" Johnny pulled a gun out from the back of his pants. "Charles told us you would put up a fight. I didn't believe him."

Well, scratch that idea. "You know Charles?" I asked, forcing my voice to shake. These men didn't scare me. Having four older brothers, one of them being in a well-respected motorcycle club, I saw shit. Death and pain. Things a person shouldn't see.

"Oh, little girl, you have no idea." Johnny sneered, scratching his temple with the end of the gun.

"How do you know him?" Coby placed his hand at the small of my back. That small movement sent strength coursing through my body. If these guys acted, we would fight. Together.

Johnny chuckled. "Oh, this is fun. He did tell me how much I would enjoy this. Charles is my brother."

CHAPTER FOUR

Coby

JOHNNY WAS CHARLES' brother. Life was sick and twisted that way. It only made sense for them to be related.

A laugh escaped me.

"What the fuck is so funny?" Johnny snapped, his back stiffening.

"You two are nothing alike," I said, goading him into losing it. He had a gun? Well, I had four brothers. "Charles at least owns his shit. You? You follow in his footsteps." I laughed harder.

"Listen, you fucking asshole …" Johnny aimed the gun in my direction. "I'll pop that grin right off your face."

"Do it," a deep voice from behind me said. "I fucking dare you."

Angel stepped up beside me, followed by Stone, Asher, and Dale. All of them were holding their own guns. Even though Asher was no longer in the military, he still stood at our back.

I smiled to myself knowing that if our boss saw this, he would shit his pants. We were military, respected. We weren't supposed to handle this on our own. Well, being in this town made you question the morals of humans. The town was small but shady as fuck.

Johnny raised an eyebrow. "You do understand that this won't end. The women will only continue to disappear. Charles will get what he wants and the head of the organization will bring this town crumbling to its knees."

"Maybe so," Asher countered. "But this is our town. I'm a jealous guy. No one is bringing her to her knees unless it's us."

One of the other men, whispered something into Johnny's ear and handed him a phone.

Johnny grabbed it, his gaze moving over the small screen before peering back at us. "You're fucking lucky."

"You see, my friend here—" the larger man standing beside Johnny pointed at him "—is a patient person, but me? Not so much. We came here for a fight." He leaned his head side to side, the tendons in his neck straining. "I'm bored. I want to play." His dark eyes met mine. "And so do you, don't you?"

A hot shiver raced over me.

Brogan was looking up at me. I knew because I could feel it. We hadn't known each other for long but there was a connection. I was an asshole, but I wasn't stupid.

My hand inched up Brogan's back to her arm. I pulled her to my side. She could handle herself but I didn't need to take that chance.

Having men's hands on her body made me see blood. I found myself craving it and it would be theirs I would bathe in.

"Huh," the man sneered, rubbing his jaw. "Someone is protective."

"Tell me why Charles targeted me," Brogan demanded.

"Why should I?" Jonny rubbed his jaw, a small smirk spreading on his lips.

"If you don't, I'll bask in the glory of seeing your guts spilling out at my feet." Brogan shrugged. "It's up to you which you choose."

Johnny looked from his men back to us before nodding once. "I'm not telling you shit."

"Fine. You fuckers need to leave," Brogan snapped. "*Now.*"

"Or else what, little girl? I could rip you apart. You would like that, wouldn't you? I can see it in your eyes as well." The bastard blew her a kiss and turned to walk away. "Until we meet again."

Shoving Brogan behind me, I lunged for him. My body vibrated, the need to hit this guy was so strong, I could taste it.

Slamming my fist into his face repeatedly, I couldn't comprehend what I was doing. I was hitting him, enjoying it and would do it over and over as long as Brogan was safe.

All of these thoughts racing through my mind, these different feelings—I wasn't sure what they meant.

"Coby," Brogan screamed from behind me.

And that drove me to hit my victim harder. Much like the people I had killed over the years, they didn't know what to expect until it was too late. If they saw me coming, it was only because I wanted them to. I wanted them to see the end of their life on the barrel of my gun.

The bastard beneath me pushed and shoved at me, trying to get a hit in. But I was bigger. I was faster. And I was definitely stronger.

Blood from his wounds coated my hoodie, spraying me in the face.

At that point, I stopped. Kneeling on his chest, I gripped his leather jacket and peered down into his one good eye. "If I ever see you again, I will cut off your skin and wear it as a coat."

Gurgling sounded from his swollen mouth.

I praised the sound.

Licking my lips, I swallowed the metallic taste of his blood and smirked. "How does it feel?"

"What?" he croaked out.

"Knowing your blood is now inside me."

"You're a sick fuck."

I only laughed.

Yes. Yes, I was.

****

(Brogan)

I never thought I would meet someone with the same darkness I had. Growing up, I was accused of being crazy, sick, twisted.

Brogan is a sociopath, bipolar, depressed ... Blah blah, fucking blah.

Finally finding a doctor who said that the wires in my brain weren't crossed right but it didn't mean I was crazy, I was able to feel somewhat normal.

But seeing Coby lose it like he had, and when he licked the blood off his lips … a part of me was turned on. I met my match. I knew it before, but tonight just confirmed everything.

Coby's brothers didn't say anything as we made our way back to the club. But he did still have a firm grip on my hand. The guy wanted nothing to do me but he was damn possessive. It didn't make sense and confused the hell out of me.

"Coby …" Dale clapped a hand on his shoulder. "You need to work it out."

"I know." Coby shook himself.

Work it out? Didn't he already do that?

"I can get some girls for you," Stone said, pulling out his phone.

Wait, what? "Are you serious right now?" I asked, but everyone kept talking. They were talking about getting the guy hookers or some shit while he had a hold of *my* hand. Fucking please.

Pulling my hand from Coby's, I clenched it at my side instead.

He reached for it again, linking our fingers roughly before I could pull it back.

I glared.

He smirked.

My heart thumped.

"What are you doing?" I asked him.

"Holding your hand," he muttered.

"I just texted Ruby. She can be on her way in five," Dale told him nonchalantly as if he were making dinner plans.

Coby only gave me a glance.

We kept walking hand in hand once we made it to the club.

"Where are you going?" Dale asked as Coby led me to the back.

"I'm going to go workout." Coby shivered, pulling me closer.

"But—"

"Have fun, brother, but I'm not fucking anyone tonight." Coby closed the door behind us once we reached the gym.

My stomach did a little somersault at his confession. Was I jealous? Hell yes. The guy was beautiful in an animalistic kind of way. Women loved that kind of thing, and I was no exception.

"Brogan," Coby snapped, pulling me from my thoughts. "I need you to hit me."

"What?" I shook my head. "Why?"

"Because if I do what I really want to do, I'll hurt you." His hands clenched into fists at his sides, flexing and unflexing. His big body was stiff, his eyes dark.

"I'm a big girl," I told him, although my voice shook. "You won't hurt me."

"Yes," he rasped. "I will."

"How can you be so sure?"

He took a second to answer, but when he finally did, I wasn't expecting the next words to come out of his mouth.

"Because it's what I want."

CHAPTER FIVE

Brogan

NO WORDS LEFT my mouth as Coby and I stared at each other. The air in the room crackled and fizzled. He wanted to hurt me. How much, I wasn't sure, but I was a fighter, and I would hit him back.

"You *need* to hit me," he gritted out, coming at me slowly.

"Are *you* going to hit me?" I knew the answer before he said it but I needed to be sure. I had been hit by men before. Doing what I did in this line of work, it was to be expected.

"No." Coby leaned his head to the side, a loud crack sounding from the joints in his thick neck. "I may be a sadistic fuck, but I don't hit women."

"Why do you want me to hit you then?" I took a step back until I hit the wall. Coby was much larger than I, standing a good foot and a half over my tiny frame but his intimidation was what got me most.

"Because I need to work it out."

"Is that what the sex is for?" Images of what it would be like for him to use me that way slid into my mind. I imagined that he would be rough, dominant, only giving me what I wanted when he felt like it. But he would make sure to give me just that. *Everything.*

"Sometimes." He closed the distance between us, placing his hands on the wall on either side of my head. "It also helps me focus on something other than death and destruction."

"You said you want to hurt me." Reaching my hands up, I allowed myself the freedom of gliding my fingers down his chest. "Why?"

Leaning his head down, his tongue peeked out to lick along the shell of my ear. "Because I know it's also what you need."

My heart jumped. "How do you know that?"

"I can see the darkness in you. I can sense it. I've been around it long enough to know that it's taking over. That's why you do what you do. But you also run from it."

"Is that why you're in the line of work you do as well?"

"Yes." He pinched my chin, tilting my head back. "We're one in the same, little one."

"Then use me."

Coby searched my face, his mouth mere inches from mine.

Just when I thought he was going to kiss me, he released me completely.

The air was suddenly sucked out of me. "What's wrong?"

"I can't do this." He rubbed the back of his neck, putting a few feet between us. "Not with you."

"But you just said ..." I shook my head. "Thanks, Coby. I really appreciate you making me feel like a fucking whore." I laughed. "God, I'm so stupid."

His brows narrowed. "You are *not* a whore."

"I know that, *asshole*," I yelled, spinning on him. "I throw myself at you. Offer to help you with whatever you need and you turn me down. Again. Well, I'm done. I refuse to beg. I am *not* that type of girl." Storming out of the gym, I headed toward my bedroom.

The club was dim, quiet. The sun had set some time ago. Not even realizing we had been in the gym for that long, I was surprised when I saw that it was now night time.

Taking a cold shower, I fought with everything inside of me not to run back to Coby. I couldn't understand why he had this effect on me. He was right, though. We *were* one in the same but something told me that his darkness was from a tragic memory. Mine was just because I was mentally ill.

As much as I wanted Coby, it wasn't worth losing myself in the end. I wouldn't beg. Not for him. Not for anyone.

***

(Coby)

When Brogan stormed off, her tight little ass walking away from me, my dick hardened to the point of pain. The first time she even hinted at being interested in me,

I had laughed like the asshole I was. But it still didn't stop her. I wasn't sure why she kept trying. She got my attention from the first moment I met her. She didn't have to do anything else.

"Then use me."

It took everything in me not to take her up on that offer but I was a private man. I wouldn't fuck her some place where someone could walk in at any time. Not the first time, anyway.

Pacing back and forth, I thought over her words. One night. One time. I could do it. I would get the satisfaction I needed without having to fuck someone else.

An old fuck, Ruby, was ready and waiting for me. One text and I could be balls deep inside her within a matter of minutes. But with her, it was never satisfying.

Brogan.

My body vibrated, my feet moved of their own accord until I reached the hall leading to her bedroom. Could I do this? Could I fuck her once and be done with it? I knew the answer before I even cared to admit it.

Brogan would be the sustenance that fed my soul when I was hungry. And right now, I was fucking starving.

CHAPTER SIX

Brogan

IT HAD BEEN an hour since I stormed out on Coby. Sixty minutes since I told him to fuck me in not so many words.

I sighed, a flush of heat coating my neck. At first when he turned me down weeks ago, it was embarrassing but now it just pissed me the fuck off. I didn't know what he wanted, but apparently, it wasn't me. I wasn't good enough. Or *he* wasn't good enough for that matter. I didn't care about his past or his demons. I wanted him. Just one night. I wanted a moment where I connected with another person and not feel ashamed for the dark thoughts racing through my mind. That was one reason why I became attracted to the guy. I could see he was hiding behind his dominant exterior when really, he was a vulnerable little boy.

Rolling over onto my back, I jumped when I saw a dark shadow move out of the corner of my room.

My stomach tumbled when my gaze landed on Coby. "What are you doing?" I whispered, my voice disappearing into the darkness of the night.

He didn't say anything. He stalked back and forth in front of my bed, keeping his eyes locked with mine. I could sense the battle going on inside of him. Should he, or shouldn't he?

Before I could answer my own question, his full mouth spread into a wicked grin. Coming toward me, he ripped the blankets off the bed, exposing my scantily-clad body.

So many questions bounced around in my head. I wanted to ask why the sudden change of heart but all I could focus on was this beautiful man standing before me.

With a firm grip, he wrapped both of his hands around my ankles and pulled me to the edge of the bed.

A gasp escaped me but I couldn't move. Even if I wanted to, I was held captive by his stare. This was it. It was finally happening. And now that it was, I had no idea what to expect.

Flipping me onto my stomach, he loomed over me. His hot breath scorched the back of my neck. Running the back of his knuckles down my spine, he gripped the hem of my tank top and pulled it over my head. His hips pushed into the flesh of my ass, strengthening that heat I had felt for him since the first time he looked at me.

I panted, arching beneath him. "Please."

"Shut the fuck up," he growled, fisting my hair in his hand and pulled my head back. His rough calloused fingers slid to my breast. Pinching and squeezing. Massaging and kneading until I was a writhing mess beneath him.

The sting from the strands of my hair being ripped from my scalp forced a smile onto my lips. Pushing my ass back against him, I reveled in the feel of him growing and hardening under my touch.

"How long has it been since you felt a thick cock inside of you?" he asked, his rough voice sliding over my body.

"Too long." I pushed up onto shaky arms, gazing at him over my shoulder. "When was the last time you felt a wet pussy sucking your dick dry?"

His eyes darkened, his grin widening. "A week ago."

"Hmm …" I continued to rub my ass against him. "Did you think of me when you fucked her?" Although I was jealous of the women he had been with already, I knew I could make him forget them.

"With every damn thrust, I thought of you," he snarled, pushing my head into the mattress.

"Good." Digging my fingers into the sheets, I waited. For him to take control. For him to give me what I had been craving since I became sexually active years before. For him to just let me be … me.

With a rough tug, Coby ripped my panties in half and pushed them into my face. "Smell how much you want me."

I inhaled, letting out a moan when the sweet scent from my body tingled into my nose. "I've wanted you for months." Rising onto all fours, I gave my hips a shake. I played dirty and I knew what I wanted. I was comfortable in my body and wanted him to know it.

Coby gave my ass a hard swat, pushing me forward, and knelt behind me. Pulling the belt free from the loops in his jeans, he wrapped the leather around my arms. Binding them behind my back, he held the buckle in one hand while sliding the other down the side of my body. "You will submit to me."

I licked my lips, my blood pounding in my ears. "Make me."

The sound of a zipper lowering, followed by a tin foil wrapper, invaded the silence in the room.

With a rough hold on my arms, he pushed my head further into the mattress before thrusting into me hard.

My eyes widened, the breath of air I had been holding leaving me on a gasp. I felt him everywhere. Every inch. Every vein. Every hard muscle. I could feel the blood pumping through his body, giving him the energy to fuck me how he saw fit.

Coby pushed into me, thrusting rough and violent. He gave me what I craved, showing me that it was okay and I wasn't the only one who held some darkness inside of them.

My body burned, stretching around him to meet his glorious size. I had always imagined that it would be like this. Intense. Dark. Dangerous. But utterly delicious.

"Can you hear your cunt sucking me, Brogan?" He leaned over me, the scruff of his jaw scratching my cheek while he stroked my hair.

"You feel so good," was all I could get out.

He grunted, pumping his dick deep inside of me.

That familiar tingle crawled from my toes, hitting me straight in the center of my core. "Harder."

"Baby, my cock is going to destroy you."

Although I had itched to touch him, I enjoyed the feeling of being restrained. Of being completely helpless, knowing he would give me the greatest pleasure in return.

"I've imagined all this time what your pussy would feel like," he whispered, his voice hoarse.

Closing my eyes, I let his dirty words wash over me and submitted.

***

(Coby)

An hour later and I had her body tightening around my tongue. Her fingers and nails dug into my hair, pulling me closer and closer. Her hips bucked against my face, begging me to push her over that edge. I could eat her for hours, spending the rest of my days between her legs. Brogan was so damn delicious, I lapped at her center like a starved man.

Growling and humming, I let the vibrations leaving my throat rumble through her.

She whimpered, thrusting her hips upward.

Releasing her with a pop, I spread the folds of her pussy. "Come all over my face, baby."

"Oh, fuck." Her eyes were wide with passion as she watched me. "Please."

I grinned, gripped her ass, and dove into her hard.

The sounds of her screams sent me over the edge but I didn't want this to end anytime soon. Knowing I wouldn't be there when she woke up in a couple hours, I would fuck her until she passed out in my arms.

Brogan's cunt continued to tighten around my tongue as I forced another orgasm out of her.

"Coby," she begged, shaking beneath me. "I … I can't take anymore."

Sucking her clit between my teeth, I lapped and pulled until another release crashed through her.

Releasing her completely, I sat back and knelt between her spread thighs.

She stared up at me with dark sleepy eyes.

Her body was covered in a sheen of sweat, her curly hair matted to her forehead.

Needing to leave her with a little something extra, I wrapped my hand around the base of my cock and stroked. Up. Down. I pulled and tugged, imagining her pretty little mouth wrapped around the tip. Her teeth sinking into me until I came hard down her throat. But for now, coming on her stomach and pussy would have to do.

CHAPTER SEVEN

Brogan

ROLLING OVER ONTO, my muscles twitched and jumped with the protest. Every inch of me was sated. Completely and utterly satisfied. Experiencing the night with Coby was something I would never forget. A part of me didn't expect it to happen again but a girl could dream. He was nothing like I imagined. He was more. So much more.

The scent of sex permeated from the blankets I was wrapped in. Snuggling into them, I inhaled deep and let out a peaceful sigh.

I remembered when he gave me a little something to remember him by. Coby coming on my stomach was the hottest thing I had ever experienced.

RUDE

A hard bang sounded on my door, startling me.

"What are you doing in there?" Creena called out, knocking on the door again.

Wrapping a sheet around my sore body, I made my way to the door and opened it an inch.

She laughed, looking down at my makeshift dress. "Good night?"

"You have no idea." I grinned. "What's up?"

"Boss lady wants a meeting. There's some more news on the clubs being blown to shit and ..." Creena sighed. "Another death."

"Fuck me," I grumbled. "Be out in five."

Slamming the door shut, I quickly took a shower. As much as I didn't want to, I washed Coby off me. God, that beautiful delicious man. One thing struck me as odd. He never kissed me. Not even a peck. He fucked and left but I didn't even remember him leaving. My stomach twisted. No. I would not get upset over this. I had been hurt too many times over stupid men. I refused to let another destroy my heart.

Once I finished cleaning myself up, I got dressed and headed out into the main part of the club. Jay usually held meetings in one of the large rooms, but when I didn't see anyone in it, I went outside.

Everyone was standing around the *Rod's Construction* trailer. It was Angel's company but since Asher had been medically discharged due to PTSD, it was now his in a way. Since Angel hired him as manager, Asher had been busy and taking on as many jobs as he could. Living in the small shithole town we did, there was enough work to last him the rest of his life.

"Brogan," Meeka called out, slipping away from Asher. "How are you?" She raised an eyebrow. "You look exhausted."

Was it that obvious? I chuckled. "It was a ..." The hairs on the back of my neck tingled.

Coby came up beside us, nodded once at Meeka and walked up to the rest of the crew. Not paying me any attention, he headed into the trailer.

"Long night?" Meeka teased, snapping me from my thoughts.

"Yes." Part of me wanted to demand Coby to talk to me but I wasn't that kind of girl.

Ignoring the raging thoughts forcing their way into my mind, I went back inside to make myself some coffee.

As I was taking a sip of the soothing liquid, everyone made their way into the club one by one. The noisy chatter was something that I would never get used to. Although we held many parties, those people weren't family. But these guys? Vice-One was now a part of our lives whether we cared to admit it or not.

"I'm not letting you stay here by yourself," Angel told Jay, brushing his finger down her cheek.

"I won't be by myself, baby." She stood on tiptoes and kissed him fully on the mouth. "I have my sisters."

"We're not leaving. You deal with your club business first and then my guys and I will join you."

"Angel." Jay placed her hands on her hips, staring up at him defiantly.

"You can argue with me all you want and insist that you'll be fine but we're not leaving. You should know by now that your protection comes first."

She sighed. "Fine. Let me talk to my girls first."

Angel kissed her forehead, giving her hand a light squeeze before rounding up the guys, and headed back outside.

"What's going on?" I asked, making my way up to Jay. Besides some shithead blowing up clubs, I could sense something else was at stake.

Jay whistled, signaling for everyone to follow her.

"As you know, Max is taking a break," Jay said, sitting at the head of the table. "I don't know when she'll be back but she's asked to step down as vice-president for the time being."

My heart gave a start. I knew it was coming but I still didn't like hearing the words.

"Dale needs to get his head out of his ass," Creena mumbled.

"I agree but that's not important right now," Jay folded her hands on top of the table. "We have to worry about Max and the baby. She's staying with Angel and me right now. The guys don't want us being alone."

"Creena and I are staying here," I pointed out.

"We'll get to that." Jay took a breath. "Brogan, I would like to have you as vice-president until Max gets back on her feet."

"Really? But I ..." I leaned forward. "I appreciate that. I really do but I don't ... I don't think it will go well with the other shit I do."

"That's why you would be perfect for the job." Jay smirked. "You're a tough little thing. Most men are scared of you and anyone who has been in your chair knows what you are capable of."

I still wasn't sure if I should have been proud of that or not. "Yeah, but you think I'm really capable of being the VP?" I was always behind the scenes. The only time you saw me with the rest of the crew was when we went on a ride. Which didn't happen often. God, I missed my bike.

Jay smiled. "I wouldn't ask you if I didn't. All the girls agree. It was Max's idea in the first place."

I looked at Creena and Meeka. They both grinned, nodding their heads in encouragement.

"Can I think about it?" I wasn't sure why I was second guessing my capability of helping with the club. It wasn't like I didn't do it in the first place. But the title alone scared me.

"You can." Jay frowned. "Is something wrong?"

"I … I just need time."

"Okay." She turned to Creena. "Can you let the guys in?"

Creena did as she was asked, holding the door open for Vice-One before taking her place back at the table.

I tried ignoring the heat crawling up my spine. I tried ignoring the way the hairs on the back of my neck stood on end. But as Coby sat beside me, all the air was sucked out of my lungs. Much to my dismay, he pulled my chair closer to his.

With a hand that had given me so much pleasure the night before, he cupped my inner thigh, giving it a light squeeze.

My body stiffened. Pushing his hand away, I crossed my legs. Whatever game he was playing, he wouldn't win.

Coby pulled me closer. "You think you can get away from me, little one?" he whispered in my ear.

"You need to keep your hands to yourself before I stab you in the dick," I threw back at him, trying to focus on what Jay was saying to the group.

"Now why would you do that?" his voice lowered. "You seemed to like my dick last night."

"Because you won't leave me alone," I mumbled.

Coby gripped my knee, digging his fingers into the bone. "I'll never leave you alone, Brogan."

I sighed, uncrossing my legs. I linked my fingers between his, stopping his hand from going any higher.

A deep chuckle left his mouth.

"What's so funny?" I scowled.

"You like it when I touch you." His words heated me from within.

Before I could respond, a heavy smack on the table made me jump.

"Brogan," Jay barked. "Problem?"

Yes. A large six-foot-five one. "No."

"Care to join us in on this little meeting?" Jay's words were meant to bite but instead, a hint of amusement flashed in her gaze.

"Sorry," I dug my nails into Coby's hand. "I'm a little distracted. What were you saying?"

****

(Coby)

I couldn't help but tease her. Her spitfire little energy amused me. My dick twitched, needing to get back inside of her tight body. This was new for me. I was a fuck them once and leave kind of guy. Unless they were paid for.

With Brogan's nails digging into my hand, the sting sent a fire roaring through my body. She played dirty, and I'd chop off my left nut just to see how messy she could get.

"My father's crew is on a rampage," Jay's voice interrupted my thoughts. "All of them have sticks up their asses about what club is going to get hit next." She let out a sigh and pinched the bridge of her nose. "I don't know what's going on, but I need you all to do what you do best and get me as much information as possible."

"I'll talk to Greyson," Brogan spoke up, relaxing her hold on my hand. "He's supposed to be coming down in the next week or so."

"Okay." Jay nodded. "Good." She turned to Angel. "When do you guys leave for your next mission?"

"In a week," Angel answered, his gaze flicking to Asher.

Asher shifted his weight in his seat.

My chest panged for my brother. If there was something I could do to make it so he could be back in the military, I would. Although it would take a couple of weeks, he was put on stress leave. He didn't want anyone knowing about his past or the demons that kept him up at night.

Meeka rubbed her hand up and down his arm, whispering softly to him.

He smiled, kissing her nose.

Turning my hand over, I cupped Brogan's and linked our fingers.

She looked up at me, her brows furrowing.

Yeah, I have no idea what I'm doing either, little one.

All I knew was that I craved her touch. Her darkness made me feel normal. Like it was okay to have an off day. She would be the light in my shadows whether she cared to admit it or not.

"Do we know what club was hit last?" Creena asked, pulling her hair up into one of those messy bun things that I could never understand.

"My dad said it was a chapter in a couple towns over." Jay pinched the bridge of her nose. "Dante's Kings are using their resources and trying to do what they can to bring these bastards down. Everyone is coming together but no one knows shit. It has to be Charles Brian and his band of merry men."

Mumbled curses sounded around the room.

Charles Brian was the epitome of evil. Running a human trafficking ring and kidnapping Asher and Meeka a couple months ago, he was first on my hit list.

"Charles has laid low since last time," Angel pointed out. "We need to find out why he targeted Brogan in the first place."

"He was probably just targeting all of us," I muttered.

"We should have fucking killed him when we had a chance," Dale muttered, cracking his knuckles.

"As much as I agree, you know we couldn't. We're already stepping out of our job description. We're Navy SEALs. We deal with terrorist shit. Not human trafficking." Angel rubbed the back of his neck. "If Vega wouldn't have brought us into this shit ..."

The air in the room became thick.

Eric Vega, our old boss, killed himself in front of Jay. He had been one of the traffickers in this organization, much to our surprise.

"And if I wouldn't have brought Asher and Meeka ..." Angel shifted uncomfortably beside Jay.

"Hey." Asher tapped his knuckles against the top of the table. "I could have said no. That's in the past. We got out. We're safe."

"Yeah, but look at you now." Angel rubbed the back of his neck again.

"Fuck, man, don't do this shit." Asher's voice became thick.

"Okay," I interrupted. "Listen to me, what's done is done. We're going to end this one way or another. There's no point harping over the past."

Dale grunted. "How come when you don't say much, the one thing you do say is always right?"

"Because it's the truth." I had always been quiet. I figured if there was nothing important to say, why speak? Although it bothered some, it seemed to attract Brogan.

"I need to go for a run," she muttered. "Or hit something."

My blood vibrated through my veins. I knew what I needed but it would have to wait until that night. Brogan would learn quickly that last night was not a one-time thing. She was my new addiction, and I would use her to satisfy this itch I had.

But she was right. I needed to hit something too. And hit hard.

CHAPTER EIGHT

Brogan

CHARLES BRIAN.

I had never met the man but I would give anything to have him in my chair. To hear his screams. To feel his body shaking beneath my touch as I tortured him with whatever instrument I saw fit.

But until that time, I would have to find other ways to work it out.

Once the meeting was over, everyone went their separate ways.

Asher and Dale went outside to continue working on the club. Jay had instructed them to tear down the wall and make that section of the building bigger after asking me to design it.

I mulled over the new blue prints spread out on top of the bar. "Jay, we should really wait until these are done before the guys work on the club."

"I just want that section bigger for now while you design the rest. I don't want the building one big construction zone where it's not even livable. So, one part at a time." She tapped the part of the blue print I had just finished working on. "You need to go back to school for this. You're brilliant, Brogan."

I grunted. "School is boring, and I hate being told what to design."

She laughed. "Well, you'll always be my architect."

"Thanks." I smiled up at her. "How are you and Angel doing?"

Her grin widened. "Wonderful." Her cheeks heated. "We have our issues, but it's much better than before."

"That's good." I gave her a quick hug. "I'm glad. Now you go take care of yourself." I winked. "And let me continue designing your … baby."

Her eyes widened. "Um …" She coughed, shaking herself. "Yeah. Okay. You … uh … have fun." She spun on her heel and made her way outside.

I laughed. I wasn't stupid. I knew something was going on with her, and I would bet my life savings that she was hiding a secret. She stopped drinking. Ate better. And she gave me an excuse every time I asked her to workout. But my lips were sealed until she was ready to announce it.

A couple hours later and I was still working away on the new design for the club. I had enjoyed making buildings come to life just from a pencil and a piece of paper. After my brothers had convinced me to go to school for it, I learned a lot but became bored and annoyed when I was told that my designs weren't modern enough. They were unique. Mixing history into today. But they never matched up to my professors' standards.

"Hey, little one."

I jumped at the deep voice in my ear.

Coby sat on the stool beside me, brushing the back of his hand up and down my bare hip.

I should have worn jeans but it had been hotter outside so I put on my favorite leather shorts. Stupid me.

"What are you working on?" he asked, reaching over the counter and grabbing a bottle of water.

"Jay asked me to design the rest of the club while you guys work on the one section that was blown to shit." I took the bottle from him and gulped down half of the water before handing it back to him.

"You're an architect?"

I scoffed. "Not professionally. I do it for fun because it's relaxing and takes me out of my head."

"I know the feeling." Coby hooked an arm around my middle, pulling me between his legs. "This is really amazing. You're talented, Brogan."

"Thank you." My body heated at being so close to him again, but as much as I knew I should have pulled away, I couldn't. "What do you do for fun?"

"Nothing really." He took the blue print from my hands. "I'm impressed."

A flush slid up the back of my neck. "You are?"

"Of course." He nodded. "Not many people can design buildings. Did you go to school?"

"Yeah, but I got bored. I didn't like being told what to do." My breath caught when I realized what I had said.

"You liked being told what to do last night," Coby pointed out, tightening his hold on my waist.

"That was different." I licked my lips, my gaze glancing down at his full mouth.

"How so?"

"I trust you."

***

(Coby)

Those three words shouldn't have bothered me but they did. I wasn't sure why. Brogan deserved better than me but as much as I felt that way, I couldn't help but need her. I craved everything about her. She was beautiful. Smart. And so fucking feisty, it made the alpha in me roar.

"Why do you trust me?" I grit out, mentally smacking myself for questioning her feelings.

She laughed. "I have no idea why." Her body relaxed in my hold. Without speaking on the subject further, she went back to drawing.

Although she didn't give me a reason as to why she trusted me, her answer made sense. This thing between us was new, unexpected. She had asked me out back when we first met. I turned her down and was rude about it but now that we had one night together, that was long forgotten.

"Hey," she said a moment later. "Want to get out of here?"

"Sure." I needed to get back inside her but that would have to wait until later.

Brogan rolled up the blueprint and stuffed it into a cardboard tube. "Come with me." She stepped out of my embrace and headed toward the door.

I followed her, wondering where she was taking me. But I found myself not caring. Wherever she went, I would follow and stand right by her side if she needed me to.

When we reached the side of the club, my heart jumped.

A couple of weeks ago, I had found her in the basement of the club, torturing some shit head in her chair. And much to my surprise, it turned me the fuck on. Her dominance. The unexpected superiority that permeated from her bones. Even though I knew back then that she was submissive in every sense of the word, when it came to protecting her club, she was one-hundred percent in control.

"I know you saw me down here a couple of weeks ago," she said, unlocking the door. "But I want you to see my room without anyone else in it."

I pushed open the door when the lock clicked free and waited for her permission to follow. It was surreal to me to wait. I had always been a take charge kind of man but I found with Brogan that I needed to allow her to have control. I dominated over her in the bedroom but outside of that, she would always have the upper hand.

"I heard that your nickname is Ghost," she said, walking down the stairs.

I grunted. "No one calls me that anymore."

"Why not?"

"Because I've threatened them and told them I would chop off their balls and shove them down their throats if they called me it."

She laughed. "Why? Ghost fits you. No one sees you from what I hear. You're good at what you do, Coby." She flicked on the light before walking over to a long table that held every tool imaginable that could do some serious damage to an unwilling victim.

"Maybe so but I'm not proud of what I do. Even though most of the people deserved everything I gave them." I leaned against the table, watching her brush her fingers over a set of knives.

"Most people," she repeated the words. "Have you ever made a mistake?"

My stomach twisted. I was human. We all made mistakes. "Yes."

She nodded. "So have I." She took a breath, turning to me. "I used to scare my parents."

I knew the feeling. "My father died when I was young. He was an abusive asshole. I remember his funeral and how I wanted to dance on his grave but my mother pulled me away before I could."

Brogan's eyes widened. "Really?"

"I went back the next day by myself. It was raining."

"And you danced."

"I did." I winked.

"Wow." She laughed again. "I shouldn't laugh but that's fucking awesome."

"Yeah. My mother didn't think so." I rubbed the back of my neck.

She sighed. "I love my sisters but I don't talk to them about ... stuff, either."

Needing to change the subject for fear that she would close up on me, I asked a typical ice breaker question. "You have siblings, right?"

"I have four brothers. Greyson is my stepbrother as you know and three by blood. Blake and Brox are twins and Benny is the oldest. My parents had a thing for names that started with *B*."

RUDE

I chuckled. "I like your name," I told her, pushing a strand of hair behind her ear.

Her breath caught. "Coby."

And *fuck me*, but I loved it when she said my name. Pinching her chin, I tilted her head. "Say it again."

She smiled. "Coby."

Fuck.

CHAPTER NINE

Brogan

I WANTED HIM to kiss me. My lips tingled with anticipation, waiting. Wanting. *Needing.* God, did I ever need Coby to put his mouth on mine. I wanted to feel his tongue sliding along mine. Dancing. Owning. Controlling me with his kiss much like he did with the rest of his body.

"You want me to kiss you," he said, his mouth mere inches from mine.

"Yes," I answered, even though it wasn't a question.

"Where?" he asked, his mouth touching the corner of my lips.

"Everywhere," I tilted my head back, my body becoming alive by that small touch.

"Hmmm … I can think of many places I've already kissed you."

Oh, dear God. I pushed out of his hold, shaking myself. There was no way I was doing this with him in this room. I made my way toward the stairs and turned back to him. "You're going to come to me tonight. Aren't you?" I knew the answer before I even asked.

"Yes," he said, closing the distance between us.

"Good." I nodded once. "Good."

We headed up the stairs but all I could think about what would happen later on. Would he restrain me with his belt again? Would he use something else? Would he let me touch him this time? All of these questions bounced around in my head with no impending answer in sight.

"Don't think about it, Brogan," Coby whispered in my ear once we were outside. "I'll take care of you." He wrapped an arm around my waist, pulling me back against him.

I let out a sigh at the feel of his erection pressing into my lower back. "Coby."

His hand travelled up between my breasts before wrapping around my throat. "I'll take care of you so fucking good that you'll forget about every other man who has been inside this tight little body."

I pushed back against him. "I'll make you forget every pussy you've fucked."

He groaned. Holding my wrists in one hand, he pulled my arms above my head. "I've already forgotten."

I grinned, rubbing my ass against his growing length. "Good."

"Fuck, you're so damn hot." His breathing picked up, sliding along my skin.

God, I wanted him. We were outside and I wanted him. Anyone could walk out and see us at any moment and I still wanted him. I didn't care. He made me throw all caution to the wind. "You need to fuck me. Right now."

"Do I?" his hand gripped my hip, moving his pelvis back and forth against me.

I moaned, leaning my head against his chest. "Yes."

"Or else what, little one?"

"I'll stick my hands down my shorts and make myself come."

He chuckled. "I don't fucking think so." His teeth sunk into the tender spot under my ear. "Your orgasms belong to me."

I let out a soft groan, liquid seeping into my panties. "You think so, do you?"

"Oh, Brogan. I know they do." Pushing his knees between my legs, he ground into me hard. Gripping my chin, he shoved his fingers into my mouth and cupped my mound with his free hand. "You like when I control you. You crave it. There's a kinky darkness inside of you that wants to come out and play."

I moaned, digging my fingers into the wall. The bite of the brick stung my hands but I didn't care. I didn't care about anything except for this man holding me in his arms.

Licking my tongue along the two fingers in my mouth, I sucked and pulled.

His breathing quickened, a deep growl rumbling from his chest.

Coby undid my shorts, sliding his fingers into the waist band of my panties. "I'm going to give you the orgasm that you crave. You're going to scream around my fingers. If you're quiet, I'll slap your cunt until you cream all over my hand."

I nodded, needing the release I knew he could give me.

His fingers slid between the folds of my pussy.

I jumped, spreading my legs wider for him.

"Keep sucking my fingers, Brogan. Show me what to expect when I fuck your mouth with my cock."

I took his fingers as far as I could go. Licking my tongue up and down them, nibbling and pulling, I imagined they were his dick.

Coby thrust two fingers inside of me, pumping hard and deep.

I cried out, riding against his hand.

"That's it. Fuck my fingers, little one." He pushed his thumb into my mouth one last time. "Come hard for me. Don't fucking disappoint me."

I smiled, lifting my hips up and down his fingers. As much as I wanted him to fuck me, I enjoyed the feeling of his hand between my legs. The shorts were loose enough that he could fit his whole hand inside them but I needed more.

Taking the hint, Coby removed his hand from my shorts and brushed his fingers up my inner thigh.

"Coby," I whimpered.

He placed me back on my feet and released me completely. "Look at me."

I did as he said and looked at him over my shoulder.

Sticking his fingers that were just inside my body in his mouth, he smirked. "Turn around."

On shaky legs, I did as instructed and leaned against the wall. Much to his surprise, I ran my hands down my body, pulling my shorts down my legs.

His eyes widened, following my movements.

"You think you control me, Coby. But I'm the type of woman who knows what I want." I tossed my shorts on the ground, leaving me standing in a white tank top, a black thong and my scuffed-up boots. "I want you. Again. And again. I want you so deep inside me, I can feel you in my throat."

His eyes darkened.

Before I knew it, he was on me.

And he was right where I wanted him.

***

(Coby)

I wanted to make her wait. I wanted to make her beg and demand that I fuck her because she couldn't take it anymore. She had me wrapped right around her finger and I couldn't say no.

When she pulled her shorts off and stood before me in hardly anything at all, I could no longer control the incessant urge to get balls deep inside her.

Throwing her over my shoulder, I slapped my hand against her ass and charged for her room.

I didn't care if anyone saw. I didn't care if anyone heard. I needed her in ways I never knew was possible. One night was not enough. She challenged every waking thought I had. Every action. Every moment.

Once we reached her room, I kicked the door closed and threw her on her bed.

She had her hands around my neck and my mouth on hers faster than I could breathe and I loved every second of it.

Shoving my tongue inside of her mouth, I ripped her tank top in half. She moaned, arching beneath me.

With shaking hands, she pulled my shirt up and over my head, breaking apart the kiss for a fraction of a second.

My fingers trailed down the center of her body before gripping the sides of her thong. "Tell me you want me," I said, releasing her mouth.

"I want you." Her cheeks were flushed, her chest rising and falling with ragged breath. "Now fuck me."

I smirked, pulling her beneath me. Kneeling between her legs, I gripped her ankles tight in my hands. "I will. And eventually, I'll fuck you everywhere."

Her eyes widened.

"Do you know what that means, little one?" I pulled her thong down her legs and kissed her inner thigh.

"Yes." She licked her lips, watching me.

"Tell me." I brushed a finger between the cheeks of her ass. "What does it mean?"

"You'll fuck me where no man has ever been."

I growled, shoving my face between her legs, and swallowed the delicious taste of her body. No man had ever been inside every part of her body? That made me feel like a fucking king. And I would damn well make sure she enjoyed every second of it.

***

(Brogan)

Coby-*Fucking*-Porter.

He used me good. Again. And again. So many times I lost track. I had never been with a man who could go for hours on end. Each time he had his own release, he would be back between my legs, making sure I had orgasm after orgasm. It became so intense, one touch and I exploded.

It was early the next morning. I lost track of time being with Coby. He made me forget everything else and focus on him. On us.

When I had told him that no man had ever been in that tight part of my body, he lost it. I would have laughed under normal circumstances but the animalistic growl that left him turned me on even more.

Throughout the evening before, my phone had rang, knocks sounded on the door, but I ignored everyone. Coby didn't leave my side until sometime during the night from what I could tell.

Rising from the bed, I savored the aches and pains from being used hard and fast the night before. I threw on sweat pants, a sports bra, and a tank top before heading out of the room to get some much-needed coffee.

The delicious scent of coffee beans permeated through the air. Who was up this early already?

Shrugging it off, I headed to the bar, poured myself a mug and went to walk to one of the booths in the far corner of the club when I saw Coby sitting there.

"What are you doing here so early?" I asked, sitting beside him.

He wrapped a hand around my inner thigh and kissed my head. "I never left."

"You didn't?"

"No." He pulled me against him and placed a soft peck on my neck. He shivered, his tense body relaxing after that small touch.

"What are you working on?" I asked, ignoring the flutter in my belly and nodded toward the laptop he was typing away on.

"I found some articles about that woman who attacked Jay. Angel asked me a couple days ago to do some more research on it."

"What did you find?" I placed the mug on the table and curled against him.

"She's everywhere." Coby clicked link after link, scrolling through hundreds of articles. "There's never any mention of her name. No one knows who she is or what she wants. Or even where she's from. I've contacted an old friend to see if he can dig something up on her."

The woman was beautiful. Long dark hair. Alabaster skin. Perfect complexion. And she looked to be tall as well. Everything that I was not. It made me wonder what kind of women Coby was usually into before he started sleeping with me. A sudden hint of jealousy twisted at my gut. *Get a grip, Brogan.*

"She's beautiful," I pointed out.

Coby grunted. "Sure."

"You don't think so?" I sat up straighter, hooking my arm around his.

"What are you getting at, Brogan?" He frowned, his gaze searching my face.

I huffed, chewing my bottom lip. "I have no idea."

He chuckled. "You're jealous and I haven't even said anything about her."

"It's not her." I waved a hand in front of me. "It's every woman. I bet all the women you've been with have been tall. Slender. Super model beautiful."

"Yeah? And all of the guys you've been with have probably been fucking normal too."

"I …" My mouth snapped shut.

"Exactly." He pulled me into his side, wrapping his arm around my waist. "If you must know, you are the only woman I am fucking. Do I think she's beautiful? No. Because I don't go for women who attack my friends."

My heart gave a start.

"She could have killed Jay and that would have destroyed Angel. He's my brother. He comes first and foremost. So, no, I don't think she's beautiful."

"Okay." I turned to him. "So, I'm the only woman you're fucking, huh?"

He rolled his eyes, shaking his head. "You are too much."

"You love it." I pushed onto my knees and kissed his cheek. "Well, you, Mr. Porter, are the only man I am fucking."

"I know." He cupped my nape and placed a hard kiss on my mouth. "I'm the only who can make you scream like you did last night."

I shivered. "You're proud of yourself, aren't you?"

"Fucking right I am." His tongue slid between lips, sucking mine into his mouth. The kiss ended all too soon. "Who are you, little one?" he whispered, kissing my nose.

"I could ask you the same thing, Coby." I turned around and leaned against him while he went back to work on his laptop.

Coby wrapped his arm around me, holding me tight against him and cupped my inner thigh. Always the thigh. I had come to know rather quickly that it was his favorite spot to touch whenever I sat near him. I wasn't exactly sure why but it made me feel safe. Owned. Although these questions bounced around in my mind, I let them rest for the moment while we sat in a comfortable silence.

"Fuck me," Coby growled a half an hour later. He continued searching through articles on his laptop, cursing every so often.

"What?"

A phone rang suddenly, making me jump.

"Yeah," Coby barked into his cell. "Shit. Hold on. I have someone with me who needs to hear this." He placed the phone on the table and hit speaker. "Go ahead, my man."

"All right," a throat cleared. "I was doing some digging on this shit since the moment you asked me a couple days ago. This organization is tight. They have firewalls up on their systems like I've never seen before. And I've hacked into the government's systems before." The man on the other end chuckled.

"Lucas," Coby demanded. "Focus."

"Fine. I'll pat my own back then."

I raised an eyebrow.

Coby shook his head. "Lucas," he repeated.

"Yeah, yeah." The man, Lucas, cleared his throat again. "You're lucky I love ya, my man. This cold is kicking my ass. Anyway, this woman is the sister to the front runner of the organization. She has a Daddy complex and the big brother takes care of her. If you get my drift."

"Um ... gross," I blurted.

"Yeah," Lucas agreed. "I'm all for fucked up shit but that's some serious fuckedupness right there. I also found that they have been running this organization together for years. They've recruited men from all over, trying to bring in as many females as possible. They've also started broadening their reach and are now going for boys."

"Shit," Coby muttered, pinching the bridge of his nose. "Do you have names?"

"Coby, Coby, Coby, what do you take me for? Some kind of chump?"

Coby pinched the bridge of his nose. "I'm not a patient man."

"So damn testy." Lucas coughed. "Tina and Zane Birch. But that's all I've found." Another cough. "I'll keep digging but I need a couple days to gather their location and all of their assets. I don't need these people on my ass. I'm trying to be a good little boy."

Coby scoffed. "Right. Talk to you soon, Lucas."

They said their good byes and Coby hung up the phone.

"Well, that was enlightening," I mumbled.

"I'd say."

I sat up, stretching my arms above my head until a crack raced down my spine. "So, who was that?"

"Someone I met years ago. He's a hacker and is quite known for his work."

"He hacked the government?"

"Yeah." Coby chuckled, shaking his head. "He got away with it too. They couldn't prove anything even though they know it was him."

"I think I read about that in the paper. He's kind of crazy."

"He is." Coby winked.

A flutter raced through my heart. A wink. It was such a small movement, I wasn't sure why it had this effect on me. Coby wasn't your typical man. He was quiet. Withdrawn. Spoke when spoken to or when he had something to say. But get him in bed? And he had tons to say. His dirty words from the night before rushed into my mind causing a flush of heat to envelope my skin.

Coby looked down at my lips. "Are you thinking about me?"

"Yes," I answered automatically.

"Good."

CHAPTER TEN

Brogan

A MONTH HAD come and gone.

Vice-One had gone on another mission, only to bring back sour moods and piss-poor attitudes.

But something was wrong. The night they came home, Coby never showed up.

Angel greeted Jay with a hard kiss.

Asher grabbed Meeka, holding her tight against him.

Dale and Stone grabbed themselves a beer each and gave Creena and I both hugs. I appreciated it. I was happy they were home safe but it wasn't enough.

"Where's Coby?" I asked, ringing my hands in my lap.

"He's not here?" Dale looked at Stone who only shrugged.

I sighed, going back to cleaning the bar. If Coby didn't want to come say hi and let me know that he was home safe, fine. Fuck him. It wasn't like we had made our time together official. It was just sex. Hot, intense, delicious sex. But sex nevertheless.

I moved around the bar, slamming bottles and taking my frustration out on the items before me.

"What did those bottles ever do to you?" Angel asked, sliding onto a stool.

"Where is Coby?" I asked, not caring about the questions that would later come with my curiosity.

"He doesn't handle missions well sometimes. So, when we get home, he usually goes off and works out or …"

"Has sex," I finished for him.

"Right." Angel frowned.

I waited, holding my breath that he would ask me why I wanted to know where Coby was. But when he didn't and left to go find Jay, I let out a deep breath.

It looked like I would just have to wait for Coby to come to me. And I was fine with that. It would be over my dying breath before I ever chased a man.

***

A soft click sounded throughout the silence of the night.

I jumped up in bed, finding Coby standing a few feet away. "Coby."

He didn't say anything.

"What's wrong?"

He shook himself and pulled off his jacket followed by his boots.

"Where were you tonight?" I asked when he climbed into bed beside me.

Coby wrapped his arms around me, pulling me tight against his hard chest. His nose brushed up the length of my neck while he took several breaths. He inhaled deep, letting the air out in a soft sigh.

I pulled back. "Where were you?"

His eyes searched my face. "I was too fucked up to come see you."

"What is that supposed to mean?"

He frowned. "Exactly what I just said."

"You could have come here."

Coby moved to kiss me but I slapped my hand to his chest, stopping him. "I'm glad you're okay but next time don't make me wait."

"Fine." He grabbed my hand, kissed my palm, and gave it a soft nibble before covering my mouth with his.

Running my fingers through his hair, I deepened the kiss.

He groaned, his lower body instantly becoming hard for me. "This is what I came home to," he whispered against my mouth.

"Coby ..." I broke the kiss. "You can't say things like that."

"I know but it needed to be said."

I sighed, pushing out of his hold, and sat up in bed.

"What is it?" he asked, grabbing my hand.

"What are we doing?"

"Why do we need to put a label on it?"

"Because ..." I chewed my bottom lip. God, I was being such a girl. "We don't."

"Good." Coby pulled me into his arms. "Because I'm enjoying this. I don't know what we're doing. But I look forward to coming to you every night." He pulled my head down to meet his mouth. "I enjoy spending every moment I can inside of you."

"Why didn't you come here earlier with the guys?" I asked, running my fingers through his hair.

"Because after a mission, I can get a little uneasy. It took everything in me not to come over here and fuck the shit out of you, but I didn't want you to think I was using you." He brushed a finger up and down my bare arm. "Sometimes I can't control myself."

"Was it a bad mission?" I mentally smacked myself. Of course it was bad.

"Well, it wasn't a good one." His jaw clenched. "Doing the shit I do takes me a little bit to get past."

"You know you can always use me. I mean if you need me to help make you feel better." I shrugged. "I'm here."

"I was worried how you would feel," his cheeks reddened. "Fuck. I sound like a woman."

I laughed, kissing him softly on the mouth. "Stop being a pussy and worrying about how I feel. I'm a big girl, and if you haven't figured it out by now, I'm not your average woman."

He scoffed. "Oh, I figured that out. I don't know many women who would tell their man exactly what they want in bed."

"You think you're mine, do you?" I teased, poking him in the ribs.

"You know it, baby," he snarled into my neck, pushing me back on the bed.

I giggled, wrapping my arms around his shoulders.

"You just giggled." He frowned. "You never giggle."

"Um …" My cheeks heated.

"Hmm …" His tongue licked up the side of my neck. "I love when you blush."

"I missed you," I whispered.

"And I'm going to spend the rest of the night showing you how much I missed *you*." And he did.

***

A soft knock sounded on my door.

A warm body shifted beside me.

It was the first night Coby had spent the full night with me, allowing me to wake up next to him in the morning.

I kissed his cheek, threw on his t-shirt, and trudged to the door. "Hey," I greeted Creena. "What's up?"

"Your brothers are here."

"What?" My eyes widened. "All of them?"

She nodded, glancing over my head at the bundle in my bed.

"Okay, give me five." I shut the door, pulled off Coby's shirt and quickly got dressed. "Coby," I said, kicking the bed.

"It's too damn early," he grumbled, stretching his thick arms beneath his pillow.

"I agree but you have to get up." This was not good. Not good at fucking all.

"What's wrong?" He sat up, scrubbing a hand up and down his face.

"Nothing," I threw his pants at him. "Nothing at all."

"Then why are you kicking me out of your bed?" He slowly pulled his pants on. Much too slow for my liking.

I huffed. "Can you move any slower? Please, Coby. Get the *fuck* out of my bed."

"What gives, Brogan?" he stood from the bed, leaving the fly of his jeans undone.

My mouth watered at the sight. That delicious V dipped between his legs, sliding beneath his pants.

"Brogan, stop staring at my dick or I'm going to fuck you with it."

My eyes shot up to his. "My brothers are here."

"And …"

"I can't explain it right now. I just need you to leave." A heavy bang sounded on the door, jarring through my body. "Shit."

"Sis, why the fuck are you sleeping so long?" The door shoved open, revealing one of the twins. "We tried calling you." Brox frowned, his gaze passing between Coby and me. "Does Greyson know he's in here?"

"Greyson," Coby repeated. "Why the hell would he care?"

"No reason," I said quickly, shoving Brox back. "I'll be out in a sec."

Brox leaned his head down, his gaze searching my face. "You're in for it, you know that, right, Brogie?"

I sighed, my heart stuttering at the childhood nickname my brothers had given me. "Whatever. Leave."

"Brogan." Coby came up behind me. "Why the *fuck* would Greyson care if I'm here? He's your stepbrother. Right?"

Shit. Shit. Shit.

"Yes." I turned around, pulled open the door and ran out into the hallway.

Coby followed me but thankfully, he kept his mouth shut.

"There's our sister," Blake came toward me and pulled me into a hug. "I heard there was a man in your room."

"Seriously?" I glared at Brox. "Already?"

Blake laughed. "We're twins, Brogie. Remember?" His deep blue eyes twinkled. "He doesn't need to tell me shit and I still know what he's thinking."

Brox clapped a hand on Blake's shoulder. "Yeah, well someone has to look out for our sister."

I shook my head. "I'm fine," I reiterated to both of them. It was funny seeing them together. They were identical twins; the only difference being was their eye color and Brox's hair was a little darker. But at a quick glance, you wouldn't be able to tell them apart.

"Are you two shitheads giving our sister a hard time?" Benny, the oldest, slowly stalked toward me. He nursed his left leg, walking with a slight limp.

"How's the leg?" I asked, wrapping my arms around his hard waist.

"Still missing and still hurts like shit," he tapped the top of his artificial knee. "Solid as a rock, though."

"I'm glad." I kept my arms around him for longer than normal. I had missed him. All of them. But Benny the most. He had joined the military at a young age and got medically discharged when an accident almost left him for dead. After losing his leg from the top of the knee down, he swore to take it easy and settle down. The settling down thing hadn't happened yet.

"Hey …" He pulled back, looking at me intently. "What's up?"

"Nothing." I pasted a smile on my face for added reassurance. "Just missed you guys."

"Are you sure?" He pinched my chin, moving my head back and forth like he could see whatever issue he thought I was having all over my face.

"I'm fine." I stepped out of his embrace. The hairs on the back of my neck stood on end, giving me that familiar warm feeling coursing through my body. I turned around, finding Coby standing a few feet away with his thick arms crossed under his broad chest. Clearing my throat, I took a breath. "Coby, these are my brothers. Brox, Blake, and Benny," I said, pointing at each of them. They greeted each other politely with handshakes and man grunts.

Benny sized him up. Being the oldest, he always did the protecting, making sure all of us were safe and stayed out of trouble. But that didn't always work.

"Where's my favorite girl?" Greyson's voice boomed from the doorway.

My stomach tumbled, my heart picking up speed.

Greyson sidestepped around Benny, glanced at Coby, and came toward me. A wicked grin spread on his face before he pulled me into a hard hug.

"Care to tell me something, Brogan?" he whispered in my ear.

"Nothing to tell," I said, giving him a quick squeeze, and pushed out of his hold.

"Really?" He frowned. "You're lying to me."

"You need to mind your own business, Greyson," I told him. "You're my stepbrother."

"That's not what you used to say when you begged for it," he bit out.

"That was years ago. You need to move on." I shoved out of his grip and took a step toward Coby.

"So, Coby." Greyson stood up. "How do I taste?"

Coby's eyes narrowed.

"You have got to be fucking kidding me," I yelled at Greyson. "Do what you came here for and leave. You got me? Stop being such a dick."

Benny pushed Greyson back a step. "You need to watch what you say about my sister."

"She's my sister too," Greyson threw back.

"That card flew out the window when you fucked her." Benny shoved him.

"She wanted it just as much as I did," Greyson said, stepping in Benny's face.

Brox and Blake both came forward, followed by everyone else. We had an audience, and as much as I wanted to drive my fist through Greyson's face, now was not the time. This was a private matter no matter how much he tried to be an asshole.

"You guys, stop," I pushed myself between Greyson and Benny. "We're not doing this here. Remember what happened last time?"

"Yeah, fucker got a broken nose." Brox smirked, shaking out his hand. "Can I hit him again?"

"No," I cried.

"All right, ladies." Angel cupped Greyson's neck. "How about we have that meeting with my fiancé. That is why you came here, right?"

Greyson grunted.

"Brogan."

I winced at the deep voice in my ear.

"You need to explain yourself before I spank it out of you," Coby demanded, wrapping a strong hand around my upper arm.

"I know." I took a breath. "Greyson, if you're not here on business, I suggest you leave." At that point, Jay came toward us.

"Grey, tell me what you found," she barked, stepping between him and Benny.

I pulled out of Coby's grip and stomped to the room we always used for our club meetings.

Coby shut the door behind him, leaned against it and crossed his arms under his chest. "You and your stepbrother fucked."

I paced back and forth, rubbing the back of my neck. "It's not something I'm proud of."

"Will he be a problem?"

I stopped suddenly. "No." I shook my head. "Whatever he thinks, nothing is going to happen again. We had sex years ago. I was bored. Our parents died a couple months before. I just wanted to feel something."

"Did it help?"

"No," I muttered. "It made me feel worse but I couldn't stop myself. Benny had just joined the military. The twins were away all the time. Greyson and I spent months together. Just him and I. One thing led to another."

"He's in love with you," Coby said, scratching the scruff on his jaw.

"Is it that obvious?" I sighed, slumping onto the couch.

"Do you love him?"

My breath hitched. I never thought about it but … "He's family. I'll always love him like a brother but I won't lie to you. Yes, a part of me loves him just a little more."

"Have you fucked him recently?"

My head snapped up when Coby didn't question my feelings. Who was this man and why the hell was he so damn perfect? "God, no. I've been with other men since him but no one has curbed this itch until …"

"What?"

"You."

***

(Coby)

I got it. It made complete sense why Brogan turned to the one person she trusted to make her feel somewhat normal during a difficult time in her life. I never liked Greyson. He was cocky and thought his shit didn't stink just because he was the president of a motorcycle club. He meant well but I was man enough to admit that I was jealous. I wanted those years with Brogan. I wanted to be close to her like he was. I wish I could have known her when she lost her parents so I could have held her and took care of her.

These thoughts racing through my mind were new and unexpected. I wasn't a man who fell hard and fast but something about Brogan drew me to her. She and I were one in the same.

When I found out Greyson fucked her, even though it had been years before, I had the sudden urge to wrap my hands around his throat. I imagined squeezing until his eyes bulged, smirking down at him until he begged for his life. A life that didn't deserve the air he needed to survive my grip.

It took everything in me not to throw Brogan up against the wall and force myself inside of her until she was coming undone around me. But I didn't. I wouldn't. I was fucked over by a woman once. It wouldn't happen again. No matter how much I enjoyed being with Brogan.

"I thought Greyson was over it." Brogan waved a hand in front of her. "I know I'm irresistible but he needs to move on."

I chuckled, sitting down beside her on the couch. What was with this woman who could make me laugh for no apparent reason at all?

"You're irresistible as *fuck*," I whispered in her ear, wrapping my hand around her throat. I loved controlling her and when she submitted to me.

Her mouth parted, her head falling back against the couch. "Coby."

"I love when you moan my name." I licked up the length of her neck, biting gently at the sensitive spot beneath her ear. "Why do you affect me this way?"

Brogan dug her fingers into my thigh. "Because I'm the only one who can make you feel good."

Fuck me, I loved how confident she was. I had never met a woman who knew what she liked in bed as much as Brogan did.

Brushing my thumb across her bottom lip, I pushed it into her mouth.

She sucked and pulled, much like she did my cock.

A hot shiver raced down my spine. I couldn't get enough of her. She was the beginning to my end, and I had a feeling that our time together had only just started.

CHAPTER ELEVEN

Brogan

I WANTED COBY. Every single thing about him. I wanted to dive into his mind and find out all his dark and dirty secrets. He hadn't shown me much. Only giving me a tidbit of the information that laid on the surface.

But I never expected Greyson to react the way he did. He never confronted the other men I had slept with. What was it about Coby that made him blow up?

It had been a couple of days since I saw Greyson. He left without a goodbye, informing Jay and the other girls that another club had been hit including, yet again, another death.

RUDE

With every fiber of my being, I knew it was Charles Brian and his men. He was proving a point. Letting us know that we may have stopped him once but it won't happen again. Or that was what he liked to think.

We had found out from an informant that Charles had Johnny and his men stir up trouble with us and the guys. But we hadn't heard from them since. I had a feeling it wouldn't be the last we would see of Johnny though. It was just a matter of when.

Coby had stayed away. He didn't call. He didn't text. He didn't email.

My fist landed against the punching bag followed by my knee. I hit. I cursed. I danced.

The more I hit the bag, the more frustrated I became. My muscles burned, aching at the torture I was causing them. But it was the only way I could feel something other than this hurt over being ignored by Coby.

Suddenly, a whoosh hit me square in the chest. I fell back, landing hard on the mat. The breath was knocked out of my lungs as I gasped for the air I wasn't allowed.

A thick fog washed over me, stars dancing in my vision. Yelling and voices sounded around me, but I couldn't make out what they were saying.

Loud screeching pierced my ear drums.

Everything hurt. My skin. My muscles. My bones.

With a shaky hand, I reached up to touch my face when a thick liquid coated my fingers. A red crimson shade dripped from the tips.

A heavy bang sounded again, debris from the ceiling falling around me.

I lifted my arms, shielding myself from getting hit in the head but the impact on my body still hurt like a motherfucker.

I groaned, pushing the pieces of cement and brick off me. "Fuck," I bit out, rolling over onto my side. The world around me tilted and wavered. Impending nausea struck me suddenly. Breathing through it, I rose onto all fours.

"Get everyone out!" I heard someone scream.

"Shit."

"Where's Creena?"

"She's outside."

"Max?"

"She wasn't in the club, thank God."

"What happened?"

"We've been hit."

Shit. Our club was the next one on Charles' list. I wasn't sure how bad the damage was but the way I was feeling, death would have been better.

"Where the fuck is she?"

My heart jumped at the new voice but I still couldn't make out who said what.

"I don't know."

"She was working out."

"Fuck."

"Brogan!"

My chest rose and fell with ragged breath but I couldn't force the words to leave my mouth. *I'm in here. Please help me. I can't move.*

Warm arms wrapped around my middle, lifting me against a hard body. "I got her," the same voice rumbled. "I got you, beautiful girl."

RUDE

The voice was gentle, giving me the solace to finally close my eyes. *Maybe this was how it would end.* And that was when the world went black.

****

"Wake up for me, Brogan. Give me see those beautiful eyes."

I groaned, my head ringing.

"Wake up." A soft mouth covered mine. "Please."

My eyes fluttered open, landing on Coby's handsome face. "Coby," I whispered, my throat raw as sand paper.

"I'm here." He brushed my hair off my forehead. "Do you remember what happened?"

I shook my head.

"The club was hit." He looked behind him, his brows narrowing in the center. "Everyone is waiting out in the hall."

I followed his gaze and that was when I realized that we were in the hospital. "Tell me."

"You're bruised up and you have a couple scratches but it's nothing life threatening," his shoulders relaxed. "You're going to be sore for a couple of days but it won't feel any worse than when we workout hard." Or he fucked me rough but those words never left his mouth. His eyes darkened.

Attempting to sit up, my arms shook beneath my weight. "I want to go home."

Coby let out a sigh. "There is no home anymore, Brogan. Not until the club gets fixed up."

"What?" My eyes widened. I pinched the bridge of my nose, attempting to ward off the impending migraine.

Coby kissed my forehead. "We'll figure out something."

We?

Just when I was about to ask what the hell he was talking about, everyone filed into the room.

I was sure that more than a couple visitors were not allowed but at that moment, I didn't overly care.

The loud chatter pierced into my brain.

"Shut up," Coby barked, silencing the room.

"Someone tell me what's going on." I sat up straighter, holding onto Coby's arm.

He shifted his weight, sitting beside me on the bed.

No one seemed to notice. If they did, they didn't anything.

I was a fool to think that I could hide my feelings for Coby from my sisters. "Someone. Talk."

"The club got hit hard," Jay ground out. "It's not livable and it's going to take weeks for it to be fixed up."

"We'll start on it tomorrow," Asher interrupted. "But even with all the help, there's no way we can make it so you ladies can live in it for at least another month or so. Anything we can salvage, we'll put away in storage."

A grumbled response sounded around the room.

"My bike," I gasped. "Is she okay?"

"Yes, baby," Coby muttered. "She's fine."

A breath left me on a whoosh. "Good." I tapped his hand. "Good. Anything else?"

"Max will continue staying with Jay and me," Angel said. "I don't want any of you by yourselves until this shit is handled."

"We can meet up at the tattoo shop," Jay added. "Saves everyone having to drive out into the country.

Vince is staying there while his place gets fumigated since Violet moved."

Vince. I frowned. Oh, right. Stone. Jay had been the only one to call him by his first name.

"Okay, that's settled." Angel nodded to Creena. "What about you?"

"She can stay with Asher and me," Meeka stated. "Brogan can as well."

"Brogan's staying with me," Coby said, his face impassive.

"Are you sure?" Angel asked, raising an eyebrow.

"Did I fucking stutter?" Coby grabbed my hand. "I said she's staying with me."

"Well …" Angel looked between us.

My cheeks heated.

"How come I am always the last to know anything?" Angel shook his head.

"You have other things on the mind, baby." Jay kissed his cheek. "Coby, you keep my sister safe."

Coby nodded once, squeezing my hand. "I will."

***

(Coby)

I had no intention of letting our group know that there was something going on between Brogan and me. I was a private man. I wasn't even into public displays of affection but knowing that Brogan could be far away from me, I jumped on the chance to have her where I could see and touch her but most importantly, take care of her. Even if she hadn't been the crossfire of the newest explosion, I would have wanted her home with me.

A couple hours later and the doctor gave the go ahead to discharge Brogan. I reassured him that she would be taken care of and that we would be back if anything happened.

While I drove us out of the small town, I glanced over at her sitting in the passenger seat. With her hand tight in mine, I could finally relax. After seeing her in the rubble, bruised and bloodied, it took me back to a time where I had feelings I couldn't control. Pain. Heartache. So much death. I could still hear the screams.

"Where are we going?" Brogan asked, sitting up in the seat. She winced but no complaints about pain left her mouth.

"I'm taking you to my home."

"Your home?" she turned to me. "I thought you lived with Dale."

"I do," I told her. "When I'm in town. But I also live in the city."

"Really?" she frowned. "What else don't I know about you, Porter?"

A shiver shot straight to my dick. God, I loved when she called me by my last name. "Many things, little one."

She harrumphed, crossing her arms under chest. "You know everything about me, yet I know shit about you."

I laughed. "Are you fucking kidding me right now?"

"What the hell is your problem?" she snapped.

"Woman, you know more shit about me than anyone." Even my fucking wife. I forced those thoughts out of my head. I would not think about her.

She ruined everything. My life. *Me*. It was *her* fault I turned out the way I did.

"Well, I find that hard to believe when you hardly talk except to tell me what to do when we're fucking."

I gripped the steering wheel. "What went on in my life before you is not important."

"How is it not, Coby?" she huffed. "I can't deal with this shit right now. Why did you even bring me with you? Is it just to control me and fuck me whenever you feel like it?"

Without even thinking, I pulled the vehicle to the side of the road. The tires screeched, the car coming to a halt as horns blared past us.

"Listen to me good, little girl," I turned to her and pinched her chin, forcing her to look up at me. "I've led a hard fucking life. I don't want to talk about it because I don't want it to taint what we have. You got me? I've been burned. Fucked over. Broken down into nothing, and I only had myself to bring me back up. The military is all that I have. I live for it. Breathe it. It's my fucking life. I will tell you when I *want* to tell you. Not before. Understood?"

Brogan glared, shoving her head from my grip. "I like you but you're being a big asshole right now."

I grunted. It was what I was known for. Quiet. Brooding. Blah blah, fucking blah.

"Be patient with me," I said, brushing my thumb over her bottom lip.

"I've been patient, Coby."

Her words struck a chord with me. She *had* been patient. More patient than most women would have been. I needed to get it together before I lost her too.

CHAPTER TWELVE

Brogan

COBY WAS AN asshole. But no matter how much of a dick he could be, it attracted me to him even more. There was something really wrong with me.

When we pulled up in front of a large apartment building, I couldn't believe that Coby actually lived in the city. Especially in one of the most expensive condominiums out there.

"You live here?" I asked, gazing out the window.

"I own it." Coby grabbed my hand and kissed my knuckles.

"You own it," I tested the words on my tongue. Somehow, I was not surprised. The man had secrets and was closed like a vault. Of course he owned the building. It only made sense. God, I was losing it.

"I inherited it from my grandfather. He owned this line of condos with some hotels and restaurants as well."

"Really?" My eyes widened.

"I'm his only grandson, so when he died, everything was put in my name." Coby rolled down his window when we pulled up to a gate guarded by two security men.

"Mr. Porter," the young man greeted. "You in for the night?"

"Yes." Coby gripped my hand.

"Have a good evening." The man motioned to his partner, indicating for us to drive through.

Coby led us down into a parking garage.

"That's some high-tech security," I said in awe.

"In my line of work, you can never be too safe." Coby pulled into a parking spot a moment later, excited the vehicle and came around to my side of the car.

What was I getting myself into? Coby was rich. I realized that I hardly knew anything about him.

"Come on, little one," Coby gently pulled me from the car. "Stop thinking so much." He petted a hand over my head, kissing me softly on the mouth.

I sighed, needing to wrap myself in his warmth but I was still pissed that he wouldn't tell me anything about himself.

My body ached with each step to the elevator as memories of what had happened that night reigned full force into my mind. I could have been killed. We all could have. Oh, God. My heart started racing. My breathing picked up.

"Hey." Coby cupped my cheeks. "Look at me."

"I ... I ..." I gasped for breath. "I almost died."

"But you didn't," he said, his voice firm. "Now breathe, Brogan."

Squeezing my eyes shut, I shook my head. I had been through so much in my life but I had never come close to dying. I toyed with death, danced around it like I was invincible. It wasn't right, but I couldn't stop myself.

"Brogan." Coby gave my body a gentle shake. "Look at me."

My eyes snapped open, landing on his handsome face.

He breathed, slow and deep.

I mirrored his movements, gripping his hands tight in my own.

"That's my girl." He kissed my forehead, letting his lips linger. "Let's get you comfortable." He wrapped his arm around my shoulders, holding me beside him when we reached the elevator.

I snuggled into his side, gripping his shirt for dear life. I had always been one to take care of myself but every now and again, even the strongest person needed help. Coby made me feel safe. Like I could do anything in this world. I felt strong when I was with him.

When we entered the elevator, Coby pushed a key into a slot and pressed the button with a P marked beside it.

"Why are you in the military if you own all of this?" I asked, praying that he wouldn't close up on me again.

"Because I need to be in control. This was all my grandfather's work. He hired me on at a young age and showed me the basics of how to run a business but it wasn't enough. I sold a lot of the businesses he left to me but I still manage a couple."

"You're a man of many talents, Porter," I said, trying to lighten the solemn mood.

"Not enough apparently," he glanced down at me. "Put me in the field and I can hide within a matter of seconds. You won't see me until I want you to. But when it comes to talking and this," he waved a hand between us. "I know jack shit."

"I'm sorry for pressuring you," I blurted, my cheeks heating.

"No," he pushed a strand of hair behind my ear. "I need to be pushed sometimes but I also need you to remember that I push back."

"I don't expect any less from you."

We stared at each other for what felt like hours, gazing into each other's eyes. My heart thumped, skipping several beats before I looked away.

Coby cleared his throat.

The elevator came to a stop when we reached the top floor.

"After you, little one," Coby said, his voice rough.

I took a breath, stepping out into a long hall.

He grabbed my hand, holding it tight in his and led us to a double set of doors at the end of the hallway. "My apartment takes up this whole floor. No one else can come up here without my key. You're safe, Brogan."

I nodded, my body relaxing at that.

"My home is your home," he whispered in my ear, unlocking the door to his place.

We had only known each other for a couple months and now I was living with him. *No. I was staying with him. Until I found my own place and got my stuff back. If anything was saved that is. Oh, God, what if I had nothing? No clothes or books. What if everything was destroyed in the explosion?* My eyes burned, my throat constricting as realization dawned on me.

"Coby." A sob escaped me.

"Shit." He pulled me against him. "It's okay. Let it out."

I cried into his chest, wrapping myself around him. "I have nothing," I hiccupped. "Everything is gone."

"You don't know that yet. But you have your life," he tilted my head back, staring intently into my eyes. "You're alive, Brogan. That's all that matters. All of you got out safe."

"I'm going to kill those fuckers who did this."

"There's my girl," Coby smirked. "But not if I get to them first."

"I think we'll all have a hand in destroying them," I muttered, stepping out of his embrace. Kicking off my shoes, I slid my toes into the soft plush grey carpet in his living room.

Gazing around the large room, I wasn't sure what I was expecting to see in Coby's home but this was not it. It was clean, bright, and modern. I took Coby for a laid-back kind of guy but it seemed that everything had its spot. Is that how he looked at me as well? I had my spot in his life. Would he get bored of me and toss me away like trash? God, what the hell was I thinking coming here with him?

"Bathroom is down that hallway," Coby stated, his eyes burning into me.

I hugged myself, nodding. "Come with me?" I didn't want to be alone. Something had switched between us over the past couple of hours. He had become darker, moodier, and me? I became more attracted to him.

I sighed, rubbing my hands up and down my arms.

"This is my bedroom." Coby pushed open the door, turning on the light. "Anything you need is in here. You're tiny but I'm sure you could fit into my boxers." He winked.

I smiled up at him. "I just want to wash tonight off me."

"Understood."

While Coby headed to the en-suite bathroom, I stayed back and scoped out his room. A large king size bed sat against the far wall. Floor to ceiling windows were hidden behind black curtains. Red throw pillows sat atop the mattress. Did he bring other women here? I imagined him on his bed, tangled in the satin sheets until he was spent and exhausted. Maybe he spent the nights here by himself. Did he touch his own body?

A wave of heat washed over me at the dirty thoughts that slid their way into my mind. All I could picture was Coby's large hand wrapped around the base of his cock.

"What are you thinking about?"

I jumped at the deep voice in my ear, my cheeks heating. "Nothing."

"You're looking at my bed. Are you imagining me in it?" Coby wrapped his arm around me, sliding his hand down my back. "You had a rough night, but yet you're still thinking those dirty as sin thoughts. Aren't you?"

"You don't know what I'm thinking," I muttered, gripping his shirt tight between my fingers.

"I don't need to know exactly what those thoughts are but I can see the heat in your eyes," he kissed the corner of my mouth. "As much as I want to spend the night fucking you in my bed, you need your rest."

Disappointment fluttered in my belly. "Being with you will make me feel better."

He chuckled. "I won't leave you and I'll take care of your beautiful pussy later. Right now? You need a bath."

****

(Coby)

Denying Brogan access to my cock was the hardest thing I had ever done. She pouted. Begging me with her eyes. But she needed rest. The doctors gave her a free bill of health but it didn't mean she should spend the night in the throes of passion.

I helped Brogan out of her clothes, leaving her standing naked before me.

Her tanned, toned skin was marred by bruises and cuts. Thankfully, that was the only damage. She would be sore for a couple of days but it wasn't anything life threatening. I didn't know what I would do if that were the case.

I caught her staring at my bed, chewing her bottom lip.

"Ask me," I told her an hour later while we were in the bathtub.

"Ask you what?" She played with the bubbles, letting them drip off her fingers.

"I saw you checking out my bed." I kissed her neck. "Ask me."

"Has there been anyone else here?"

"You mean, have I brought another woman home and fucked her in my bed."

"Yes." Her cheeks reddened, the flush traveling down between her breasts.

"No. You are the first." I brushed my thumb back and forth over the base of her throat.

"Can I ask why or will you shut me out?"

I wanted to laugh. I wanted to tell her that I wasn't this dark and brooding man. I wanted to tell her that I didn't get married at a young age only to have my wife run away with my child. I wanted to tell her all those things but it wouldn't be true.

"I didn't want to taint my home by a woman's wrath," I muttered, leaning my chin on top of Brogan's head. "This apartment is mine and mine only. It doesn't have a woman's touch. It's cold and modern, and it's fucking mine."

"Um ... well, someone's a little bitter." Brogan sat forward, turning in my arms. "I had a crush on this guy in high school. My brothers found out and scared the guy off. It happened so many times to me over the years that I just gave up and started having one-night stands instead."

"No serious relationship for you?"

Brogan scoffed, tapping the side of her head. "I've been accused of being crazy my whole life. Who wants a girlfriend who tortures people for a living?"

I did. Clearing my throat, I rubbed the scruff on my jaw. *Crazy.* It was a horrible word. Brogan wasn't crazy, not in the sense some would think. Being in the military, you see things. Most come out of it needing professional help. They can't control the demons.

"I don't think you're crazy," I told her, running my finger down her bare arm. "I think we all have our own shit to deal with. If that makes us crazy, well, then so am I."

She smiled. "Thank you. Just … thank you."

***

(Brogan)

Coby didn't think I was crazy. Well that was good to know. Too bad the rest of the people I knew didn't think that way. They never said but they didn't have to. I could see the judgement in their eyes every time I came up from the basement or brought a guy home. Sex was the only way I could silence the noise in my head.

After the bath, Coby gave me a pair of his boxer shorts and a t-shirt. I threw on the shirt but not the shorts as I wanted to feel his hands on me. I figured wearing something only on top might be a big enough hint. He had told me to rest but I couldn't. I tossed and turned, mulling over the last couple of hours in my head.

Coby had never brought a woman home. Not to this apartment. Everything in me told me that he had been fucked over by a female but I didn't know how. There had been rumors going around the group but no one said for sure what his issue was.

Sometime during the night, I had woken, restless and unsure. It was almost three in the morning but no sign of Coby anywhere.

I left the bedroom, sore and stiff. My bones felt like they were grinding against each other, fighting for their place inside of my body.

"Coby?" I called out, trudging down the long hallway.

RUDE

A deep voice sounded from the kitchen so I headed there. The closer I got, the clearer the words became.

"It's too soon," Coby said. "I know."

He must have been talking on the phone. I shouldn't have eavesdropped but the tremor in his voice concerned me.

"I'm not sure. We leave in about a month but no date has been set. Yeah. She can stay here. I know. I never thought I would live with a woman again."

Again?

"No. I know she's nothing like her. No, I don't miss her. I don't miss anything about her," Coby growled. "She was a fucking whore but she was carrying my baby."

Baby? Holy shit on a stick.

What the hell was going on?

I spun on my heel, heading back to his bedroom. My hands shook. I didn't know much about Coby but he had a kid? That was a big fucking deal.

A throat cleared from the doorway.

Turning slowly, I found Coby standing a few feet away. A dark shadow slid over his face, forcing my stomach to drop.

"How much did you hear?"

Too much.

"I should leave." I grabbed my clothes and headed to the bathroom. "I shouldn't be here." I was rambling but my thoughts couldn't focus.

"Brogan." Coby blocked my path, wrapping his fingers around my arm. "You can't leave."

"I ... I ..." I stammered. God, this man. What was it about him that made me lose all train of thought? "You have a baby."

Coby's jaw clenched, his eyes darkening to the point of black. "No. Not anymore I don't."

"Not anymore?" My heart jumped. "Oh, God, I'm sorry."

"It's nothing for you to be sorry about." Coby's voice was hard. "But I am not talking about this. You shouldn't have been listening."

"I couldn't sleep. I was looking for you."

Coby pushed me back, pulling the clothes from my arms. "Yeah? Why? Did you want something, Brogan? Were you looking for me to fuck you?"

"Yes." I glared up at him. "I wanted to feel better. I knew you could do that but you're standing here being a fucking asshole like you always are because I accidentally overheard your conversation. If it was so fucking private, maybe you shouldn't have been out in the open."

"Little girl, I will remind you that this is *my* fucking home. I will talk where I want and when I want."

"Then don't get mad at me if I accidentally walk in on your conversation," I threw back at him. "God, I'm so stupid." I stormed out of the bedroom. If he wasn't going to give me my clothes, then I would leave wearing the shirt he leant me.

"Where the hell do you think you're going?"

"I'm leaving, Coby. I'm sick of your moody shit."

"You're not leaving." He came up behind me, grabbed my arm, and spun me around. "I won't let you leave." Holding me against his hard body, his hands trailed down my back before cupping my ass. "Please.

My heart gave a start at the desperation in his voice. I didn't know what was going on but his mood changed suddenly, and it made my head spin. "Coby."

"Please. You can't leave." He pushed his face into the crook of my neck, inhaling deep. His body relaxed.

"What is going on with you?" I asked, letting him hold me but not returning the hug either.

"It's the anniversary of their death," he mumbled in my ear.

"Their death?"

Coby released me, heading to the couch. "My wife committed suicide. She was pregnant. She took my baby with her. And as much as it pains me to say this, I've never forgiven her."

***

(Coby)

The words left my lips, taking away the control I had fought so hard for these years. I finally told someone about her. The monster who destroyed me and everything we had worked toward.

"Coby," Brogan knelt in front of me, taking my hands in hers. "Tell me what happened."

Under normal circumstances, I would have thrown her over my knee for being so demanding. But I knew it needed to be said. I wasn't sure how much I could get off my chest but maybe a couple words here and there would help.

"When I was a child, I was diagnosed with bipolar," Brogan confessed. "But that also depends on which doctor you speak to." She winked, trying to lighten the mood.

Speak, Coby. Tit for tat. But I didn't. I couldn't. No one knew except for Dale. That's what happened when you get drunk and spill your secrets.

"What happened?" Brogan asked, determined to get the answers she was looking for.

I brushed the back of my knuckles down her cheek. "I fell in love."

CHAPTER THIRTEEN

Brogan

HIS WIFE COMMITTED suicide, taking their baby along with them. My chest ached for Coby. What he had gone through made my problems look teeny tiny.

I now understood why it was hard for him to talk about it. Instead of asking more questions, I sat beside him on the couch, holding him as best I could while we watched TV. Neither of us were really watching it, though. We got lost in our thoughts, traveling to a past that we never had any control of.

Was I mentally ill? I wasn't sure. I never went back to the doctors to find out.

A phone chimed.

Coby reached for his cell, his gaze moving over the small screen.

"Angel wants to meet up in a couple of days. He'll let us know the location when the time comes."

"A couple of days?" I asked, looking over Coby's shoulder at the text.

"Yeah, something about they want everyone to take some time to deal with this shit," Coby grumbled.

"Okay." I took a breath, hoping for the best that my next question wouldn't cause Coby to lose his temper. "Why did you bring me here?"

Coby stiffened beside me, rubbing the back of his neck. "I like you, Brogan. When I'm not with you, I miss you like I've never missed anything before. But I can't put a label on it yet. I need time."

I nodded. "I like you too," I whispered.

"Be patient with me." He brushed his nose up the side of my neck and pushed me onto my back. His heated gaze roamed down the length of my body. "I can't begin to tell you what you do to me. I don't talk. Never have. But with you, it comes easy. Even though I don't talk about my past, I have no problem talking about my future with you."

I cupped his cheek, brushing my thumb over his bottom lip but I couldn't say anything. I didn't know what to say to him. All I knew was that I would be there for him. Even if whatever this was that was happening between us didn't grow into something more. Right now, it was sex, and I would take advantage of that.

***

(Coby)

"So, you and Brogan, huh?"

My back stiffened at Angel's question. It had been a couple days since the explosion at the club and all of us were finally meeting up. We had decided on a central location and met up at Jay's tattoo shop. Business had been slow so she closed it up while we sorted out this shit.

"It's about time," Asher chimed in, stretching his arms over his head. "I've seen the way you look at her."

"You don't know shit," I told him, taking a long swig of my water. I loved my brothers but I wasn't about to tell them anything when it came to Brogan.

"Coby has been moping around the apartment for years," Dale joked. "He finally got laid by the pussy he couldn't have."

I smacked him across the head. "Respect, my brother. Or I'll smack you harder next time."

"Fucker." Dale rubbed the spot I hit. "You know it's true."

Maybe so. Brogan was the one thing I had craved even before meeting her but I wasn't about to admit that to the man who couldn't control his own actions when it came to women.

"Are you happy?" Angel asked. He didn't know my history, and a part of me felt bad for that but none of us talked about the shit we'd gone through before meeting the Harlots.

"No," I admitted. "I won't be happy until Charles Brian dies by my fingertips."

Dale chuckled. "That's my brother. Listen, if you fuckers want to go track him down …" He waggled his eyebrows. "I'm game. I need something other than sex."

I knew the feeling. "All of those women not cutting it anymore?"

"Fuck you," Dale muttered, crossing his thick arms under his chest.

"Maybe you should man up and approach the one woman who won't put up with your shit," Stone suggested, taking a swig of his beer.

Dale shoved to his feet, forcing the chair to fall back. "Listen, asshole—"

"All right," I grabbed him by the back of the neck. "Let's take a walk."

"No," he shoved out of my grip. "All of you can judge me but I know you've done your own shit to push women away. Leave my situation out of it."

"Let's take a walk," I said, my voice firm.

Dale stomped out of the makeshift kitchen.

"Something bad will happen before he gets his shit together," Stone said. "I've seen it before."

"I love you, man, and I respect you, but when it comes to Dale, you don't know shit." I followed Dale outside, the cool night air caressing my skin. "Dale?"

"I'm an asshole," Dale muttered, leaning against the brick wall.

"We all have our moments." I stood beside him, mirroring his pose.

"I don't know what I'm doing. When I muster up the courage to talk to Max, words come out of my mouth before I can even think about them and then we have a fight. God, I'm such a dick." His voice grew thick. "I'm scared."

"I know."

He slid down the wall, landing on his ass. "I want to be with her but a part of me doesn't. What does that say about me?"

I sat beside him, stretching my legs out in front of me. "It means you're human."

"I'm not ready to be a father."

"Most people aren't."

"Do you think about her?" Dale asked, leaning his arms on his bent knees.

"No, but I think about the baby she took from me."

"Does Brogan know?"

"Yes, but not everything. I have the same problem you do. She tries to get me to open up and then I explode for no reason at all."

"It fucking sucks, doesn't it?"

I chuckled. "Yes. It does."

***

(Brogan)

"Can you be in love with someone and hardly know anything about them at all?" I asked Meeka, curling my feet under me.

"Um …" Her eyes widened with excitement.

"Don't." I pointed at her. "I'm not labeling anything yet. I'm just asking." I didn't want to think about my feelings for Coby and jinx it. We had become close, even more then it just being sex but we needed to take our time. I had a jealous stepbrother to worry about and Coby had his past.

"I think the heart wants what it wants," Jay chimed in, handing me a water. She sat down beside me on the couch in the waiting area of the tattoo shop and rubbed her lower belly.

"Are you going to make us wait or are you going to admit it finally?" I asked, nodding toward her stomach.

She smiled, her cheeks reddening. "Yeah. I guess it's time, isn't it?"

Meeka giggled.

"I'm pregnant and scared as shit." She laughed. "Angel is more excited than I am."

I glanced at Max.

"I'm fine," she said, catching my stare. "Don't worry about me. I want Jay to be happy. God knows, she deserves it. Both her and Angel do."

"Thank you," Jay whispered, her eyes glossing over.

"Wow. This pregnancy is going to turn you into an actual human being," Creena joked, laughing.

"Shut up," Jay pouted. "I am not a human."

"Seriously?" I raised an eyebrow. "Pregnancy hormones have you losing your mind too?"

She laughed. "I guess so." She took a deep breath. "I love you girls. I don't say it enough."

"Have you talked to your sister?" Max asked, taking a sip from her water bottle.

"Yes. We talk every chance we can. I miss her but I understand that she needs to lay low for a while." Jay sat up, massaging her lower back.

"You have pain already?" I asked, helping her by kneading my fingers into the tight muscles of her tail bone.

"Yeah. We went to the doctors, and I'm almost four and a half months."

"Are you sure you're not further along?" Max asked, pointing at the small bump of Jay's lower abdomen.

"Um …" Jay shrugged. "The doctor mentioned twins because of Violet and I but I thought it skipped a generation. And since we don't know anything about Angel's history, we're only guessing right now."

Angel had been in foster care his whole childhood. I couldn't imagine how difficult it was to not know where you came from. My brothers drove me nuts but they were a part of me. I would be completely lost without them.

"Either way, as long as you and the baby or babies are healthy, that's all we care about." Creena took a swig of her beer. "How does it feel not being able to drink?"

Jay snorted. "It fucking sucks."

We all laughed, enjoying the somber mood of not talking about Charles Brian even though I knew we were all thinking about him.

At that moment, the guys appeared. Asher pulled Meeka from the chair she was sitting on and sat on it himself before lowering her to his lap. She kissed his cheek, wrapping his arm around her waist.

Angel leaned over Jay, kissed her hard on the mouth, and sat beside her on the couch.

She blushed, smacking his hands away from her hips but gave up after a couple seconds. Giggling, she leaned into his side.

He kissed her head, whispering something in her ear.

She nodded.

He grinned, shaking his head.

His gaze met mine. He gave me a wink before looking back at his fiancée.

My neck heated at being caught staring but I couldn't help it. Two of my sisters were finally happy. After all the shit they had been through, it was about damn time.

"Are you staring at your friends?" Coby whispered in my ear, running his hand over my lower back.

"Yes." I didn't even realize he had sat beside me. "I'm happy for them."

"Me too." He nodded toward Dale who stood off to the side and Max who looked pale. She sat on the other couch, holding her lower belly. I knew she hadn't been feeling well the past couple of days. I just prayed everything was fine with the baby.

"Have you talked to Dale?" I asked Coby, enjoying the feel of his hands on me.

"Yeah, but that shit takes time," he grunted. "He's more closed up than I am."

"Is that even possible?" I teased, poking him in the ribs.

He grinned, grabbing my hand, and kissed my knuckles.

My breath caught in my throat at the public display of affection. Coby wasn't that type of man. I knew it even before we started sleeping together. "Coby."

He winked.

"Have you heard anything from the insurance company?" Meeka asked Jay.

"Insurance should get back to us in a couple days," Jay explained. "I'm just happy that we're safe. As much as it annoys the shit out of me, it could have been worse."

Several grunts and sounds in agreement went around the room.

"Has Greyson said anything? Did he contact his resources?" Jay asked me.

"I haven't talked to him in a couple of days," I confessed, shifting in my seat. "But I'll call him. I know he's still in town."

"Call him now," Jay demanded. "I'm getting antsy."

Coby's eyes burned into the side of my head but there was nothing I could do about that now. No one needed to know that Grey was an issue in my personal life.

Doing as I was told, I dialed Greyson's number.

"So, you're talking to me now?" Grey answered almost immediately.

"I'm not calling over that," I snapped. "The club got blown to shit." I explained what had happened and that we all got out safely but the club wasn't livable in its current condition.

Greyson let out a string of curses. "Fine."

I placed him on speaker phone and put the phone on the table. "Go ahead."

"I've been dealing with shit in New York," he explained. "Even though I'm not there, people like to think I have something to do with the explosions."

"How could you have something to do with it?" Jay asked, sitting forward. "Or are you telling me that you did? If I find out—"

"Fuck. It wasn't me," Grey cursed again. "Listen. My sources are telling me that this is some underground shit that's going on. Charles Brian is doing everything he can to make it so this doesn't point back to him."

"It has to be him," Angel countered. "He's pissed because he got caught. He took my brother and his fucking girlfriend. I'll end him before he even knows what hit him."

"And to add that he knew Vega," Dale pointed out. "All of them need to go down. All of the customers, every single bastard that has something to do with this business."

"We need to get to the top," Stone added. "This isn't our job but it's hit too close to home for us to stop."

"Too many people have died already." Jay shook her head. "I'm not letting anyone else get hurt or worse."

"We'll stop this, baby," Angel reassured her.

"How? We have no idea how this even began," she cried. "Fuck, I hate not having control," Angel scoffed.

"Shut up." Jay playfully pushed him. "You know what I'm talking about." She turned back to the phone. "Greyson, you need to help me out here. I need to avenge my sisters.

"You're not avenging shit," Angel argued. "But, Grey, you need to contact all of your sources."

"I have my guy looking into things as well," Coby added.

"Really?" Dale raised an eyebrow. "Since when do you have a guy?"

"Since always." Coby shrugged. "You just never asked and we haven't needed him until now."

I stifled a laugh, enjoying his honesty.

"Okay." Angel frowned. "Who is this guy then?"

"He's an old friend. I should have told you this before but we've been kind of distracted. The leader of this shit has a sister. Zane and Tina Birtch. She's the woman who attacked Jay," Coby explained. "They're close."

"In more ways than one." I shivered.

"Fuck me." Stone rubbed the back of his neck. "So, you're telling us that this woman is the sister to the front runner of this organization and they're more than just siblings?"

"Yes." Coby nodded. "But we still don't know if it's him or her who is the leader in all this shit. The sister has Daddy issues. It's your typical story of the children being abused who grow up to be psychopaths. My guy is still looking into it further."

"I'll start looking into that as well," Greyson added. "If there are two of them, someone is about to slip up and reveal things they never meant to. Do we know where Charles is?"

"He ran and hasn't made himself known yet but we know that he's the one who is controlling these explosions," Asher said. "When we catch him, I'm going to end that fucker."

"Not if I get to him first."

"I can't wait to watch the life leave his eyes."

"I'm going to rip off every piece that touched me."

Everyone spoke at once, agreeing in the end that Charles needed to die. I would give my left arm to have him in my chair but I didn't say it out loud. These people meant everything to me but I had a feeling that they wouldn't appreciate my honesty.

"Are we all good with staying where we are?" Angel asked, voicing his leadership role like always.

We all said yes and that we would check in when we could as well, letting each other know that we were safe.

"Are you good with living with me?" Coby whispered in my ear.

A hot shiver raced down my spine. "Yes."

"Hmm … that makes me hard," he purred.

"Coby," I groaned.

He chuckled. "Let me take you home, little one."

CHAPTER FOURTEEN

Coby

BROGAN WAS GOING to be the death of me. Her strength. Her determination. Her need to make me open up would bring me to my knees, and I would submit willingly. I wanted to give her all of me. To show her that I was a good man or that I at least had good parts. Everyone had a dark side to them. Whether you acted on it or not was up to you. In my line of work, that darkness needed to come out every so often. It needed to be shown to these evil bastards that there was something way worse than them. But before they could comprehend that, they would die at the tip of my rifle.

RUDE

It had been a couple of days since the meeting at Jay's tattoo shop. We all met up at the club, doing our best to fix it up as quickly as possible. The girls cleaned, throwing the debris in the trash while my brothers and I put up walls.

Brogan worked hard on the blue prints, deciding that it was time for a change anyway.

Every time I walked by her, a knowing glance would pass between us. I had spent the night before inside of her, wrapped in her warmth until we both passed out from utter exhaustion. It was a perfect way to go to sleep. But no matter how wonderful our time together was, I knew it wouldn't last. None of my relationships did because I would get scared and push women away. I was a fucking pussy.

"How are you doing, brother?" Dale asked, coming up beside me, and clapped a hand on my shoulder.

I grunted in response.

He laughed. "That good, huh?"

"How are *you* doing?"

He frowned. "Same old shit. Max won't talk to me, and I'm still an asshole." He shrugged. "Nothing I can do about it."

"Do you believe that?" I picked up a slab of wood and placed it on the cutting board. "Have you tried talking to her?"

Dale helped me line up the wood to the saw. "I've waited too long."

I looked over my shoulder to where Max was talking to Jay. Her pregnant belly had become more pronounced over the past week or so. It pained me for the baby I missed.

My chest tightened. Clearing my throat, I glanced back at Dale.

"Yeah," he sighed. "I know."

I didn't even have to say anything and he knew what I was thinking. I needed the next mission we were going on to come fast. Although I would miss Brogan, I needed to shoot something and do what I did best.

A sudden rumble of an engine sounded from far away, the noise becoming louder as it neared the club.

I recognized the bike as it pulled up into the parking lot, followed by a black SUV.

Greyson parked his motorcycle, climbed off it, and stretched.

Brogan's brothers stepped out of the vehicle, all four of them coming toward us.

My fists clenched at my sides, needing to punch that smug look off Greyson's face.

He caught my stare and headed to where Brogan was standing. Before she could protest, he had her in his arms, his hands a little too close to her ass.

She pushed out of his hold, glaring up at him, and I took that as my cue.

"Coby." Angel clapped a hand on my shoulder, stopping me. "We need him."

"He's an asshole," I growled.

"Yes, he is, but he's Brogan's family, and he's helping us end this shit." Angel placed both hands on my shoulders, gripping them tight. "You tell us to think first before we act. Take your own advice, Coby."

Fuck.

I took several calming breaths before I nodded.

Angel let me go but continued to watch me as I headed to Brogan and Greyson. The bastard needed to be taught a lesson when it came to touching my woman.

My woman.

RUDE

Fuck yeah. My woman.

***

(Brogan)

"You need to stop touching me," I snapped at Greyson. "Just because you can't have me doesn't mean you need to be a dick about it."

Greyson chuckled, his eyes darkening. "Yes, it does. You think Coby can give you what you need?"

"That is none of your business." I glared up at him. "I love you but as a *brother*. You need to get that through your thick head."

"What's going on here?" Benny demanded, coming toward us, followed by Brox and Blake.

"Nothing," I bit out. "We're just having a friendly chat, aren't we, Greyson?"

His brows narrowed. "Yeah, sure." He looked over my head, the corners of his lips turning up into a wicked smirk.

My heart stuttered. I knew who was behind me without even looking. I didn't have to. My body was already in-tune with Coby's, like it knew where he was before my brain was able to catch up.

"Well now, isn't it the man who ruined it all?" Greyson gripped my shoulders, spinning me around. "Does he take your breath away like I did?"

My jaw clenched. "You need to stop this or I will let him do what he wants to you."

"All right, Grey." Benny pulled Greyson away from me. "This shit ends now or I will let the twins after you."

"I'm going to go work on my bike," I mumbled. "At least that didn't blow up." I headed to my baby, my girl, the only thing in my life that didn't make me question everything I knew. I walked up to the beauty, grateful it didn't get caught in the explosion. It was a little dusty but other than that, it was perfectly fine. Minus the parts I had to fix from years of wear and tear.

I sat on the ground, grabbed the cloth from my pocket and went to work on shining the beautiful machine. I could spend hours waxing and polishing her, making the blood-red paint glow in the sun. The white skull on the fuel tank stared up at me. I remembered the day it had been painted. Jay had designed it for me and Max had done the painting, giving me a piece of their art forever.

I heard his boots on the gravel before he came to me.

I waited.

"What's wrong, little one?" Coby asked, sitting beside me.

"Everything." I shrugged. "I'm getting impatient."

"About Charles?"

I nodded.

"Are you sure that's what really is bothering you?"

"What do you want me to say, Coby? That my stepbrother is a dickhead and should mind his own business about what goes on in my life?"

"He *should* mind his own business but I get where he's coming from."

My mouth dropped. "Excuse me?"

"I get it. I don't like the guy but I understand. He's in love with you. It's not something that one can easily get over."

I huffed. "Well, he needs to, because I don't want him. We had one summer together. We were kids. It was stupid of us to even start sleeping together in the first place."

"Did you lose your virginity to him?"

My head whipped around. "Why do you want to know? So you can be more pissed and act all alpha that it wasn't you who fucked me first?"

Coby only stared at me.

"Yeah, that's what I thought," I grumbled. "Between the two of you, I don't know who's more possessive."

"I'm only possessive when it comes to something that belongs to me. You don't belong to him. You never have."

"And I belong to you?" I scoffed. "Come on, Coby. We both know that this isn't going to last."

"Why do you say that? Are you fucking psychic now, Brogan?" Coby gripped my arm, pulling me against him.

"No." I shoved out of his grip. "I'm being realistic. I have commitment issues and so do you. We're fucking and that's it. Nothing more."

He stared down at me, the muscles in his jaw clenching.

"That's what I thought," I went back to polishing my bike. "You know I'm right."

"Baby, you don't know shit," he snarled in my ear. "I wanted you and now you're mine. You can deny it all you want. You want more. You want all of me."

"And you're going to give me all of you?" I shook my head. "Come on, Coby. You're not that dumb."

"Listen, little girl." He snaked his hand around my throat. "I'll give you one chance to stop being a fucking bitch. I don't care if we have commitment issues. I'm not going anywhere, and neither are you. You're stuck with me and you crave my dick just as much as I crave your cunt. You got me?"

"Or else what?" I breathed, shivers trembling through me at the rough hold he had on me.

He grinned. "You like it when I force you to do things. You submit to me and you don't even know it." His mouth brushed over the corner of my lips. "You need me just as much as I need you, baby."

"I can't help but submit to you, Coby."

"Yeah? Then stop being a little bitch and give me what I need, and I'll give you everything in return."

I swallowed hard.

"No judgments." He kissed my mouth. "Remember?"

"When I see everyone looking at me, questioning when I'll snap, it's hard not to judge." A breath of relief washed over me at my sudden confession.

"I go through the same thing, Brogan," Coby pushed a strand of hair behind my ear. "Everyone does, but you need to trust me, and I will do the same."

"You will?"

He winked. "Yes. I know you want to know everything you can about me but I'm not ready to talk about it. I like you. I like you a lot but I've liked women before and got fucked over in the end."

"You need to trust that I'm not like those women."

"And you need to trust that I'm not like the men you've been with. I'm not your parents. I won't leave you suddenly."

My throat burned. "That's different."

"Is it? I see the pain in your eyes, little one." He kissed me again. "Know that I am here for whenever you are ready to talk about it."

"I'm here for you too."

RUDE

"I know." He cupped the back of my neck. "I know," he whispered.

CHAPTER FIFTEEN

Coby

BROGAN HAD COMMITMENT issues. Well, that sure as hell explained a lot. *Looks like I met my match.*

After doing some more repairs on the club, we all called it a day and headed to Angel and Jay's home in the country. But what I wanted to do was take Brogan back to my own home. Not even for sex. Just to hold her. To show her that what we had going on meant more to me than I could ever say. She didn't think this would last. Hell, I didn't even know if it would but I would spend my last breath proving to her that I wanted something … anything out of what we shared.

Fuck it.

I handed Brogan my phone. "Text Angel, and tell him we're going to be late."

She frowned. "Why?"

"Because I said so." I needed to work off this frustration before I lost my damn mind. "Just do it," I demanded when she didn't move.

She huffed, sent Angel a quick text, then handed me back the phone.

I shoved it in my pocket.

"Why are we going to be late?"

So many questions that I had no answers for. No words left my mouth so I would show her instead. Pulling off the road, I drove us down a narrow path. Having to take this route for years, I learned the tricks and secret hiding spots. It was quiet and secluded. No one would hear her scream.

"Coby." Brogan sat up, staring out the window ahead of her. "Where are we going?"

"You ask a lot of questions, Brogan," I told her, gripping the steering wheel tight in my hands. Truth was, I didn't know where we were going. Not exactly, anyway. It had been years since I took a woman to this spot. But if I remembered correctly, it was private enough that it would give me everything I needed to truly dominate her.

***

(Brogan)

To say I wasn't a little bit nervous would be a complete lie. I wasn't sure what Coby had in mind. Was it sex? Is that what he wanted? Hell, I knew I could always use a good fucking. It hadn't even been twenty-four hours, and I already craved him.

"If you're taking me out here to murder me, I hope you at least use your imagination."

Coby chuckled, putting the vehicle into park and turned to me. "Get out of the car."

"Okay, Coby, seriously. What is going on?"

He leaned his head from side to side, a loud crack reverberating around the silence of the car. "I'm going to fuck you and your screams are going to die in the silence of the night."

"Well." I swallowed hard at the coldness in his tone. "All you had to do was ask."

"I don't ask," he opened his door. "I take. Now do as you're told and get the *fuck* out."

Well, this was going to be fun.

I slid from the vehicle, shutting the door behind me.

"Come here," he demanded, standing a few feet away from me.

My body shook, my bones tremoring beneath the deep sound of his voice. The cool night air slid over my skin, sending a wave of goosebumps over my skin.

I closed the distance between Coby and myself. Staring up at him, my stomach tumbled. The moon cast an eerie glow around him.

Brushing a finger down the length of my jaw, he pinched my chin. "Do you have any idea what you do to me?"

"I could take a guess," I breathed. "Probably the same thing you do to me."

"And what's that, little one?" He leaned down toward me. "Do I make you wet?"

"Yes." As much as I wanted to touch him, I kept my hands at my sides, needing him to take me further into the desire I knew he could grant me. With him, I would fall into the greatest depths of ecstasy.

"Hmm ..." he purred, licking up the length of my neck. "Your sass makes me fucking hard. Every time you argue with me, I want to throw you up against the wall and dive into your sweetness."

"What else?" I breathed, leaning my head to the side.

His teeth sunk into my neck. "I have to control myself when I'm with you. I'm not into public displays of affection but every time you talk to a man, I want to fuck you even harder."

"God, I never thought hearing something like that would turn me on."

Coby grinned, pushing me back until I hit a tree. The sharp jagged bark dug into my skin but it only heightened my senses.

"When I tell you what to do, it turns you on." He kicked my legs apart, forcing my arms above my head. "Why?"

"Because I know that I'm safe and ... and I need it." I arched against the tree, restrained by his touch.

"Yes, you are." Pulling his belt from his jeans with a snap in the wind, he threw the one end over a thick branch. "If you fight, this will hurt." He kissed my forehead. "But you won't, will you? There's a kinky girl inside of you that wants to come out and play."

"Fuck, yes."

Pushing his way between my legs, his thigh brushed against my core.

I moaned at the contact, needing more and everything he had to give me.

Coby circled the belt around my wrists, pulling tight so my feet could barely touch the ground.

The leather stung, digging into my skin but the idea of being completely bound made the pain disappear.

"You like that," Coby stated.

It wasn't a question, but I nodded my head anyway.

He stared at me for a moment, his gaze taking on a faraway look like he was remembering a time long ago.

"Coby?"

He shook himself, his face shadowed by a darkness that matched my own. Inching his fingers under my tank top, he pulled it up my torso, over my head, and up my arms.

The cool air kissed my skin.

"You are so fucking beautiful," he muttered, grazing the back of his knuckles down my stomach. "I could devour every inch of you."

"Do it," I begged, mentally scolding myself. I had never begged. I was always the one who did the controlling. Men would beg *me* but nothing compared to Coby-Fucking-Porter.

"I love it when you beg." Coby pulled a switch blade from his back pocket.

My heart jumped.

Taking the tip of the knife, he gripped my shorts and popped the button off with a flick of his wrist.

As much as I liked these shorts, I wanted to see what he would do next and just how kinky he was.

"You like my knife, baby?" Coby slid the dull side down the center of my stomach.

My breathing picked up.

"You like knowing that I'm in full control and there's nothing you can do about it." Grabbing ahold of the waistband of my shorts, he sliced them down the middle, leaving me in only my thong and bra.

RUDE

Licking his lips, he slid the knife beneath my panties, pushing the dull side of the blade over my clit.

I gasped, the cool metal sending a jolt of electricity racing through my body.

Coby smirked, ripping the material free from my body and lowered to his knees. Placing the knife beside him, he hooked his hands beneath my legs and circled them around his shoulders. "Fucking perfect."

Before I could question him, his mouth was on me. His tongue was so deep inside of me, I could feel him everywhere.

"Oh, fuck," I cried out, shaking against him.

He released me with a wet smack and slapped my inner thigh. "You will not come until I give you permission, do you understand me?"

I nodded quickly, needing his mouth back on me before I screamed out in frustration.

"Say it. Tell me you won't come."

"I won't come," I panted.

"What do you want, baby?"

"Your mouth on me."

Coby growled, thrust his tongue back inside me and dug his fingers into the flesh of my thighs. He lapped and sucked. Pushed and massaged. But his tongue never went to where I needed him most.

My clit ached, needing the release my body so desperately craved but I wouldn't beg. Not yet. Not again.

His hands massaged into the cheeks of my ass, pulling me forward and back until I was riding his mouth. The scruff of his jaw scratched at my center.

Euphoria started tingling from my toes but I took a breath, forcing the impending orgasm back until Coby gave the okay.

"*Fuck.*" My hands shook against the restraints. "Please, Coby."

He sucked harder, fucking my pussy with his tongue.

I trembled and whimpered, moving my hips against his mouth.

"Come for me," he finally said. "Scream my name."

I took that as my cue and let every emotion, every feeling, every action take over. Coby tongue-fucked my pussy, and I rode him like it was his cock. Every movement brought the orgasm higher and higher until I was screaming his name. Stars danced in my vision, my voice cracking under the pressure. Everything I had thought would happen, did. I came, and I came hard.

Coby released me but not before sinking his teeth into my thigh.

I yelped, jumping.

He kissed the spot and rose to his full height.

I stared up at him, tugging on my restraints.

"Oh, little girl." He brushed a hand down my arm. "You think I'm going to let you go just yet?" A wicked smirk spread on his face before he lifted me in his arms and wrapped my legs around his hips. "I'm only getting started."

I licked my lips, needing him inside of me. "Then fuck me, Porter."

Spreading my thighs, he undid his jeans.

Much to my surprise, he had gone commando. Everything beneath his pants was all him. Every hard, throbbing inch. It was all Coby Porter.

"Do you like what you see?" Coby pinched my chin, tilting my head back to meet his stare.

"Yes." I shivered. "Please."

"What do you want?" He leaned down, sucking my bottom lip into his mouth and gave it a gentle nip. That small touch sent a jolt straight to my clit. "Tell me," he demanded, tapping the tip of his cock against my mound.

"I want to cum all over your dick," I purred, digging my heels into his ass.

"Fuck me." Coby wrapped his hand around his straining cock and pushed the tip through the soaked folds of my pussy.

I moaned, arching against the tree.

With both hands gripping my thighs tight, he thrust into me hard, knocking me back.

I cried out, shaking against him. He was deep inside of me. He took my breath with every aching pump, owning me with each thrust of his hips.

"Harder," I pleaded, taking him as deep as possible.

"Shit, Brogan," he dug his fingers into my rear, sliding me up and down his cock. "Feel that? Do you feel how hard I am for you? Can you feel every inch?"

"Yes, oh fuck yes." I threw my head back, watching the leather of the belt dig into the skin of my wrists. All of these new sensations washed over me. Pain. Lust. But a sense of calm settled deep inside of me. Coby took me to new heights, not pushing me over the edge until he was right there with me.

"Faster," I begged. I had never had sex without a condom until I met Coby but something inside of me needed to feel every hard ridge of his cock. I needed to feel him take ownership of my body when he came inside of me.

"Baby." He wrapped his body around mine, brushing his face into the crook of my neck. "Come for me, sweet girl. Come so hard, I can feel you break."

"Fuck me harder, Coby," I insisted, the release brewing from my toes.

He snarled, his thrusts turning violent. The tree branch cracked, the belt moving back and forth with each deep pump of his dick inside of me.

The ecstasy slammed into me. "Harder," I screamed, forcing him to lose all control.

He yelled out, my name leaving his lips as his body released hot jets of liquid into me.

I moaned, taking all of him in as I came down from my euphoric high.

Coby panted, running his hands up and down my sides. He fell from my body, did up his pants and unhooked the belt from around my wrists. Pulling me into his arms, he held me tight against him and rubbed the tender flesh. He pet my hair, raining kisses on my face, and brushed his nose into the crook of my neck.

I pulled my tank top down and covered his mouth with mine. We may have had issues speaking to each other and getting over our commitment issues but my kiss was sure to pass on something. Even if it was only to thank him.

CHAPTER SIXTEEN

Brogan

WHEN WE FINALLY arrived to Angel and Jay's, I stood back, waiting for Jay to meet me in the foyer.

Coby brushed a hand down my cheek, kissed me one last time and went to join the rest of the group.

"Hey," Jay greeted me. "What's wrong?"

"Do you have something I can wear?" I asked, holding up my ripped shorts.

She laughed, shaking her head. "Of course. Not that anything I have will fit you."

"That's okay." I laughed with her. "I just don't want to have to wear Coby's coat all night."

"Is that why you're late?"

"Yes," I said, following her down a long hall. "We needed a moment."

Jay nodded once. "I understand that. These men are hard deal with at times. They've been through so much, in the military and outside of it. They think they can handle everything on their own and don't know how to ask for help."

"I knew Coby had a past but I didn't know … I didn't know it was that awful."

"That bad, huh?" Jay pushed open a door at the end of the hall. "I'll give you a pair of old shorts that are too small for me. Or did you want sweats?"

"Sweat pants, please." I didn't want to have to explain him tearing into her shorts either since he seemed to like cutting them off me.

Jay handed me grey sweats and leaned against the dresser. "He likes you a lot, you know."

"Yeah." I pulled on the pants, happy they were only a little long. "I like him too but it's difficult."

She grunted. "It always is. I'm sure he'll come around. But I need to ask you. What the hell is up with Greyson? I've never seen him act like that. He's usually always happy to see you."

I sighed, rubbing the back of my neck and told her about the summer Grey and I had spent together after our parents died.

"Are you shitting me right now?" She laughed, shaking her head. "And the ass is jealous because you got over him and he clearly didn't?"

"I guess so. He's never given me issues before when it came to other men but something about Coby he doesn't like." I shrugged.

"I know why." Jay smiled, nudging me gently in the shoulder.

RUDE

"Why?"

"Because you're in love with Coby. That's why."

***

(Coby)

I had wanted to argue with Brogan and demand that she stay in just her thong. Knowing her beautiful ass was bare and all I had to do was open my coat she was wearing made me hard as fuck. But she needed to be comfortable. So, I would get over it. For now.

"So …" Dale peeked at me over the neck of his beer. "You were late because …"

"And why would I tell you?" I snapped, smirking and crossed my ankle over the opposite knee.

"Because I'm your best friend." Dale pouted, feigning a dramatic sigh. "It hurts that you don't tell me these things anymore."

"You're such a drama queen." Asher smacked him across the head, pulling Meeka onto his lap when she went to walk by him.

"Hey, that hurts, you know." Dale rubbed the spot Asher had hit, his lips curling into a smile.

"That's the point, fucker." Asher leaned in for a kiss from Meeka but she placed a hand on his mouth instead.

"Apologize," she demanded, crossing her arms under her chest.

"Are you serious?" Asher raised an eyebrow.

"Yes." She stabbed a finger at his chest. "I am."

Dale grinned, and I bit back a laugh.

"Apologize to him," she repeated.

"You know what this means, right?" Asher asked, his voice taking on that tone that I knew all too well.

Meeka swallowed hard. "Yes, I do." Her cheeks reddened. "But I still want you to apologize."

"Fine." He turned to Dale. "I'm sorry you're a pussy and me hitting you hurt."

"Asher," Meeka cried, laughing. "That's not what I meant."

He chuckled, pulling her in for a kiss.

They shared a moment, kissing and petting.

I looked away, not wanting to intrude on their private moment.

"Fucker doesn't know how to apologize and still gets kissed for it," Dale muttered, his mood turning dark.

"Leave it alone," I told him. "Have you talked to her?"

He took a hard swig of his beer and rose to his feet. "I need another beer." And with that, he headed back into the house.

He hadn't talked to Max yet. Jay had said that she was sleeping when Brogan and I had arrived. This pregnancy was taking its toll on the poor thing.

Angel came out of the house and sat beside me, handing me a bottle of water. "Dale's in a mood."

I grunted in response and took a gulp of the cool liquid that I had come to love over the years instead of beer. As much as I missed alcohol, it had caused too many problems that I could never get myself out of. So, water it was.

Laughter sounded from inside the house making my dick twitch. I knew that laugh anywhere.

Brogan and Jay came outside, smiles on both of their faces.

Jay sat beside Angel, snuggling into his side and Brogan sat on the love seat beside the chair I was sitting in.

She caught my gaze and patted the spot beside her.

I shook my head, patting my lap instead.

Brogan raised an eyebrow, challenging me.

I chuckled and moved to the spot beside her.

"Do you always come when I call?" She waggled her eyebrows.

"How old is that saying?" I laughed.

"Old enough." She giggled, wrapped her hands around my arm, and pulled it onto her lap. "Is this okay?" she whispered.

"Yes." I didn't need to show our friends that I had feelings for this woman. They already knew. Whatever was going on between Brogan and I, we were taking it slow but any slower and I was afraid that it would push her away.

"I don't want to talk business tonight," Jay said, breaking the silence. "But I just need to know if Greyson or your contact, Coby, has said anything."

"No, he's been quiet. I'll call him tomorrow and see if he's made any new progress on this shit." Lucas was a hard man to get ahold of.

"And Greyson?" Jay asked, looking at Brogan.

She shifted beside me. "No. I haven't heard from him."

My body relaxed at that. I had to keep my thoughts to myself when it came to Greyson. I knew that but whenever he touched her, knowing that I was watching, it made me want to drive my fist through his face even more. Her brothers are different. I could like them. Especially knowing they didn't care for Grey much.

"Are your brothers still in town?" Angel asked, cupping Jay's lower belly.

"Yes, it's the twins' …" Brogan clapped a hand to her mouth. "Oh, shit."

"What?" I asked, turning her toward me.

"I forgot their birthdays. It's today, and I haven't called them yet." She rose to her feet. "I have to call them." She ran back into the house, leaving the warm spot beside me to turn cold.

***

(Brogan)

When I ran into the house, my phone rang. Taking a breath, I answered. "Blake, I am so—"

"Save it, Brogan," Blake snapped. "We came down to see you and yet we haven't seen you at all."

"You know the shit that's been going on. It's not my fault," I cried, slumping onto the couch.

"But you make time to see that guy. Coby, is it?"

My chest tightened. "I'm sorry." I took a breath. "Happy birthday."

"You can't butter me up with that sweet shit," he grumbled.

"Is that Brogie?" Brox yelled from the back ground. "Hey, Brogan," he greeted, taking the phone from Blake. "You forgot our birthday."

"I didn't forget." I squeezed the bridge of my nose. "I just forgot to call earlier."

"That's the same thing, isn't it?" he covered the mouthpiece and mumbled something to Blake. "Yes," he said, his voice clearer that time. "Brogan, we're not happy that you haven't called all day and that you've been ignoring us but we get it. Your club is important.

139

We're just glad that all of you are okay. And yes, we're glad that Greyson is fine as well."

I scoffed. "I'm sure you are. But, seriously, I am sorry. And happy birthday to you as well, Brox."

"Thank you. We need to meet up before we head back into the city."

"I would like that."

CHAPTER SEVENTEEN

Brogan

COBY AND I had been living together for a week. The club was coming along nicely but I could sense that Jay was nervous about it. She didn't want us living there for fear that it would be another target. We had all agreed that we would visit in pairs or a group but not spend the night. We also had some of our resources check out the place regularly while we weren't there. It paid to know bikers.

"Daddy, I'm fine," Jay said one afternoon, pacing back and forth in front of a table lined with blueprints. "I'm sorry I never told you. It's been a little crazy here. Yes. I know. Angel is taking good care of me. Don't worry. No, Tyler hasn't been by. He got the hint since the last time. I know. Please stop worrying so much. It's not good for your heart." She stopped suddenly. "Are you serious? Are you sure that's a good idea? I know, I know. I'm just saying it might be too soon." She sighed. "Okay. I will back you in whatever you decide. Yes. Please stop by. I miss you." She hung up her phone, placing it in the back pocket of her pants. "My dad wants to kick Tyler out of the club."

"Are you fucking kidding me?" My eyes widened. "There is no way Tyler would let that go easily."

Jay rubbed her temples. "I know."

"We got this." I pointed to her belly. "You have to take care of you and that little bundle first. Let the rest of us worry about your dad and Tyler."

"Okay." She nodded. "I'm so fucking tired, I can't even argue right now."

I laughed. "Well, I expect all the arguments to happen after the baby comes."

She swallowed hard. "I don't want to think about that right now. It scares the shit out of me."

"As it should. You're growing a human being, Jay. That's pretty fucking amazing."

Her smile widened. "Yeah, I guess it is, isn't it?"

"Definitely." I went back to my table and mulled over the blueprints. The club was going to look epic when we were done with it. Too bad we couldn't use it for a while. Not when Charles and his fucking goons were out there.

"Need any help?" Coby asked, coming up beside me.

"Yes, keep my friends safe." My voice grew thick. I never let these situations get to me but after months of dealing with it on end, it kind of got to a person sometimes.

"Hey." Coby pulled me into his arms, hugging me tight against him. "They'll be fine. I promise."

"No, don't promise something like that." I pulled from his grip. "You can't. That's how I lost my parents. They promised me they would see me again and then they were ripped from my life. I almost lost my brothers too because of it. So, don't you dare promise me that shit."

"Okay." Coby wrapped his arms around my shoulders. "I am sorry."

"My parents said they would see us later but they never did." My eyes welled but at that point, I no longer cared. "I didn't see them again."

"Shhh …" Coby turned me in his arms, hugging me against him. "Let's take a break and go for a drive."

"To have sex?" I asked, rolling up the blueprints.

"Is that what you want?" He handed me the tubes.

I stuffed the blueprints into them and let out a heavy sigh. "I just want all of this shit to end."

"We can head back to my place. We can do whatever you want. Sex. Eat. Sleep. Workout. Doesn't even have to be in that order."

I laughed, hugging him tight. "Thank you and yes, all of that sounds wonderful."

We told everyone that we were leaving and that they should probably do the same. There was no point wearing ourselves out over something we couldn't live in or use for a while.

An hour later and we were headed into the city when Coby got a call.

"Shit, it's the head office."

"Head office?" I asked, stepping out of the vehicle.

"Yeah, something to do with one of the apartments I own flooding. Will you be fine here if I leave you alone for a little bit?"

"Just give me your key," I said, holding my hand out. "And I'll make myself right at home."

He grinned, kissing me hard on the mouth. "Good girl. If you leave, text me, just so I know where you are if I get back before you."

"I will," I called out, blowing him a kiss, and headed inside the large building. Once I made my way into the elevator, I changed my mind and decided to go for a walk instead. Needing some fresh air, I made sure to text Coby and stay around the area since I didn't know the city that well. I found a large bookstore a couple blocks away with a coffee shop built into it. It was heaven and smelled even better.

"Can I help you, miss?" a young girl asked, greeting me at the door.

"No, thank you." I smiled. "Just looking around."

She nodded, holding the door open for me.

I thanked her and went in search of the romance section. It was my guilty pleasure. A lot of the stories would never happen but there were some that I liked to hope would. And the heroes in the books? Even better. But Coby was my real-life hero. He took me from myself and we had only been spending time together for a few weeks, a couple months at the most. I lost track of time when it came to him.

"You looking for a good book?" a young man asked, pulling a paperback off the shelf. "I hear this one is great. My sister loves this author."

The cover caught my eye. A flogger. A whip. And a belt? Yum.

"Thank you." I smiled up at the man, my breath catching in my throat when I really looked at him.

His hair was dark, shaggy and unkempt. He wore a tailored suit, fitted to his strong body and his eyes, God, they were beautiful. So green they looked like emeralds.

I cleared my throat, looking away. Guilt sat heavily in my stomach over gawking at the guy when Coby had been so good to me. But I was human and the guy was beautiful. If you went for that sort of thing.

"You're welcome." The man smiled, although it never reached his eyes. "I also hear that this one is good too." He pulled another book from the shelf, this one featuring a cowboy on the front.

"I'm not really into Western romances but I'll give it a shot."

He nodded once. "Are you from around here?"

"No. I'm staying with my … friend." I realized then that I didn't even know what to call Coby. Not like I could say that he was my fuck buddy to a complete stranger.

"Well, your friend picked a perfect place to live. I love this city and all it's about. It holds so many different cultures and walks of life. It really is surreal."

I noticed after listening to him for a couple of minutes that he held a hint of an accent, but I couldn't place where it would be from.

"Well—" he checked his watch "—it looks like my time is up. Thank you for the chat." He turned and walked away.

Well, that was odd. I placed the books back on the shelf even though he had recommended them. Something about this situation felt off. I should have just stayed at Coby's in the first place so I made my way back there. Almost accidentally turning down a dark alley, I hightailed out of there before I could get myself in another situation like a couple weeks ago. I remembered back to that night when Coby had saved me along with his brothers. I should have known then that something more would come out of our relationship whether we both cared to admit it or not.

When I arrived back at Coby's, he was sitting on his couch with a tumbler in hand. It held dark amber liquid and every so often, he would take a sip.

"Everything okay?" I asked, slipping out of my shoes and noted the liquor he was falling into. I had never seen him drink before knowing it wasn't something he had done in a long time.

"Where were you?" he asked, ignoring me.

"I texted you. I went to the bookstore and then I got lost." I sat beside him, cupping his knee.

"You should have stayed closer to home."

Home. He said it like it was mine too but it wasn't. I didn't have a home anymore thanks to the bastards who blew it up.

"I'm sorry. I didn't think it was an issue." I rose from the couch and went to leave when Coby grabbed my hand. He pulled me down beside him, cupping my throat.

"I got worried," he breathed into my ear.

"There's nothing to worry over," I reassured him. "I'm fine. I promise." Although, the conversation I had with that man was a little odd.

"What's wrong?" Coby asked, pulling me onto his lap.

"Nothing, really. I just had a strange conversation with a man at the bookstore," I said, telling him about what had happened. "It just seemed different to me."

"Well, if it seemed that way then it probably was. I've learned over my lifetime to always go with your gut."

"True." We sat in silence, enjoying each other's company but I still couldn't get over the man I met at the bookstore. It bothered me to no end that he had this effect on me. It was unnerving the way he had stared at me like he was looking deep within my soul.

"You're still thinking about him, aren't you?" Coby asked, interrupting my thoughts.

"Yes." I sat forward. "I'm bothered by it because I feel like he had wanted something. Or maybe to say something to me but never did. He scared me in a way I'm not used to."

Coby searched my face. "I don't want you leaving here without me."

I rolled my eyes. "You can't make me stay. I have to work on the club."

"We'll go together."

"I need to have a life, Coby. You know that."

"Then have a life with me but if that guy made you feel uncomfortable, I don't want to take the chance that you'll see him again."

I sighed, rubbing the back of my neck. "I know. I shouldn't be bothered. It was just ... weird."

Coby kissed my forehead. "We leave soon. I'm not sure exactly when. This could be last minute shit."

"Fuck."

"I got the call before you came back."

My heart sunk, dropping into my feet like heavy weights. "How long?"

"I'm not sure. We've tried convincing our boss to let us focus on the human trafficking ring but it's not what we do. We're SEALs and we deal with terrorists."

"Hasn't Charles done terrorist shit too?"

"Yeah," Coby grunted. "He's a man of many talents. It makes me wonder if there is even another front runner. Maybe he's the brother to the woman. It wouldn't surprise me. He is sick and twisted like that."

"Meeka told me what happened to her and how she was sold to Charles." I shivered. "He needs to die."

"Asher won't talk about it."

"It makes me wonder who will be next."

***

(Coby)

I wanted to scream that she was wrong. That she was crazy to think that way but it made sense. Jay had been taken first. Then Meeka and Asher. Jay's sister, Violet, had been taken years before. Who *would* be next?

I didn't want to think that way but it was hard not to when Charles was going through all of us. Taking from us what was rightfully ours. Destroying the girls' club and home, a piece of their lives they had grown accustomed to for years.

The fact that Brogan had left my place earlier that night when I wasn't there left me pissed off and on edge. Every fiber of my being needed to protect her and remind her and everyone else that she belonged to me. But did she really? My thoughts were a jumbled mess.

Leah did this to me. I was normal when I met her. Not bitter and hating the world. Not miserable in any way. She had mental health problems her whole life and one day, she just couldn't deal. I blamed her for so many things in my life but taking my baby from me was the final thing that broke me.

While Brogan curled against me, I brushed my hand up and down her bare back. Nothing else came of tonight other than talking and spending time together. No sex. As much as we needed it, getting to know each other would be a harder task for each other. Brogan needed sex as much I did. It took us out of our heads and let us just feel that familiar connection we had with each other.

I wasn't sure why exactly, but I fell hard for this woman lying beside me. No, I knew why and I was an idiot for denying it all along. I had been missing something since Leah died and Brogan would be the one who could fill that void. She understood where I was coming from. Craved the darkness inside of me. Although she had been accused of having mental health problems her whole life, she wasn't Leah. I knew that, but sometimes the words leaving my mouth said different.

"Coby." Brogan stirred beside me. "Are you okay?"

"Yeah." I kissed her head. "Can't sleep."

"Do you want to talk about it?" she asked, resting her chin on my chest.

I shrugged.

"Did you have a bad dream?"

"More like a bad reality," I grumbled. "My wife's name was Leah. She was happy when she found out she was pregnant but she was so far gone in her head that she couldn't control her thoughts or actions."

"She had mental health problems?" Brogan's eyes widened.

"She did. For her whole life. She had told me over and over again how scared she was that our baby would end up like her." My throat tightened. "But she never gave it the chance."

"Oh, Coby." Brogan hugged her arms around me. "I'm so sorry. It must be hard being with me then."

"No." I cupped her cheeks. "Never."

She sighed. "I was never diagnosed with anything but I've always known something was off."

I didn't respond. There was nothing more I could say. Leah had been my one true love. Or so I thought. It was funny how different she was compared to Brogan. They were nothing alike but stole every part of me just the same.

"Let's talk about something else." Brogan rolled onto her back. "How about ... sex? Why do you need to be in control?"

I chuckled, appreciating the change in subject. "It's just how I am. I can't control anything else in my life, so sex is my way of taking that back. I love my job but it has shitty aspects that I can't stop. But when it comes to sex, controlling your movements and actions, your orgasms, even the breaths that leave your mouth—it turns me on and leaves me very satisfied."

"Have you always been like this?"

"With other women, you mean?"

"Yes."

"Why? Would you be jealous?" I teased, knowing the answer before she even told me.

"Yes, just like you're jealous of Greyson." She snapped her mouth shut. "I mean ..."

I pulled her under me, cupping her throat. "You think I'm jealous of your stepbrother? You think I'm jealous over the fact that he fucked you first and it wasn't me you lost your virginity to? Yes. Is that what you want to hear? I *am* jealous. You fucking hear me?

I'm jealous of every man who has given you an orgasm because all of them belong to me. Past. Current. Future. Your orgasms are mine."

"When it comes to Greyson, you have nothing to be worried about." She pushed my hand off her. "You need to trust me."

"I do trust you." I kissed her hard on the mouth. "It's him I don't trust."

"I know that but there's nothing I can do, Coby."

I stared down at her. She was right. God, I was such a dick sometimes.

Flopping back down beside her, I wrapped her in my arms. "I'm not a good guy, Brogan, but you make me want to be one."

"Where is that coming from?"

I yawned, my eyelids getting heavy. "Just trust me."

Coming home to find out my wife had committed suicide was not something anyone could prepare for. I had been away on a mission for the past six months. Tired and hungry, sore and in need of a warm body and hot shower, I craved Leah's arms. But when I walked into our bedroom and saw her sprawled out on the bed with a pill bottle in her hand, I knew.

The military had turned me into a hard man to deal with. It wasn't something I was proud of but I couldn't control the things I had seen. Leah had been good for me. She was happy that I was making something of myself. Happy that I could prepare our baby for the future. But she took that from me.

I stood in the doorway, a bouquet of roses in my hand, expecting to be greeted by her but instead, I was hit by her death.

I didn't cry. I didn't yell and scream. I only stood there. Frozen in place. Stuck in a time where I didn't know whether to move forward or back. How could she do this to me? How could she take away something I never even had a chance to love?

RUDE

Suddenly, I fell to my knees, the roses dropping to the floor. A wail left my mouth. I didn't need to touch Leah to know that she was gone. Her vacant eyes stared at me from the bed. No longer showcasing the life she had lived.

"How could you do this to me?" I asked the still form. "How could you take away our baby?" My voice rose as each question left my lips. "How could you destroy me?"

I rose to my feet, charging for the bed. Grabbing Leah's body, I pulled her against me, cursing and shouting into her deaf ears.

Our relationship had been toxic, dangerous but she came to me at a time in my life where I needed her most. And now this.

My chest ached, my body convulsing with each sob that left my mouth. Tears burned down my cheeks.

Fisting her hair in my hands, I pulled her head back and stared hard at her beautiful face. It no longer held the flush of life.

My body shook but my voice remained calm and even. Pulling the phone from my pocket, I dialed 911 and reported the suicide. Not giving the operator any more information than needed, I hung up and threw the object across the room.

"This is your fault," I told my dead wife, already feeling the changes in my personality her death was causing. Reaching between us, I brushed the back of my hand over her swollen belly. Our baby never stood a chance.

"I don't know you but I love you nonetheless," my voice cracked. "I'm so sorry you were never given the chance to survive. This world is evil but I knew going in that once I held you in my arms, it would make everything worth it but now ..." I could no longer speak as reality dawned on me. I was now a widower. No wife. No baby. What was the point?

***

(Brogan)

The next day, I decided to make Coby breakfast. Since Benny had cooked in the military to gain some more experience, he taught us everything he knew. Now if only I could figure out how to cook for two people and not five.

"Are you making me breakfast, little one?" Coby asked, kissing my neck.

I laughed. "I'm trying to. Think you can eat a lot?"

"I'll eat whatever you put in front of me." He playfully smacked my butt. "This smells fucking fantastic."

"Thank you. Benny taught me. He calls it his magic eggs 'cause they taste so damn good but you have no idea how he does them."

Coby chuckled, leaning against the island behind me. "I enjoy watching you in my kitchen."

"And I enjoy being in your kitchen. I love the club but it was too small to do anything so we ordered in a lot. I hope with these renovations that Creena and I can move around the kitchen without spilling something on each other."

"How's she doing?"

"Good. We're keeping her on. We don't look at her as a prospect anymore but with everything that's been happening, we haven't had a chance to make it official." I made a mental note of reminding Jay of that next time I saw her.

"I like her. She seems like she has a good head on her shoulders."

I turned around. "Since when do you care about my friends?"

"What the hell is that supposed to mean?"

"I mean, you've never asked before. So why now?" I poked a finger against his chest. "Don't get so defensive."

"I want to get to know you and if knowing your friends helps me know *you* better, then that's what I'm going to do."

My heart stopped.

"What's that look for?" he asked, raising an eyebrow.

"Nothing." I turned back around and flipped the omelet before it burned.

He nudged me gently. "Talk to me."

"I just don't know why you want to get to know my friends when this isn't serious anyway."

"You're honestly standing there telling me this? Maybe it's not serious now but even with all our commitment issues, I know we both want something out of this.

"Yeah, you think so, do you? And how do you know that?"

"Because I know you feel it. I have only felt it one other time."

Squeezing my eyes shut, I shook my head. "Don't do this. Not now."

"Stop lying to yourself, Brogan."

"I don't want you to hurt me and you could. If anyone was to rip out my heart, it would be you, Coby."

"I would never do anything to hurt you. I have no intentions of that."

"Most people don't." I turned off the stove and placed his omelet on a plate. "Here you go."

He sighed but took the plate from me. Forking a mouthful between his lips, he chewed and chewed, swallowed, and took another bite.

"Well?"

He didn't say anything until every last bit was gone. "That was fucking delicious."

I laughed. "Took you long enough to tell me."

"I think you should come here."

My cheeks heated. "Yeah? And what do I get out of it?"

"A couple orgasms … or ten."

And for the next couple of hours, Coby lived up to his promise, satisfying me in ways I never even knew was possible.

CHAPTER EIGHTEEN

Brogan

I WAS IN love with him. It made sense. It was the only reason I was pushing him away. Even though I wasn't sure if it was actually love, I did care for Coby. A lot. I missed him when he wasn't around. I craved his touch and the way he saw inside my head, read my thoughts and never judged me. He was the part of me I had been missing my whole entire life.

I needed to talk to someone about this. I wasn't the type of girl who sat with my friends and discussed guys but I needed answers. Or someone to set me on the right path at least.

Coby was still sleeping so I headed out to the living room and called Meeka. She had been the one person in my life to not put up with my shit, and I loved her even more for it.

Sitting on the chaise by the window that overlooked the city, I dialed my best friend and waited in bated anticipation.

"Hello?"

"Hey, Meeka," I greeted, gripping the phone tight in my hand.

"Hey, girl, what's up?"

My heart stuttered. "I …"

"Brogan?" Meeka paused. "Is everything okay?"

"Yes. I just have a question." I took a breath. "Now before you jump to conclusions and make a big deal out of it, just hear me out."

"Okay …"

"When did you know you were falling in love with Asher?" I asked all in one breath. I winced, waiting for her badgering of questions but when they didn't come, I thought maybe she had hung up. "Meeka?"

"Um …" She cleared her throat. "Wow. Okay. My situation is a little different than yours. I've known Asher my whole life. A part of me has always loved him but the first time he kissed me, it opened up something else entirely. It's a feeling I never even knew existed before."

"Did you just know?"

"Yeah. I guess I did. He never made it easy but relationships take work. They take time. It's not always hearts and flowers but we have each other. He saved me, and I like to think that maybe I even saved him a little."

"I think you did more than that, Meeka."

"He has a history. A very dark one. But I'm glad that I was able to help him deal with that."

"It's like all of these men have dark pasts," I muttered, remembering Coby's story.

Meeka sighed. "They do but that's what makes them human. I'd rather a broken man than one who acts all perfect. They are the ones you have to watch out for."

"True enough."

"Who are you talking to, hummingbird?" Asher asked in the background.

"Brogan." Meeka covered the mouthpiece, her voice muffled. She giggled.

My cheeks heated. Afraid I was imposing on their private moment, I quickly said goodbye and hung up the phone.

"Brogan."

I jumped.

Coby stood at the end of the hallway, frowning. "What are you doing on the floor?"

I looked around me, not even realizing I was no longer sitting on the chaise. "I'm not sure."

Coby came toward me and sat on the floor beside me before grabbing hold of my hand. He brushed his thumb back and forth over my pulse point. "Your hands are as calloused as mine."

Not quite sure what he was getting at, I didn't respond.

"Most women I've come across in my life have soft, perfect hands. But not you."

"Are you insulting my hands, Coby?" I raised an eyebrow.

His lips twitched. "No. I'm complimenting the fact that you're a hard worker. You protect what's yours and you'll go through anyone and do anything to make sure those you love are safe."

"Well—" I pulled my hand from his grasp "—it doesn't seem to be getting me anywhere but thank you for noticing." I crossed my arms under my chest, looking out the large floor to ceiling window. It was early morning. The sun had risen, kissing the tops of the buildings in the city.

Coby brushed a strand of loose hair behind my ear. "Why are you up so early?"

"I couldn't sleep." I shrugged. "I don't sleep much anyway." My body took that as a sign, forcing a yawn out of me.

Wrapping an arm around my shoulders, Coby kissed my head.

"What was that for?" I asked, my heart fluttering.

"No reason," he muttered, his hot breath heating my skin.

We sat in silence, reveling in each other's company for what felt like an eternity. It was comfortable, quiet, needed. All of the guys in my past always wanted just one thing. I was okay with that. Now I felt like I was waiting for this. For Coby.

"What were you talking to Meeka about?"

My heart jumped. "That depends. What did you hear?"

"Enough."

Chewing my bottom lip, I held back the urge to run away. I had feelings for him. Hard, deep feelings but it still didn't mean that I was ready to admit them out loud. Yes, I may have asked Meeka about falling in love and I was thankful that she didn't question it further but I couldn't talk to Coby about it. Not yet.

"Brogan, talk to me."

"There's nothing to talk about." I went to stand when he gripped my arm, stopping me.

"You will tell me," he demanded.

I scoffed. "Not right now I'm not. And besides, no matter what you heard, it's not important."

"Like fuck it's not. I heard what you asked Meeka."

The back of my neck heated. Of course he did. The guy was stealthy and heard everything. I had no idea that he was even listening.

"We're not talking about it," I grumbled, pulling from his grasp.

"We're going to have to," he reminded me.

My head whipped around. "Why, Coby? It's not like anything is going to come out of this." Although I said the words, I didn't believe them myself. I was so damn confused. We needed to get this shit with the human trafficking settled first before we could think about having a relationship. Right? Wouldn't it be selfish of us to be happy when so many others weren't?

"What are you scared of?" he asked softly.

"Everything," I snapped. "You. Us. What you went through should make you second guess everything but you're the one sitting here demanding for me to tell you my feelings. Why?"

"Because I know what we have is stronger than what I had with Leah."

"Do you miss her?"

Coby thought a moment, rubbing the scruff on his angular jaw. "I miss parts, yes. I loved her. I know I did. I may talk bad about her but in all honesty, I met her at a difficult time. Her ending her life only made it worse."

My heart pained for him. "How so?"

"My mom wanted me to amount to something more than being in the military. It got to the point where we stopped talking for years. When Leah died, I saw her at the funeral. We hadn't talked for five years before that."

"You must have been really young when you joined the military," I said in awe.

"I was. I joined when I was seventeen."

"You can do that?"

"Well … I did it." He smiled.

"You truly are inspiring, Coby." I chewed my bottom lip, looking intently into his eyes. "I know you want more from me but right now, I'm enjoying this."

"I just want your happiness." He cupped my cheek, leaning his mouth toward mine. "And I want your soul."

A flush of heat washed over me. "Yeah? What else do you want?"

He grinned and placed a soft kiss on my lips. "Just you."

I sighed. "You have a way with turning me on just from your words, Porter."

Coby chuckled. "You have a way of bringing them out of me."

"Really?" I raised an eyebrow. "I thought you were always like this."

"Well …" He shrugged. "It depends on the woman I guess."

"What do you mean?"

"If the woman isn't submissive in any way, then I don't bother, but with you, I found that I needed to control you even before I knew you would submit to me."

Sexually submitting. God, it was delicious.

"I have to be in control everywhere else in my life. I figure submitting in the bedroom would give me a break."

"Have you submitted to another man before?" Coby asked, cupping the back of my neck.

"No." I knew all through my sexual experience that I would end up submitting. All through my life, men had tried to dominate me but it never worked out. They were too shy. Timid. Scared that I would be mad or some shit. There should be only one pussy in bed, and it belonged between my legs.

"As much as I like that you've submitted to me, it gives me greater satisfaction that you trust me and that you know when to tell me to stop."

"I don't think I could ever tell you to stop, Coby."

He grunted but didn't say anything else.

It was the same response I got from him time and time again. I wasn't sure what more I expected from the guy. He had been through a lot. Lost everything in a short amount of time but a part of me was jealous over the fact that Leah had stolen his heart first. I tried convincing myself when I first heard about her that I wasn't jealous but I was human. It only made sense. But I would like to hope that I could steal part of his heart as well. If he let me.

***

(Coby)

I could sense the jealousy in Brogan. She didn't like hearing about my past with Leah but she asked questions anyway. Leah had taken part of my heart, loved it for a short time, and squeezed it to the point of death shortly after.

"I didn't know Leah was ill when I first met her," I said, needing to break the silence. "She hid it well."

"She never took her medication, did she?" Brogan grabbed my hand, brushing her thumb back and forth over my palm.

"No." I chuckled to myself, remembering the toxic fights we had and no matter what Leah had said to me, I still loved her.

"Looks like you can't get away from women who have issues." Brogan shook her head, her shoulders slumping with a heavy sigh.

"You don't have issues," I snapped, sick and fucking tired of her putting herself down. So, she interrogated men in the basement of the club for years. So, she fucked her stepbrother. She was human. She made mistakes. Just like every other fucking person in this shithole we called life.

"I *do* have issues, Coby," she said, her voice calm although I was raging on the inside. "As much as I love submitting to you in the bedroom, I'm sadistic at heart." She rose to her feet, stretching her arms above her head. "I should go."

"Go where, Brogan?" I followed suit and pulled her against me. "You have nowhere else to go."

"Thank you for that wonderful reminder, Coby," she cried, pushing me back. "You don't think I don't know that? You think I forgot that I lost everything?"

Rubbing the back of my neck, I only stared down at her.

She huffed, crossing her arms under chest. "I need to head back to the club to see if anything was salvageable. I'm sure the basement is fine." She shivered, chewing her bottom lip. "I don't think anything could get rid of it."

"Why do you say that?"

"Because it likes to remind me of what I've done," she muttered. "It holds my demons, Coby, and there's not a damn thing I can do about it."

CHAPTER NINETEEN

Brogan

EVERYTHING IN ME told me to run away. Coby was getting too close. I lived and breathed him for the past couple of months and as much as I didn't want it to change, these new feelings were suffocating me. They squeezed my lungs, forcing the air to stop its course through my body.

He never fought me. Even after all the shit he had been through with Leah, he never once tried pushing me away. Did he have the same feelings that I did?

Coby had disappeared into his office, and I found myself itching to go back to the bookstore. Although that man I had met not too long ago bothered me in a way that left my nerves on edge, the imaginary worlds called out to me. Reading was my solace, and I was ashamed to admit that I hadn't delved into a good book in a long time.

Heading to Coby's office, I took a breath, knowing he wouldn't want me to go out alone. I knocked on the door, waiting.

"Come in," he called out.

Opening the door slowly, I peeked my head in. "You busy?"

"Not at all." He sat back in his leather chair. "What's up?"

"I don't mean to bother you." I walked further into the room, shutting the door behind me.

"You never bother me, little one." He held out his hand. "Come here."

My heart gave a start at the rough demand and I did as I was told. Sitting on his lap, I wrapped his arm around my middle and kissed his cheek. "Working hard?"

He smirked. "Always. Now what's going on?"

"I want to go to the bookstore."

Coby stiffened. "Why?"

"What do you mean *why?* It's a bookstore. That should be a good enough reason."

"What if you see that man again?"

"I can't live life like that, Coby. I've seen a lot of men in my day that should scare me or bother me but I choose to ignore them." Although that man had something about him that set me a little on edge, I wouldn't let him stop me from going to the bookstore. "And besides, I'll be in public. Nothing will happen."

"I don't like this," Coby muttered, holding my hand tight in his.

"You need to trust that I can take care of myself. What do you think I did before I met you?"

"That's beside the point." He turned me in his arms. "I don't like that fucker who talked to you."

"You don't even know who he is, Coby. And you wouldn't have even known about him if I didn't say anything," I reminded him. "I promise I'll stay at the bookstore and be in an open area. He won't get me alone. He probably won't even be there." I kissed Coby softly on the mouth. "I promise."

Cupping my nape, he deepened the kiss, sliding his tongue between my lips.

I moaned, opening to him and gave him my every breath. Wrapping myself around him, I straddled his lap, pushing my hips into him. All thoughts of the bookstore were long forgotten.

His body grew under my touch, hard and rigid, begging me for my touch. It was a battle of who would break first. As much as I loved when Coby controlled me, I found at this point that I wanted to play. I wanted to see how far I would have to go to make him beg.

"Tell me what you want," he demanded, brushing his mouth down the length of my jaw. "Tell me you need me."

I smiled, tilting my head and ran my hands through the short hair at his nape.

"Tell me you crave my cock." His deep voice rumbled over me, sliding through my body like the blood that gave me life.

I *did* crave him. Every inch. Every hard vein.

"Brogan." The rough plea that left his mouth set my body on fire.

RUDE

Circling my hips against him, I pushed and pulled, taking from him what I wanted until even *I* couldn't control it.

"You like teasing me." He pulled my head back, staring intently in my eyes. "You want me to beg."

Shit. "Will you?"

His lips curled up into a wicked grin. "I don't beg for anything. Especially not from a little girl who thinks she can bring me to my knees just from her touch."

I smiled, licking up the length of his neck. "You won't have to beg, Coby. Your cock will do it for you."

He chuckled, pushing me back against the edge of his desk. Pulling a knife from his back pocket, he ran the blade down my center.

My breathing picked up, watching the metal sparkle in the dim light of the room. "Your knife doesn't scare me."

Coby raised an eyebrow. "I know it doesn't." With a flick of his wrist, the soft cotton of my shorts fell to the floor.

Cool air washed over my naked bottom half. "Coby." I arched, hinting, needing him inside of me. Some part of him. His cock. His fingers. His tongue. I didn't care.

"Spread your legs," he said, his voice rough. "Show me how wet you are."

I did as I was told, spreading my knees and ran my hands down my inner thighs. My fingers sent shivers down my spine as I opened myself to him, showing him exactly what he did to me and the effect he had on my body.

He licked his lips, his dark gaze watching my movements. Holding the handle of the knife tight in his hand, he ran the butt of it over my mound.

My heart jumped, my skin igniting on fire. One move and he could cut me.

Coby kept his gaze on mine, watching me, waiting for a hint that I wanted him to stop. But I didn't. I needed him to take me past the point of seduction. To show me that it was normal to crave the dark side of sex as long as it was consensual. That there was nothing wrong with being kinky if we were both safe.

"Trust me." Coby pushed the butt of the knife against my pussy, pumping slow over the opening.

Throwing my head back, a low moan left my mouth.

With his free hand, he grabbed hold of mine. "Let go for me, Brogan." He pushed the end inside of me, filling me until all I felt was the handle and his fingers.

I gasped, shaking around the hard object. This was wrong but felt so damn right at the same time. "Oh ..." A coherent sentence couldn't form on my mouth. I had been experienced but nothing compared to this moment. This time and place with Coby. Him fucking me with a knife.

****

(Coby)

My balls were going to fucking explode.

This knife and I had been through a lot. Threatening those who wronged me, slicing a few dozen or so necks, but never had it been inside a woman.

Brogan's moans and purrs slid into my ears as I thrust the butt of the knife in and out of her sweet pussy. The heady scent of her desire wafted into my nose, making my mouth water.

Pumping hard and deep, I wanted her orgasm. I wanted her to come all over my knife and when she did, she would beg me for more.

"Coby," she whimpered, lifting her hips up and down the length of the handle.

My cock hardened, pushing against my pants.

"I … *fuck.*" Brogan pushed me back, crashing her mouth to mine and rode the object between her legs. "Harder," she begged. "Show me how much you want to own me with every object possible."

Fuck me. Lifting her in my arms, I dropped her onto the desk and pumped the object in and out of her. Rough. Hard. It bordered on violent, reminding her of what my cock was about to do. "Come for me. Come like the kinky little whore you are."

She grinned, her pupils dilating. "Fuck me."

"I am." I shoved the butt of the knife into her as far as it would go.

She cried out, shaking beneath me. "Oh, yes."

"Scream my name, Brogan."

"Fuck," she shouted, her orgasm crashing through her.

Throwing the knife on the floor, I had my pants lowered and my cock free before she could take her next breath. Shoving myself inside of her, I bellowed out her name.

Brogan shook, gasping for air as I owned her with each pounding thrust.

Digging her heels into my ass, she pulled me tighter, taking all of me in. Grabbing my hand, she smirked and licked her tongue up the length of the cut in my palm.

My cock twitched.

Her grin widened. "Like that, baby?"

"Fuck me," I groaned. "You're a dirty little girl, aren't you?" I licked down the length of her jaw. "And you like it when I'm nice and deep, don't you?"

She moaned, her eyes fluttering closed. "More than you'll ever know."

I chuckled. "Oh, I think I know already." Slowing my hips, I pet a hand over her head. "You crave my cock. You enjoy the feeling of being owned." I enunciated each sentence with the movements of my hips, taking her higher and higher until she shattered around me. "I can feel your body ripple with pleasure as I force orgasm after orgasm out of you."

"Yes," she whimpered. "God, yes."

"Hmmm …" Pulling out of her, I flipped her onto her stomach.

Brogan smiled, licking her lips and gripped the edge of the desk.

Towering over her, I slid back inside her and covered her completely. It was slow. Rough. Pure delicious torture as I brought us both to the brink of passion. I wanted to fall over the edge of ecstasy with her. We used sex as a way of communicating, speaking through our bodies. And with Brogan, I could talk forever.

CHAPTER TWENTY

Brogan

COBY SMILED AT me.

I smiled back.

He looked away.

So did I.

A slight burn tingled on my cheeks as the memories of what we had been doing for the past hour melted into my mind. Coby fucked me with the handle of his knife. My heart jumped, although my body heated. It had felt amazing and he had instigated it but a part of me wondered if he expected me to push him away. It couldn't be normal for me to enjoy that dark side of kink.

"Brogan." Coby pinched my chin, forcing me to look at him. "What's wrong?"

"Nothing." I stepped into a new pair of black leggings I had purchased a couple days before, the soft material hugging my toned thighs.

"You're chewing your bottom lip like you haven't eaten in years. Tell me what's wrong."

I touched my swollen lip, not realizing I had been munching on it. "It's no big deal, Coby."

"Yes," he grabbed the tank top from my hands and slid it over my head. "It is."

Smacking his hands away, I smoothed the material down my center. "It's fine. Don't worry about it."

"Brogan."

"What, Coby?" I spun on him. "I'm embarrassed, all right? Is that what you wanted to hear?"

"Why are you embarrassed?" he asked, frowning.

"Because I let you fuck me with the handle of your knife. I'm all for kink but even that was new for me."

"You're ashamed."

"No. Yes. I don't know." I shook my head. "I have no idea how I feel about it."

Coby grabbed my hand, pulling me to the edge of the bed and sat with me in his arms. "What we do is strictly consensual between you and me. I won't do anything that you don't want me to do."

"How did you know that I wanted you to keep going?"

"I could read your body language. If I thought in any way that you were uncomfortable, I would have stopped. Next time I'll give you a safe word. That's my own fault. And for that, I'm sorry."

"A safe word?" I raised an eyebrow. "Seriously?"

He winked, and I swore my insides just melted.

RUDE

"You know I like my kink, Brogan. It's not just from reading and doing research. I have experience and want to learn as much as I can. I know what to do and what not to do. As long as you are safe and you trust me, that's all I care about." He kissed my shoulder and patted my butt. "I have some more work to do." He rose to his full height and placed a hard peck on my mouth. It was a silent reminder of who I belonged to and for that, I would never complain.

***

It was a cold blustery day as I made my way to the bookstore. I was somewhat surprised that Coby was okay with me going. I had invited him to join me but he stated he had too much work to do.

I couldn't understand why, but I was nervous to see that man again. And as I walked into the bookstore and saw him standing by the section of books I frequented, that nervousness only heightened.

"Ah, it seems we meet again," the beautiful man stated, catching me staring.

My neck heated, and I silently scolded myself for thinking he was attractive when really, he scared the shit out of me. Which wasn't easy to do.

"I guess so." I smiled, attempting to be friendly.

"Something's wrong," he said, frowning.

"No." I shook my head. "Sorry."

"You're lying." He turned to me. "Do I make you uncomfortable?"

"You're intense. Like my boyfriend."

Something flashed in the man's gaze over this new-found information. But he didn't say anything about it.

"Do you come here to buy books or are you psychic and know when I'm going to show up?" I crossed my arms under my chest, frowning, and embraced the sass that Coby had come to enjoy.

The man chuckled. "Paranoid a bit, are we?"

"What do you expect in this day and age? Maybe it's just a coincidence but every time I'm here, so are you. So, tell me, Mr. ..." When he didn't give me his name, I huffed and continued. "Anyway ... why are you here?"

"Isn't that a loaded question?" He grinned. "I could tell you but then I'd have to kill you and we wouldn't want to ruin that pretty face of yours."

"Right," I said slowly. Little did he know, that I could kill him just as quick. One thrust of a hardcover book in his temple and he would drop. I just had to him hard enough and he would fall to my feet. *On that note* ... "I think I should go." I grabbed a random novel, headed to the cash register, and checked out. When I looked to see if the man was following me, he was nowhere to be found. Odd. Definitely fucking odd.

Something about him bothered me and set my nerves on edge. Maybe Coby was right in his warnings and that I should stay away from the bookstore. Although, he would like it if I just stayed with him instead.

My phone rang, jarring me from my thoughts as I ran across the street. Noticing it was Brox calling me, I halted suddenly when I reached the sidewalk. "Brox."

"You need to get to the hospital," he demanded.

"Oh, God." I clapped a hand to my mouth. "What happened?"

"Benny. He's been shot."

CHAPTER TWENTY-ONE

Brogan

MY WORLD FELL out from beneath me. It was cliché to say but it was true. Benny was my everything. He was the glue that stuck our family together. We had issues, never having it easy in life and he was the one who remained positive. He already lost his leg. God needed to give him a break.

With shaky hands, I dialed Coby's number.

"Brogan? Where are you?" came his deep reply.

Tears welled in my eyes at the concern in his voice. "I'm standing outside your building. I need you to drive me to the hospital. Please."

"I'm on my way." And with that, he hung up.

Pacing back and forth, I didn't have to wait for Coby long.

His SUV pulled in front of me. "Tell me what happened," he demanded as I sat in the passenger seat.

"Benny was shot." I scrubbed a hand down my face. "I don't know anything else yet."

"Okay." He grabbed my hand, squeezing it hard. "I'm here."

We headed to the hospital. Apparently, the one in town was full from a bad accident that happened on the freeway so Benny was flown to the city. Either way, I didn't care where he was. I just wanted answers.

When we arrived at the hospital, I jumped out of the vehicle before Coby had a chance to put it into park.

"Yeah, we're here," Coby said into his cell. "Okay. Got it. See you later, brother." He followed me down the hall until we reached the elevators. "Give me your phone."

I did as he said, not thinking straight and prayed that he could get the answers for me.

Coby linked his fingers in mine, giving me the strength I needed.

I didn't know what had happened. I didn't know why or how or what the hell was going on. All I knew was that I would kill whoever hurt my brother.

"You'll get through this, little one," Coby said, leading me into the elevator. He pressed a button on the panel before giving my knuckles a gentle kiss.

"I can't deal with this shit," I whispered, my heart hammering in my chest.

"You won't have to deal with it alone." Coby placed a peck on my forehead when the doors opened. "Your brothers are just down the hall."

"How do you know that?" I asked, frowning.

"I've been texting Brox on your behalf."

A sigh of relief left me, thankful that Coby was the calm one between us, because if it would have been me, I would have freaked out first before getting the answers I needed.

"Brogie." Blake came around the corner, followed by Brox and Greyson.

I ran toward Blake, wrapping my arms around his hard waist. "Do we know anything yet?"

"Not yet," he said, returning the hug.

Brox pulled me from Blake's arms and enveloped me in a hard embrace. "I'll fucking kill whoever hurt him," he growled in my ear.

"I'm thinking the same thing," I told him.

He grunted, releasing me, and disappeared down the hallway into what I could only assume was the waiting area.

"Can I give you a hug?" Greyson asked, coming up beside me.

My gaze flicked to Coby who stood off to the side.

His jaw clenched but other than that, no other movement or emotion flashed on his face.

"Sure," I told Grey, turning toward him.

He smirked, pulling me against him and wrapped his arms around my middle. He inhaled. "You smell like sex."

My stomach dropped. Shoving out of his grip, I stomped down the hall where Brox had gone. It wasn't the time and place for me to yell and scream at Greyson. I wouldn't let him win. I loved him. He was my stepbrother but he was also an asshole.

"Do we know anything yet?" I asked Brox, slumping down in the chair beside him.

His hands curled into fists on his lap.

"Brox?" I touched his shoulder. "Talk to me."

At that point, Blake and Greyson joined us, sitting in their own respective seats. Greyson sat across the room from me, his brow crinkling in the middle. I knew I needed to talk to him. We needed to sort this shit out and move past what happened years ago.

"Someone needs to tell me what happened," I demanded. "Please."

A throat cleared from the doorway. Coby nodded toward me. "Can I talk to you?"

Letting out a heavy huff, I followed Coby out into the hallway and leaned against the wall.

"I talked to Blake," Coby said, standing beside me. "I didn't get much information out of him but he said that your brother was drunk."

My stomach somersaulted, bile rising to my throat. "I'm not surpruised," I muttered.

"Is that a problem?"

"I might as well tell you. Benny is an alcoholic. He started drinking heavily after getting discharged from the military. Losing his leg almost cost him not only his life but his sanity as well and swimming in the bottom of a bottle was the only thing that could stop him from going over that edge."

"I know how he feels." Coby shifted beside me, grabbing hold of my hand.

"You do?"

"I let myself go after Leah died. Alcohol and sex was the only way I felt somewhat normal but even then, it didn't do shit. I fell into my work and got hired on to do things no human being should ever be asked to do."

"Shit."

"Yup," he grunted. "Looks like all of us are all kinds of fucked up."

"It comes with the territory I guess." I scrubbed a hand down my face, sliding down the wall until I landed hard on the floor. "I love my brothers but they like to protect me as much as they can. They won't tell me shit until I scream and beg."

"What did Greyson say to you?" Coby sat on the floor beside me, not caring in the least that we were in a public setting.

"I don't think it's the time to talk about that," I mumbled.

"Maybe not, but, honestly, right now, I don't give a fuck. I'm tired and sick of losing control. So, tell me or I'll beat it out of him until he does."

Pulling from his grip, my head whipped around. "Just because you can control me in bed, doesn't mean shit, Coby."

"Yeah? Listen to me good, little girl." He pinched my chin, forcing me to look at him. "I've fallen to my knees for you. It may be inconsiderate of me to bring this up during a hard time but Greyson is the one who started it. So, tell me. *Now*."

"He told me I smelled like sex." I shoved from his grip. "Happy now?"

"Not one fucking bit."

***

(Coby)

When the time was right, I would kill him. Or drive my fist through his face at least. The fact that he made Brogan uncomfortable was enough to drive me mad.

I walked her back to the waiting room, leaving her with her brothers and stood off to the side. Watching.

Waiting. Ready for the time when she needed me. Until then, I would keep quiet.

"You need to tell me what happened," Brogan demanded again, staring each of her brothers head on.

"Benny got drunk." Brox pinched the bridge of his nose, exhaling a deep sigh. "He's been doing good but fell off the wagon."

"Why?" Brogan asked softly.

"We don't know." Blake shoved to his feet. "We don't know shit, and it's driving me fucking nuts."

"There has to be a reason for all of this," Brogan glanced my way, her eyes pleading with me for help. "I need to know what happened so I know who to kill."

There she was. I bit back a smile.

"Are you the Tapp family?" a young man dressed in white came into the room, looking down at his clipboard. "Benjamin Tapp?"

"It's Benny," Brogan said, rising to her feet. "He goes by Benny. Is he okay?"

The doctor glanced around the room. "You're all family?"

"Yes, we're his siblings." Greyson came up beside Brogan, placing a hand on her shoulder.

I knew it shouldn't but that small move irritated the fuck out of me. Everything in me told me to charge for him and push him up against the wall. I had to fight the urge to rip off every part that had touched her in the past.

"Please," Brogan pleaded. "Tell us if he's okay."

The doctor smiled. "He's fine. The surgery was a success. He had his stomach pumped due to the excessive amount of alcohol he drank but the bullet missed vital organs."

RUDE

The air had switched in the room, a collective breath of relief leaving Brogan and her brothers.

Brox, Blake, and Greyson gave each other the respective hugs required when someone finds out good news. Even though Greyson was the black sheep of the family, during something this difficult, they all pulled together like nothing had happened.

Expecting Brogan to hug each of them, I was surprised when she came toward me.

"He's fine," she whispered, wrapping her arms around my middle.

"He is." I returned the embrace, reveling in the feel of her warmth enveloping me but something still wasn't right. There was that familiar darkness in my gut that meant this family wasn't out of the clear yet. I had learned over time that anything could switch in a matter of a second. Benny needed to heal and get out of the hospital first before I believed that he was truly okay.

"What's wrong?" Brogan asked, staring up at me.

"Nothing." I kissed her forehead. "Why?"

"You're stiff." She frowned. "Talk to me. Please."

"I don't like hospitals." Which was somewhat the truth.

"Fine." She turned in my arms. "Can we see Benny now?"

***

(Brogan)

I wasn't sure what to expect when the doctor gave us permission to go see Benny but seeing my brother lying still in the hospital bed forced me to take a step back. My brothers greeted him, hugging and joking while I stood off to the side and waited. For what, I wasn't sure, but I couldn't find it in me to celebrate his safety. It didn't make sense. I knew that. But doing what I did for a living, anything could happen in a split second. I was happy he made it out of surgery but I would be even happier if he could go home.

"How are you feeling?" Brox asked him.

"Like I got shot." Benny winced as he tried to sit up. "Damn thing hurts like a bitch."

"The doctor said you lost your leg," Blake pointed out, nodding toward his leg that no longer had the prosthetic attached.

"Yeah." Benny scrubbed a shaky hand down his face.

"What happened?" I finally asked. He had been shot. He was missing his leg. And that was all I knew. What all anyone would tell me.

My brothers looked my way, none of them saying anything to me.

At that point, a laugh escaped my lips. "Wow. This is fucking great. Benny gets shot, loses his prosthetic leg in the process, almost dies, and no one will tell me shit. I thought Coby was closed up like a fucking vault." I shook my head. "If no one will tell me anything, I'll find out myself. You know I will and you also know how."

My brothers looked away, one by one, glancing down at Benny.

He met my stare head on, the only one of my siblings who wouldn't back down from my fight.

"Tell me," I demanded. "Or I'll find someone who will."

"Leave us," Benny told our brothers.

"Are you sure?" Blake asked.

"Did I stutter?" Benny snapped. "Leave. Or I'll let Brogan make good on her threat."

The guys left, shutting me in with our oldest brother.

"Come here," Benny demanded once we were alone. He pushed himself higher up the bed and patted the spot beside him.

As much as I was mad that no one would tell me anything, my feet moved of their own accord, and next thing I knew, I was sitting beside him.

"He's making you feistier," Benny said a moment later, breaking the silence.

I scoffed. "No one is making me do anything."

"That's my sister," Benny sighed, pinching the bridge of his nose. "You're probably disappointed in me."

"I haven't been told shit so I don't know if I'm disappointed or not because I don't know anything."

"I got a tip that Charles had shown up at a bar in the next town over."

"Wait." I spun on him. "Are you sitting here telling me that you know of Charles Brian?"

"Just because I'm no longer in the military, doesn't mean I don't know things."

"I respect all of you and what you've done for our country but I fucking hate all the secrets," I mumbled, slumping back beside him.

Benny wrapped a strong arm around my shoulders, holding me tight against him. "I know. Trust me, if I could tell you everything, I would but you know that it's classified."

"You're no longer in the military. Why does it even matter?"

"I can still get in trouble." He let out another sigh. "I was special forces. My team was supposed to bring down the terrorist part of the organization that your boyfriend is dealing with."

"He's not my …" I waved a hand in front of me. "Never mind … go on."

"When I arrived at the bar that Charles was supposedly at, I had a moment of weakness and let myself go."

I swallowed hard, knowing he had been struggling with alcoholism for years.

"Anyway, that's not an excuse. I saw Charles. He started spewing shit. He didn't know who I was but before I could get anywhere, I wound up here. I don't remember much else. I'm just thankful Greyson was with me."

"He was?" I sat up, turning toward Benny.

"We had gone to the bar together. He tried convincing me not to drink but it was the anniversary of my accident." A dark shadow passed in front of his face.

God, I completely forgot. "I'm so sorry. I forgot."

"It's fine." He shook his head. "It's not something I like reminding people about."

"I know." I pointed to his leg. "So, what happened there?"

"I got so drunk, I took it off and threw it at Charles." He shrugged. "Not my finest moment."

"Under normal circumstances, I'm sure it would have been funny." Ringing my hands in my lap, I let out a heavy sigh. "I'm just glad you're okay. Things could have gone very differently." I made a mental note to thank Greyson for saving our brother's life.

"Well, once I get my new leg, things will be back to normal. I'll head home and live life to its fullest." Benny rolled his eyes.

I laughed, rubbing the back of my neck. "Right. And I'll do the same."

Benny smiled softly. "You're in love with him."

My mouth fell open. "I have no idea what you're talking about."

"Sure you don't."

"Either way, no matter how I feel, Coby will be the first one to know. No one else." I wasn't ready to admit my true feelings for Coby when I had no idea what would come out of our relationship. We were fucking. That's how it started and that would be how it ended. But even I didn't believe those thoughts. I wanted him. For as long as I could have him, but he was so broken and torn over the loss of Leah and their baby, I wasn't sure if I would ever be able to get inside his heart.

"Good." Benny nodded once. "I like him. He's quiet and can't stand Greyson."

"Greyson's a good guy."

"When he gets his own way," Benny reminded me.

"Maybe." I glanced at the door.

"Hey." Benny grabbed my hands, holding them tight in his large palm. "Whatever happens, I'm here. I will always be here."

My heart sped up. "Why do you say that like you're going away?"

"Because life is fucking hard and we have no idea what tomorrow will bring."

"But you can't think like that," I told him. "Life is hard but you'll drive yourself crazy worrying about tomorrow. Live in the now. Who taught me that?"

"Thank you for throwing my words back at me," Benny mumbled.

"Listen." I grabbed his hand. "I love you. I love all of you but I don't appreciate you guys keeping things from me."

"I told you what happened, didn't I?"

"Yeah, after I yelled at you," I huffed. "You can't protect me forever."

"No, but I can sure fucking try." Benny shifted. "Brogan, you and your brothers are all I have. Forgive me for trying to keep you safe."

"What about Greyson? He was with you last night. What makes him so damn special?"

Benny didn't say anything.

"It's because he's a man, isn't it?" I laughed, shaking my head and rose from the bed. "Because he's the president of Hell's Harlem. Oooo ... so fucking scary." The time had finally come. I lost my damn mind.

"Brogan, you know that's not fucking true."

"No?" I cried, spinning on my brother. "Then tell me, Benny. Tell me what really happened last night."

"I was weak, all right?" he yelled. "I lost my shit. Every anniversary of my accident, I lose myself a little more. Excuse me for being fucking human. I'm a gimp. I'm single. No woman wants a broken man."

A bubble of laughter escaped me.

"What?" he scowled. "What is so damn funny?"

"You said no woman wants a broken man."

"I know what I said."

I glanced at the door leading out into the hallway. "You clearly don't know Coby," I whispered. "I love you, Benny, but I should go and let you get some rest."

Benny rubbed the back of his neck. "Come here."

"You're so demanding," I grumbled, my lips pulling up into a smile. I gave him a hug, holding him a little longer than what was necessary but I found that it was needed. I needed it more than anything.

"Go home, Brogie," Benny muttered, squeezing me one last time before letting me go.

I kissed his cheek and left the room.

I wasn't sure why but it felt like I had just told my brother good bye. For good.

CHAPTER TWENTY-TWO

Brogan

A ROUGH CALLOUSED hand cupped mine, holding and squeezing it tight. I poured all the strength it could muster into that small touch. It gave me everything I needed to find the courage to move on and get past this. Something was wrong. I couldn't quite place it or even understand why I had been feeling this way since Benny got shot but I couldn't get these thoughts out of my head.

It was late into the night. Coby was wrapped around me, holding my hand in his, and was breathing deep and even against my neck. He fell asleep not too long ago after he gave me everything I needed to get out of my head. My body was sore, aching and tired but the pleasure he granted me pulled me out of myself.

The phone rang, jarring through my thoughts.

Coby shifted. "Yeah."

My body remained still, my eyes staring into the darkness of the room.

"Are you sure?" he asked, his voice deepening.

I knew.

My stomach tumbled.

My heart sped up.

My breathing quickened.

But I still didn't move.

No tears. No sounds.

"Okay. I'll let her know. Yeah, we'll head down shortly." Coby hung up the phone, placing it back on the end table. "Brogan?"

"Don't," I whispered, my throat parched.

"Baby." He pushed the hair off my nape, kissing my shoulder. "I'm sorry."

"No," I swallowed hard, but still, no tears fell. Maybe something was wrong with me that I couldn't cry. I knew when I left the hospital that things could still take a turn for the worse but I had prayed that God would grant me this one pass.

"Benny got a blood clot. It was unexpected. I'm so fucking sorry, little one. They did everything they could to save him. He didn't make it."

Coby held me, rubbing his hand up and down my arm but all I could do was lie there. No words. No sounds. Nothing left my lips as he explained to me how my brother had died. I didn't care. I didn't care *how* he died. I didn't care about anything. I only cared that he would no longer be with us. He would no longer be the glue that held our family together. The one who set Greyson straight whenever he gave me shit for not returning the love he had for me. Benny would no longer give me a hard time for always forgetting the twin's birthday. He would no longer have to worry about being single or that he lost his leg. He wouldn't see me fall in love. He would no longer be there. For us.

A sob broke through me, stuttering into a silent cry of anguish.

"That's it, Brogan." Coby squeezed me. "Let it out."

My body trembled, tears finally falling down my cheeks.

Benny was gone.

And I hated him for it.

****

(Coby)

Not being able to do anything for Brogan slowly destroyed me. She cried in my arms but she wouldn't talk. She didn't say anything while she broke. She didn't talk while I dressed her and washed the tears from her cheeks. Words didn't leave her mouth as I put shoes on her feet and walked her to the elevator. No sounds escaped her lips as I held her hand in mine and reigned soft kisses all over her knuckles. Nothing slid between us when I told her that I loved her.

I loved her.

My heart gave a start. It had been so long since I allowed myself to feel any emotion toward a woman that this new revelation made me uneasy.

Brogan fell into herself.

I didn't want to take her to the hospital only for her to hear the words that I gently gave her. The doctor would explain the medical shit. Her brothers would probably lose it and demand other answers the doctor wouldn't be able to give.

And Brogan would plot revenge.

I knew because it would be what I would do.

When we arrived at the hospital, I pulled Brogan from the passenger seat and kissed her softly on the mouth. She didn't kiss me back. She was frozen. A shell of herself. She hid behind the mask of pain and utter agony of losing her brother.

She would come around. She would shatter. And I would be there to pick up the pieces.

***

(Brogan)

He loved me.

When Coby said the words, I said them back. But when he didn't respond, I knew I had only said them in my head. Understanding molded his handsome face into a dark solemn shadow. I was beside myself, looking down at my body from far away. I wanted to crawl inside my head and disappear. I didn't want to deal with this. I didn't want to hear the words Coby had said to me. I didn't want to know the details on how Benny died. I didn't want to deal with my brothers and see the sorrow on their faces.

A heavy hand rubbed my back in smooth circles. I had been sitting in the waiting room at the hospital for what felt like an eternity. I couldn't remember how we got there. I didn't remember Coby walking me through the doors that would now be my own personal hell. But I especially didn't want to remember that Benny died. That he left me. That he gave up and no longer fought to survive. He had been through so much. I craved the day I could avenge him.

Voices sounded around me, calling my name and pleading for me to talk. But I didn't. I couldn't. What would I say? I didn't want my brothers to see me break. I didn't want them to see me officially lose it. The only man who would see it would be Coby and I knew that he would be there to put me back together. I wished I could return the favor when he had found out his wife had died so many years before.

"Coby?" I whispered.

"Yeah, baby?" he kissed my knuckles. "I'm here."

"Did you have someone there when Leah died?"

"No." His face softened. "I didn't."

I looked up at him, cupping his cheek. "I'm sorry."

He gave me a small smile. "Don't worry about it. My brothers have been there for me even though they don't know what happened."

"But Dale does?"

"He does." Coby kissed my forehead, his lips lingering. "Don't worry about that, though."

"Was he there for you?"

"When he found out, yes."

I nodded. "I'm glad." I leaned against him, gripping his hoodie in my hand. The scent of musk and fresh mint, wafted into my nose, making my heart stutter.

"Now what?" Brox asked, slumping down beside me. He grabbed my free hand, curling his fingers in mine.

"We start making arrangements." Greyson sat on the wooden table in front of us with Blake sitting beside him. "We ..." He swallowed. "Move on, I guess."

"Fuck." Blake shoved to his feet, storming out of the room.

"Take care of him," I told Brox, squeezing his hand. "Please. I can't do this without you guys."

Brox nodded, kissing my head. "Take care of our sister," he told Coby. "Please."

"I will." Coby cupped my thigh, giving it a gentle squeeze.

Brox left the room in search of Blake.

"I'll go after them," Greyson muttered, pushing to his full height.

Coby released my hand and stood from the chair.

Grey took a step back, his brows narrowing in the center. His eyes were red; the corners wrinkling like had aged in a matter of hours.

Coby stared at him for what felt like years before he pulled Grey into a hug. It wasn't that clap a hand on your shoulder type of hug. It was a full-on bear hug.

Grey's body stiffened before his shoulders relaxed and he returned the embrace.

I could hear quiet mumbling from Coby but I wasn't able to make out anything that was being said.

Greyson nodded every so often, fresh tears rolling down his cheeks.

My eyes burned.

Coby released him, holding him at arm's length. "I meant what I said."

"I know," Greyson said, his voice thick.

"Come here, little one." Coby held a hand out for me.

I wasn't sure what exactly was going on but I did as I was told and slid my hand in his.

Coby kissed the back of it and pushed me toward Greyson. "I'll be out in the hall," he whispered in my ear. He stopped at the doorway, glancing back at me.

Thank you, I mouthed to him.

He nodded once, disappearing around the corner.

"Brogan."

At the sound of my name coming from Greyson, I threw myself in his arms.

We fell to the couch, silently crying between us.

"I'm so fucking sorry," he muttered into the crook of my neck.

"Don't," I pleaded. "It's in the past."

"But—"

"Please, Grey," I pulled back. "Let's move forward. It's what Benny would want."

"I don't know if I can," he scrubbed his hands down his face, roughly wiping the tears from under his eyes. "But I now know that it's done between us."

I held my breath, waiting for him to make a snide remark.

"He loves you, and I know you love him. I'll step aside and stop being a dick but I will always love you too. You can't stop that."

"I know." I wrapped my arms around his neck. "And a part of me will always love you a little more."

***

Depression had settled in. I tried to stop it and push it away but losing a sibling was something I wouldn't even wish on my worst enemy. Shadows darkened my soul. Enraged thoughts traveled through my mind, threatening to control me and take over that last bit of hope I had.

RUDE

Coby had done everything he could to help me feel better. He held me. Put up with my random screams during the night. And kept me close by whenever we weren't in his bedroom. I wouldn't hurt myself. He knew that. *I* knew that. But he still felt the need to keep me within touching distance.

If he was working in his office, he would keep me on his lap. If he had to go into the office, he would bring me with him. I was like a child who couldn't take care of themselves and needed to be watched constantly but I didn't know how to bring myself out of this.

Benny and I had been closer than I was with the rest of my brothers. Even though he was the oldest and I was the youngest, we bonded in a way that I couldn't with the others. When he died, he took a piece of me with him and left behind a bitter woman who couldn't fend for herself. The only way I ate and showered was if Coby forced me. I could see him age before my eyes but no matter what he did, I couldn't snap out of it.

It had been a month since Benny passed away. We did the funeral and burial thing, no thanks to me. My brothers had been a Godsend.

I couldn't stop myself from freaking out when I watched Benny being lowered into the ground. The fact that I would never see him again or hear his deep soothing voice pushed me over the edge until I threw myself on top of his casket.

Coby had been the only one who could pull me off it, holding me against him as I sobbed uncontrollably in his arms.

"Little one." Coby kissed me softly on the mouth. "Your sisters are stopping by," he told me one afternoon.

"Really?" I sat up, rubbing the kink in my neck.

His eyes brightened. "Yes, baby."

I looked around me and then down at myself. I was wearing Coby's boxers and t-shirt. He had fed me. Washed me. Took care of me when all I did was lay around like a lump.

"I'm …" I swallowed hard. "Thank you."

"You don't need to thank me." He smiled softly. "I invited everyone over."

My head fell in my hands, my shoulders shaking. It had been a whole month. Thirty-one days. All my thoughts traveled back to the day Benny was put in the ground. The first pile of dirt landing on the casket. My screams. My rage over Benny leaving us. My brothers couldn't console me. My sisters couldn't. The only person who could get through to me at all was Coby, and even then, I wasn't sure if it was enough.

"You'll get through this." Coby kissed my head, rising to his feet.

"I don't want to," I whispered, my words falling on deaf ears.

***

(Coby)

Once everyone stopped by, I found that I had to take a step back. Voices chattered. Hugs were passed. Brogan attempted to smile even though her eyes showcased pain and heartache.

"How's she doing?" Angel asked, coming up beside me and leaned against the wall.

"Not good. She's hiding but this is the first time I've seen any light in her eyes since Benny died." I rubbed the back of my neck. "How's Jay and the baby?"

Angel cleared his throat. "Good. Healthy. Sorry I haven't officially announced it."

I grunted. "We all have shit going on, brother."

"How are *you* doing?"

"I'm fucking perfect," I grumbled, needing a drink.

"What happened to your hand?" Dale asked, nodding toward me.

"Just a paper cut," I answered, biting back a smirk at the bandage wrapped around my hand.

"I'm losing my whole team," Angel interrupted.

"I'm still around," I reminded him.

"For how long?" Angel asked, rubbing a hand down his face. "Listen, I love you, all of you, but we all have our own shit going on. You, Stone, Dale, and I are all that's left in Vice-One. The boss is riding my ass to add more to the team."

"Really?" My head whipped around. "How long do you have?"

"He's giving me until after the baby is born."

Which was only a couple of months. "If you need help, you know where to find me."

Angel clapped a hand on my shoulder, squeezing it lightly. "I know." He stepped in front of me. "Do we know who did this?" Meaning, did we know who killed Brogan's brother.

"Not yet."

"We're going to find out, aren't we?"

"You bet your fucking ass we are," I told him.

Angel grinned. "Good."

***

(Brogan)

My sisters huddled around me. My brothers sat nearby. Vice-One stood off to the side, watching and waiting. And Coby? He was nowhere to be found but the hairs on the back of my neck tingled, so I knew he was close by.

"How are you doing?" Brox asked, holding my hand tight in his.

I shrugged. I had no fucking idea how I was doing. I had no idea how I would move on from our brother dying.

My sisters talked amongst themselves, looking my way every so often. Much like everyone else, they were waiting for me to snap.

Rising to my feet, I headed to the kitchen in search of alcohol. Something. Anything to take me away from this pain etched into my heart.

"There's no alcohol here," Coby said, standing in the doorway.

Tears welled in my eyes. "I need to forget."

"Alcohol won't do that, little one." Coby stepped up behind me. "Trust me, I know that from experience."

"Then do something, Coby," I pleaded, gripping his shirt tight in my hands. "Do anything to take away this pain. Please. I can't deal with it."

Coby wrapped his arms around me.

"I can't ..." I hiccupped, falling to my knees. "Make me forget."

"It will take time, Brogan," Coby said gently, rubbing his hand up and down my back.

"No." I shook my head, pulling at my hair. "Make me forget now." Throwing myself in his arms, I crashed my mouth to his.

"Brogan," he groaned, kissing me back. But then he did the unexpected and pushed me back, cupping my face. "Don't."

I fought against him, needing to feel something other than pain. I needed to feel the connection he and I shared that allowed me to get out of my head. "Please, Coby."

"No," he said, his voice firm.

Shoving from his grip, I didn't listen and continued trying to kiss him. Running my hands over his growing erection, I reveled internally that his body listened to me. It would give me what I needed whether his mind was for it or not.

"Brogan." He pushed me off him. "Stop this. Right now."

"Coby," Dale said from the entryway to the kitchen.

"Leave us," Coby boomed before aiming his fury back at me. "You're coming with me." He pulled me to my feet, dragging me behind him until we reached his bedroom. Slamming the door behind him, he pushed me onto the bed. "You want me? Is this how you want to forget?" He was on me before I could comprehend what was going on. His tongue forced its way into my mouth, shoving and sliding against mine until I was writhing beneath him. His hands slid down my body, rough and needy, bordering on desperate. He released my mouth, staring down at me with dark lust filled eyes. "You want me to fuck you until you pass out and forget all the shit that's happened?"

Tears welled in my eyes, rolling down my cheeks. "I can't deal with this," I sobbed, covering my face with my hands.

"So, you think fucking me will help?" He pulled me to the edge of the bed, towering over me.

"Yes," I whispered.

"Baby." His face softened. "It doesn't work that way."

"I just need to feel something other than this pain. This agony." I gripped my chest. "It hurts, Coby. It hurts so damn much." The cries wracked through me, shattering from within.

"You can't cover this pain with alcohol or sex." Coby knelt between my legs, pulling my hands from my face. "You need time. All of you need it." He wrapped his arms around me, holding me in his lap. "Let it out, little one. Let it all out."

***

(Coby)

Before I met Brogan, if a woman begged for me to fuck her, no matter the situation, I would have. I would have drove so deep inside her body she would forget that she ever begged in the first place. But with Brogan, my little one, I wasn't able to do it. As much as my body desired her begging, it wasn't right.

After Brogan passed out from exhaustion, I kissed her cheek and petted her hair. I covered her face in soft kisses, holding and touching her. I tried everything to give her the strength she needed to get through this.

A hard knock sounded on the door.

"Come in," I said, holding Brogan tighter against me.

"Hey." Dale opened the door slightly, peeking his head into the room. "We're going to head out."

I nodded. Kissing Brogan's cheek one last time, I let her go and rose from the bed.

"Where are you going?" she asked, her eyelids fluttering open.

"I'll be back in a couple minutes."

"Okay." She curled her body around the comforter. "I love you," she whispered.

My heart stuttered.

Letting out a heavy sigh, I left the room and quietly shut the door behind me.

"How's she doing?" Dale asked, his brows furrowing.

"Fuck." I slid down the wall, dropping my head in my hands. I didn't know how to be there for her when no one had been there for me when I needed them most. I didn't know how to deal with this shit. "She's losing herself."

Dale sat beside me. "We'll find the bastard who did this."

"Her brothers are saying he was just in the wrong place at the wrong time but with all of the shit going down, I have to be sure. I need to get justice for her."

"I know, brother."

"Hey." Angel came from around the corner. "We're meeting up tomorrow morning."

"You think that's best?" Dale asked, stretching out his legs in front of him.

"We have no choice," Angel muttered. "Greyson thinks this has something to do with Charles."

"Fuck me," I growled.

"Are you sure? How the hell would he even know who Benny was? He's never even seen Brogan." Dale rose from the floor. "None of this shit makes sense."

"I know," Angel came toward us, keeping his voice low. "The girls don't need to know yet. I'm trying to keep Jay as far from this as possible until the time is right." He paused. "We head out on Friday."

"Are you fucking kidding me right now?" I snapped, pushing to my feet.

"It's your job, Coby," Angel narrowed his eyes at me. "Did you forget that?"

"No," I rubbed my neck. "Fuck." I looked between my brothers and the door which Brogan hid behind. She was wrapped up in my bed, her scent covering the sheets. My body stirred. A part of me wished I would have listened to her pleas and cries for me to fuck her and make her forget. I would. But not yet. And especially not when our friends were over. She wasn't thinking straight, but I would never judge her for that.

"I understand that Brogan needs you right now but she has her sisters and her brothers," Angel said. "*We* need you, Coby."

My chest constricted. All of these years, I had never been told I was needed by someone else until Brogan came into my life.

"I don't know what to do," I muttered, rubbing my hands up and down my jean-clad thighs.

"Be there for her." Angel cupped my shoulders, leaning his forehead against mine. "And be there with us so we can give her and her brothers the justice they deserve. Help us find Benny's murderer."

"I'll kill him," I confessed. "I'll rip off every limb and piss down his fucking throat."

"We'll be right there behind you, brother." Stone came up beside us, followed by Asher.

"We all will." Asher crossed his arms under his chest, his face twisting into a wicked grin. "And we'll enjoy every second of it."

"I love you guys," I whispered.

"Aww." Dale kissed my cheek. "Don't get all soft on us now."

"Lay off, fucker." I pushed him, rubbing the spot where his lips had been. "Who knows where that mouth was last."

"Ha! You are so damn funny, aren't you?" Dale hooked an arm around my neck, kissing me again.

I didn't push him that time, savoring the feel of being around my brothers.

"We love you, man, and you know that we'll do anything to make sure that girl of yours is safe. We'll avenge her and her brothers and show these bastards just how nasty we can fucking get." Angel winked. "I love my job."

CHAPTER TWENTY-THREE

Brogan

A COUPLE DAYS passed since everyone had shown up to Coby's apartment. Dealing with Benny's death didn't get any easier. Especially when I went to pick up my phone to call him. But spending as much time as I could with my brothers helped. A lot. Greyson had been easier to deal with. He and Coby were civil to each other which was all I could ask for. I loved them both. I knew that now. And both of them helped me during two of the hardest things I had ever gone through. The only difference between Coby and Greyson was that I didn't want things to end with Coby after I felt better.

I woke one night, alone. I had been staying with Coby for what felt like forever but his place still didn't feel like my home. Even though he had taken me shopping and his closet and dresser now held some of my clothes, it wasn't enough. I couldn't put my finger on it but the apartment was missing something.

Sighing, I rolled over onto my back. Coby had also left me alone while I mourned the loss of my brother. He had been there for me, taking care of me as much as he could, but we hadn't had sex since before Benny died. Coby may have been okay with that, but I wasn't.

Rising from the bed, I went in search of the man I craved. I needed his taste on my tongue. His skin shivering beneath my touch. His scent on my body.

I pulled on one of Coby's black t-shirts, the fabric hitting just above my knees and trudged out into the hall. The apartment was lit up, but there was still no sign of him.

When I reached his office, a shiver trembled through me. I went to knock but hesitated. What if he turned me down and told me I needed more time? No. I swallowed hard. He wouldn't do that. It had been long enough. I needed him.

Instead of knocking, I pushed open the door and saw him sitting behind his desk.

"Hey, little one." He smiled softly. "What are you doing up?"

I closed the door behind me, leaning against the hard wood, and waited.

He sat back, his eyes filling with lust. "What do you want?"

My body buzzed at the rough vibrato of his voice.

Coby rose from the chair and stalked toward me, the heft between his legs proving that he wouldn't turn me down tonight.

I still didn't say anything as I only stared him down.

Brushing the back of his hand down my cheek, he pinched my chin and tilted my head to meet his mouth.

A sigh escaped me and that was when all bets were off. I growled, pushing him back and jumped in his arms. When my mouth crashed to his, I knew this was where I belonged. This was the only thing that would be make me feel better.

Coby didn't even hesitate and fisted my hair in his hands, deepening the kiss.

We landed hard on the couch, with me straddling his lap and his hands roughly roaming up the length of my body.

Lifting the shirt over my head, my mouth was back on him before he could ask me again what I had wanted.

His fingers inched between us, running through the folds of my pussy before thrusting into me hard.

I whimpered, riding his hand, and licked up the length of his neck.

Our breathing quickened. Our hands never stopped touching. God, I loved this man and how he made me feel.

Sinking my teeth into his collar bone, I cried out when his thumb brushed over my aching clit.

Coby still didn't say anything. I realized then that he was letting me be in control. He knew I needed him.

He inserted a third finger into my shaking body, the sounds of my slick heat filling the room as I fucked his hand.

I wanted his dick inside me but I couldn't stop. My hips moved back and forth, riding his fingers.

Laying me onto my back, he petted my hair and pumped his hand between my legs. No words were said. The only sound was his hand pleasing my body.

Coby released me, brought his hand up to his mouth, and sucked a finger between his lips. A wicked grin spread on his face when he reached back between us.

I watched a forth finger enter me, his hand filling my lower body. A slight tingle of pain heated my skin at being stretched wide, but the more he thrust, the more it turned into a roaring pleasure.

"I'm going to fill every inch of you," he whispered, sucking my lip between his teeth.

Arching beneath him, I panted, hinting and waiting. Wrapping my hand around his wrist, I stopped him from giving me the release I craved.

"I want to come with you," I said, my chest rising and falling.

Coby sat back, pulling me into his arms.

With shaky hands, I reached into the waistband of his pants and pulled out his straining cock.

His breath hitched, his eyes fluttering closed. "Fuck, Brogan."

I took that as my cue and dropped my body down the length of him.

His eyes popped open, his hands moving to my hips, stopping me from riding him.

My heart jumped at the dark sadistic look in his gaze. "Coby?"

He pushed me off him and rose from the couch before slipping his pants down his legs. He stood naked before me, all male. All Coby Porter. "Turn around and hold onto the back of the couch."

I did as I was told.

He came up behind me, wrapping his arm around my waist. His hot breath scorched my neck. "I'll give you what you need, little one. Don't ever forget that."

With his free hand, it inched between us, rubbing over my center.

I purred, a hard moan leaving my mouth.

Coby circled his hand around my throat, holding me tight against him when his finger brushed over the tight hole between the cheeks of my ass.

My eyes popped open. "Coby."

His hand tightened. "Trust me. Trust that I'll make you feel good."

I nodded, swallowing hard and gripped his arm that was wrapped around my body.

Coby slid his finger into the tight puckered area.

A groan escaped me, my hips bucking back against him.

Pushing me forward, he moved his hand from around my throat and wrapped his arm around my middle. His lips placed kisses on my cheeks and head repeatedly, his hot breath heating me from within.

When his finger was replaced with the tip of his cock, I waited. I needed all of him. I needed him to take me to new heights and make me forget all the shit that had happened. All the shit I had done in my life. I wanted to be in the moment with Coby and just feel *him*. That was it.

Coby used the lubricant from my body, running his fingers from my pussy up to my ass and back down again. "I love you, little one," he whispered in my ear, thrusting a finger hard into my body.

I cried out, shaking beneath him. "I love you too," I moaned, gripping the cushion tight in my hands.

A cold liquid slid between my ass. I didn't even get a chance to ask what it was when the tip of his cock pushed into the tight opening.

He pushed.

I breathed.

He thrust.

I moaned.

"That's my girl," he breathed hard against my neck, placing a soft peck on my shoulder. "Take all of me."

Pain singed into a dull roar but was soon replaced with an undying lust. He filled me. Every inch. And he was now in a part of my body where no man had ever been.

***

(Coby)

Brogan was tight as *fuck*.

Her beautiful ass wrapped around my dick, squeezing, begging. Hinting for me to move. When she didn't say anything, I almost stopped but her unexpected moans of pleasure gave me the sign that I needed.

I kissed her shoulder one last time, leaned back and gripped her hips. She needed me. I knew it as soon as she walked into my office. It had been over a month and I would spend the night making up for lost time.

"I'm going to fuck you now," I told her, landing a hard swat on the right cheek of her ass.

She whimpered, pushing back against me.

"Do you want me to move?" I asked, brushing the tips of my fingers down her spine.

She shivered, nodding and looked at me over her shoulder. "Fuck my ass, Coby."

God, I loved her.

Digging my fingers into her hips, I pulled most of the way out of her body and thrust so hard, she screamed. I could feel the juices from her body, running down my balls and that only gave me the edge to pump harder and faster.

Her screams turned wild, her head thrashing from side to side.

She was going to break and I would be there to pick her up.

"Come for me," I bellowed, hammering my hips against hers.

She whimpered, meeting me thrust for thrust.

When she still didn't let herself go, I pushed her forward and reached a hand around her.

Brogan gasped once I made contact with her swollen clit. Her head fell back against my shoulder, her mouth opened in a silent scream.

"That's it, baby." I kissed her neck and cupped her forehead, keeping her head back. Stroking her clit and fucking her ass, I forced the orgasm out of her.

She shook, incoherent sounds leaving her lips until my name fell from her mouth on a violent scream.

My hips sped up, my fingers pinched and pulled until she was shaking and trembling beneath me a second time. I would give anything to make her forget all the wrong doings that had happened in her life. If I couldn't make her forget forever, I would make her forget for at least the night.

"Come again, beautiful girl." I kissed her cheek, thrusting my fingers into her soaked pussy. "Let that orgasm rip through you."

She moaned, licking her parched lips. "I love you," she whispered.

"I love you." I nibbled the soft spot behind her ear. "But right now, I'm going to fuck you like that inner slut of yours wants."

She grinned, pushing back against me. "Then have at it, baby."

And I did.

For the rest of the night, I fucked her until there was nothing left. And I loved her even more for it.

CHAPTER TWENTY-FOUR

Brogan

THE NEXT MORNING, I woke with a heavy body wrapped around mine. I was sore. Achy and stiff. And definitely sticky. Very sticky. It was damn delicious to say the least.

Coby shifted. The hair on his legs scratched at mine, sending a hot shiver racing through me. The heavy weight of his cock rested against my ass, reminding me exactly where it had been a couple hours before. It was heaven. It was everything I had ever needed. Coby took me to new heights, forced me to break in his arms and put the pieces of me back together again. He Humpty-Dumptied the fuck out of me.

I sighed, stretching my arms out in front of me, and lifted my head.

Coby smiled, kissing my forehead. "Mornin'."

I shivered at his deep gravelly voice. "Morning."

His hand ran down my naked back before cupping my rear.

My lips turned up into a grin. "I think someone has a thing for my ass."

"Fuck," he groaned. "You have no idea."

I laughed, kissing him hard on the mouth.

Coby pushed me onto my back, snarling into my neck.

Giggling, I wrapped my arms around his shoulders, hugging him against me. "Thank you for last night."

He lifted his head, brushing my hair off my forehead. "And this morning?"

My cheeks heated. "Oh, yeah."

He chuckled, placing a soft peck on my mouth before sitting back. "We leave on Friday." He turned to me, leaning his head against the headboard. "I don't want to go."

"It's your job, Coby. I understand." As much as I would miss him, I knew he needed to get away. It was a driving force that kept him going. "Besides, you have some bad guys to get."

"Yeah." He smirked. "I do." He pulled me into his arms, running his hands down my back. "Does it turn you on?"

My breath caught. "What?"

Coby cupped my breast, taking the nipple between his lips. "That I'll be dressed to kill. Hiding. Waiting. Ready to pounce like a cobra stalking its prey."

I moaned, running my hands through his dark hair and tugged his head back. "Knowing that you'll be dirty, dressed in that hot as fuck uniform, and saving our country? Damn right it turns me on."

"Then prove it, my kinky little girl." Coby lifted me and dropped me on his cock. "Prove how much it turns you on."

I cried out, the size of him invading my unprepared body.

"Don't sit there and whine like a little bitch." He cupped my nape, forcing me to look at him. "I know how your body works, Brogan."

My pussy turned slick, my body sliding up and down his length.

He grinned. "See?"

"You're an asshole," I breathed out.

"Yeah, but you love me." His hand moved to the small of my back. "Now ride me and fuck the shit out of my cock."

God, I did love him. His controlling demeanor. His incessant need to demand things of me. But I knew he would never hurt me. He would never force anything of me that I didn't want to give him in return.

Circling my hips against him, I cupped his jaw and bit his bottom lip.

He growled, the deep sound rumbling from his chest. "You play fucking dirty."

"And you love it."

***

(Coby)

It was Friday. It was the day that lead us on a mission for who the fuck knew how long. This would be hell but it would be even worse this time around because I left a hot little thing alone in my bed that morning.

RUDE

Brogan and I spent three days wrapped in each other's arms. I took what I needed from her and gave it back tenfold.

My body still hurt.

"I don't like this," Dale suddenly said, his knee bouncing up and down.

We were briefed and thrown to the wolves. It usually took a day or two but we were already on our way to what I liked to call my home away from home.

"You never like this," Stone pointed out, rubbing the scruff on his jaw.

Angel only grunted before turning back to Henley Jinx, one of the new members of Vice-One. He was just a kid but passed through the military faster than Dale went through women. I didn't know his story but Angel trusted him, and that was all I cared about.

"First time?" Dale asked Lian Wolfe, a large fucker who had a slashed scar across his cheek.

"First time with you," Lian answered, his voice rough like he had gargled with broken glass.

"Touché." Dale huffed, running his hands up and down his thighs.

"Stop trying to make small talk," I told him. "We can do that shit when we get home."

"Something's wrong." Dale shook his head. "I don't care what you fuckers think. You know I'm right."

He was. I felt it too. It was that familiar itch inside of my gut. It was the driving force behind my incessant need to put a bullet in the bastards' heads who threatened everything we lived for.

"Coby," Angel barked.

I raised an eyebrow, challenging my brother head on.

He shook his head. "You trust us?"

"With my fucking life." I looked at each of them. I didn't know Henley and Lian as well yet but Angel recruited them. "You trust me?"

Several grunts and nods later, a breath of relief washed over us.

"We need to say a prayer," Stone said finally.

In a time like this, even if you didn't believe in a higher power, hearing a prayer, any sort of prayer, gave you the courage to fight. It brought us together and forced us to work as one. We were Vice-One. Brothers. Saviors. And I would have each of their backs until this shit ended for good. Something told me that we wouldn't make it out of this one without a fight. We brought down terrorists, but with the human trafficking shit, it all mixed as one when it was so close to home.

"I love you guys," Angel said.

Dale smirked. "I love you fuckers too."

CHAPTER TWENTY-FIVE

Brogan

WHILE THE GUYS were away, the girls played. We hung out at each other's respective homes, taking turns each night. We didn't want to be alone and even though Creena had her own apartment, we wanted her nearby. That was Stone's orders.

"How come Stone is the only one who goes by his last name?" Creena asked one afternoon while we were doing dishes.

"I don't know." I shrugged. "I call Coby by his last name sometimes." *And that usually ended up in sex.* For whatever reason, Coby loved it when I called him *Porter*.

"Maybe I'll just start calling him Vincent." Creena winked. "See how he likes that."

I laughed, shaking my head. "You two go out yet?"

She scoffed. "No. He's a nice guy but …" Her gaze took on a faraway look. "Anyway … I'm not ready to settle down."

"I thought the same thing." I playfully elbowed her in the side.

"You and Coby seem cozy," she pointed out, placing a plate in the drying rack.

"Yeah … it's weird being here without him, though." My body buzzed just remembering our conversation from a couple nights ago. Wherever he was had just enough reception that we could video chat and we could watch each other come. It was the fastest I ever had an orgasm from my own hands. With Coby controlling everything I did just from his words, he had me wrapped right around his finger. And God, when his large hand closed around his—

"Brogan."

I jumped, my gaze landing on Jay. "What?"

"I was talking to you." She frowned, her eyes holding a hint of amusement.

"Sorry." My cheeks heated. "I'm a little distracted."

"I can understand why." She sighed, leaning against the counter and nodded toward Max and Meeka who were sitting on the couch in the living room. "I worry about her."

I followed her gaze.

Max laughed at something Meeka said but the smile never reached her eyes. It had been the same thing with Jay a couple months ago when her ex wouldn't leave her alone.

"How are your brothers doing?" Jay asked, grabbing a towel.

"They're dealing with Benny's death the best way they know how." I dropped a plate in the rack.

"By drinking?" Creena raised an eyebrow.

"Yeah. As much as I don't like it, I understand why. I just wish they would use something else to help them deal with it instead of alcohol." It was too close to home. Benny might not have been shot if he didn't get drunk and ended up at that shady bar.

"How are *you* doing?" Jay nudged me gently.

I shrugged. "When Coby was home, I would use him since I don't drink much, but now that he's not, I sleep. A lot." His bed smelled like him, even after I washed the sheets. It also reminded me of all the times we had spent in it together. Everywhere I looked in this apartment reminded me of things we had done and where we had done it.

"You love him," Jay pointed out. "A lot."

My cheeks heated. Again. "Yeah. I do."

"Aww. My bestie has fallen in love," Meeka teased, coming up behind me. "It's about damn time too."

I laughed. "What's that supposed to mean?"

"It means that we're happy that you are happy," Max said softly.

"God, I love you girls," my throat tightened. "And here I am getting all emotional and shit."

They laughed.

"We love you too." Jay smiled. "But we will help you get whoever killed your brother."

My heart jumped, the light mood in the air turning dark and dangerous. "You will?"

Creena clapped a hand on my shoulder. "We're family, and when one of ours is hurt, we fight back."

"As one," Meeka added.

"Right now, I can't do shit." Jay rubbed her swollen belly. "But after this bean is out, if nothing happens before then, I'll rip up this fucking town with you."

"Oh, God."

All heads turned to Max.

Her eyes were wide, shadowed by a tremor of fear.

"Max?" Creena took a step toward. "What's wrong?"

"Something doesn't feel right," Max said, her face twisting with pain.

"Okay," Creena gripped her shoulders, guiding her to a chair at the table. "You're almost seven months pregnant, Max. Things can start to feel a little different."

"No," Max said through gritted teeth. "It's the baby. Please. God."

"Call 911," Creena demanded, holding Max's hand tight in hers. "Okay, Max. Come on, girl. You got this. You're strong. Breathe."

"It's too soon." Max's chest rose and fell, a sheen of sweat coating her brow. "It's too soon."

Meeka called for an ambulance.

Jay knelt at the other side of her best friend, trying to keep her as calm as possible.

Suddenly, a scream tore through Max. It was so loud, I had to cover my ears. It was a sound I never wanted to hear again.

***

(Coby)

My brothers huddled together, closing in on a bunker that held four underground terrorists that no one knew about until that morning. Except for us of course. Our new boss was nothing like Eric Vega. He went by the book most days but then there were some when he just wanted shit done and over with.

Lian leaned against the wall, holding up four fingers and indicated for one of us to go around back. Dale took that as his cue and slid around the building.

I was holed up, a few yards away and waited for any sign that they needed my help. But this team worked well together. Even with Asher no longer being in Vice-One, he had met Lian and Henley briefly. I didn't even know we were getting new recruits until I saw them on the plane. What didn't sit well with me was that Asher was no longer a part of this team. Even though his PTSD stemmed from a difficult childhood, I would end these mother fuckers just for him.

"Fucking fuck," Angel growled.

Shit. "What's going on?" I asked into the radio.

"There are more than four bastards in here."

Pop. Pop.

Gun shots rang out, sending my blood soaring through my veins. This was what I lived for. Bringing the bad guys to justice. Knowing that these fuckers were behind the women who were being taken, gave me a brief moment of hope.

"Coby, watch our backs," Angel instructed.

He didn't have to tell me twice.

I was ready and waiting. My fingers twitched, itching with the need to end these bastards before they took anymore innocent lives.

Jay's sister was still holed up somewhere unknown, Jay being the only person who knew, and even then, I wasn't sure how much they saw each other. It was a rocky relationship and also none of my damn business. What the hell was wrong with me? *Focus, Coby.*

Zeroing my gaze on the old ratty shack, I waited. It was one thing I loved about being the sniper. I had control. I protected and remained alone until further instructions. I was never one for surrounding myself with people until I met my brothers but I would still rather do things my way. At least then I knew it would be done right.

"Coby, get your ass in here."

I loved Angel but sometimes he was even more demanding than me.

Picking myself up off the ground, I made my way down the stairs, staying alert and aware of my surroundings.

"In here," Dale said, pushing open a side door.

"Did you get any information?" I asked, bending over one of the bodies and searched the jacket the man was wearing.

"We have a couple wallets." Henley handed me one. "Nothing out of the ordinary, though. But shit got real when they fired at us first."

"You all are all right?" I made a point to look at each and every member of the team.

"Yeah," Stone grumbled, rubbing his jaw. "One of the fuckers hit me."

"We're good, brother." Angel clapped a hand on my shoulder. "We called it in but there's something you should see." He handed me a business card. The address on it was embossed in red lettering but what caught my eye was the location.

"This is only a couple blocks from my apartment," I said, handing the card back.

"All of the men have one of those cards," Lian added. "And we found this," he said, holding a picture in his hand.

RUDE

I took it from him, letting out a string of curses when I saw who was staring up at me.

(Brogan)

"How long has your boyfriend been in the military for?"

My eyes popped up over the cup of coffee I had been nursing for the past half an hour and stared at the man sitting across from me. I still never got his name even though we had met several times already at the bookstore.

"Quite a while," I answered, taking a sip of the steaming liquid.

"Good for him." The man leaned back, crossing an ankle over the opposite knee. "It's a respectable job. Not many can do it."

"Well, many think they can do it but fail," I corrected, placing the cup on the table between us. "Why do you make it a point to talk to me whenever I'm here?"

The man raised a dark eyebrow. "Can't a man be polite?"

I scoffed. "Please. I'm not stupid. I see the way you look at me."

"And how do I look at you, little one?"

"Don't call me that," I bit out.

"Why not?" A hint of amusement flashed in the man's dark eyes.

"Because only one man is allowed to call me that, and it's certainly not you."

"You have some fire behind your tiny size."

I rose to my feet, suddenly aware of how little I had on. Shorts and a t-shirt later and I still felt fucking naked. "I'm leaving."

"Wait." He grabbed my hand, stopping me. "Don't go."

I shoved out of his grip. "I have to make a phone call." Before the guy could stop me again, I ran out of the bookstore. It was weird having coffee with another man. But it wasn't my fault. He just sat down at my table and started talking to me. I huffed, pulling my phone from my pocket and made my way across the street. "How's Max doing?" I asked Jay when she grumbled her hello.

"Still grumpy and still on bed rest," Jay mumbled.

I sighed, heading back into Coby's apartment building. "She needs us now."

"I know. Listen—" Jay cleared her throat. "If you talk to Coby, you need to tell him what's going on so he can let Dale know."

I stopped suddenly. "Really? Wouldn't it make more sense to wait so Dale isn't distracted?" The doctors gave Max instructions to stay off her feet and told her that the baby was stressed. Rightfully so. The father wanted nothing to do with the situation.

"I don't know," Jay cursed. "Max doesn't want me saying anything but I can't help but wonder if it would make Dale fight harder."

The elevator dinged, the doors opening a moment later. "I'm not sure, boss, but whatever you want, I will do."

"I know. I haven't been able to get a hold of Angel." Jay's breath hitched. "I'm worried."

My stomach twisted. For her to be worried told me something. It said that this shit was real. I knew it was all along but when the person who was easy going was concerned, it didn't sit well with me.

"Have you heard from Coby?"

"No." My chest constricted. God, I missed him. His touch. His scent. His voice. I had never been in love before. If I would have been told that this was what it felt like, I would have let myself fall in love with him sooner.

We continued talking about how we missed the guys, how Max was beside herself with worry over the baby, how life was evil and liked to laugh in our faces. So much fucking fun.

An hour later, I had said goodbye to Jay and hung up the phone and sat there. So much had happened in the past couple of weeks but something was still missing. I needed to go to the basement at the club. Since the most recent explosion, I hadn't stepped foot into that solitude I had allowed myself for the past couple of years. I wasn't sure what it said about me but I craved the control over the men who sat in my chair.

"Don't let it bother you," Benny had said to me months back. *"Anyone would be lucky to sit in your chair. At least then they're still alive."*

He was the only other person outside of the club who knew what I did. Until Coby came along and I realized that he enjoyed watching me give those bastards what they deserved.

After the most recent events, we weren't any closer to finding out where Charles was or who the head of the organization was. We only knew it was a brother and sister duo who were closer than siblings should be.

Suddenly, a loud bang on the door sounded throughout the apartment.

I jumped to my feet, a cold shiver racing down my back at the unexpected noise. "Someone there?" I mentally cursed myself. Not like the person would answer.

Giving myself a much-needed full body shake, I headed to the door and looked out the peephole. Not seeing anyone standing behind the door, I opened it and peered out into the hallway. No one was allowed on this floor without a key. Coby had reassured me of that but no matter how much security you had, it wasn't one-hundred percent fool proof.

The bang sounded again, but this time, it came from inside the apartment.

"Listen, fucker," I called out. "You're playing a very dangerous game."

No response came, except for another bang.

I sighed, not having the patience for this shit, and shut the door. "I don't know how you got in here," I said, following the banging. For an apartment, Coby's was huge. I didn't realize how many places there were to hide until this very moment. A tremor of fear mixed with the delicious taste of excitement, coursed through my blood. Pulling a chair from the dining room table, I slid it to an empty space in the foyer. If this became messy, at least it wouldn't be close to where we ate.

The banging repeated.

Tap. Tap. Tap.

Instead of searching out the noise, I stood back and waited.

A couple minutes later, a large shadow appeared in the hallway, revealing the man from the bookstore.

My heart jumped. I had known all along that there was something off about the guy.

He held a baseball bat in his hand. "You don't seem surprised to see me," he said, leaning against the wall opposite me.

"I'm not," I gripped the edge of the back of the chair. "I know a fucked-up person when I see one."

"Ah," he pointed the bat in my direction. "You waiting for me to sit?"

"Nope." I sat in the chair. "I figured I might as well get comfortable while you tell me why you're here and all that shit."

The man raised an eyebrow. "You're not scared?"

I sighed, feigning a yawn. "I'm bored."

"Is that right."

"Listen, clearly you know that I'm alone. I have no idea how you got in here but I can only imagine that you paid the security guard off. Or you killed him." I shrugged. "Either way, you didn't come here to chat. So, tell me what you want."

The man started pacing back and forth, tapping the bat against the floor with each step. "My sister warned me that you wouldn't budge easy."

"Your sister?" I repeated, realization dawning on me. "So, you are the head of the organization." I laughed, shaking my head. "Lucky me."

The man sneered. "You know who I am."

"I'm not dumb, Zane. I know a brooding asshole when I saw one but I have a feeling that it's your sister who truly runs the show."

He only stared at me, not moving, not budging, not showing any hint of emotion.

I was right. I knew how it worked. They had a sick and twisted relationship thanks to the abusive home they grew up in. This guy tried to be in control, letting everyone on the outside think that was the case when really, his sister was the true master mind.

"So, tell me. Does your sister do this shit because she's jealous? Having an abusive father can really fuck you up." I pretended to check out my nails. "Does it make you hard, knowing that she's the one who is truly in control?"

"You have no idea what the fuck you're talking about." Zane took a step toward me, his body rigid and stiff.

"No? You think I don't know what it's like to have an unhealthy relationship with your sibling?" I laughed. "At least I wasn't related to mine."

His brows narrowed. "What I do with my sister is none of your damn business."

"It is when you come into my home uninvited." I crossed my arms under my chest, lifting my chin defiantly. "So, tell me. What the *fuck* do you want?"

"Hmmm … someone is getting a little impatient." Zane scratched the dark scruff of his jaw. "I want you to tell whoever you work with to stop searching us out."

I scoffed. "Like that's going to happen. You take innocent women, girls, and throw them into a life far worse than hell. Why would we stop?"

"Not just women."

"Excuse me?"

"We don't take just women," he smirked. "Not anymore."

"So, you take men too." I shook my head. "What the fuck ever."

"We tried taking your brother." Zane tapped the bat against the floor. "But he refused."

"Wait." Blood rushed to my head, forcing me to grab hold of the chair I was sitting in before I fell over. "What the hell are you talking about?"

"Your brother," Zane repeated slowly. "He may have been in the wrong place at the wrong time—" He waved a hand in front of him "—but, really, it gave me the idea that maybe we need to up our ante. People would pay for men. Boys. You don't hear about it often so we decided to give it a shot. Your brother would have been the first."

I swallowed past the lump that had formed in my throat. "Why?"

Zane shrugged. "I was bored. I wanted a new toy to play with and my sister wouldn't let me touch her anymore."

"You're a sick fuck," I bit out.

"Oh, I know." A wicked grin formed on his face. "But you know how that feels, don't you? You see, we're cut from the same cloth, you and I."

"No." I shoved to my feet. "We are not. Now tell me what the hell my brother has to do with this."

"That brother of yours would give us the push we needed to make some extra cash. To reach a new clientele. But when he refused, I had to end him. I couldn't let him go to the authorities."

Oh, God. "You … You killed Benny. It was you. You took him away from me." The words left my mouth, falling on deaf ears as he continued walking back and forth in front of me.

"He would have been a good one too. My sister could have used him up and turn him into the best little toy possible."

A sob escaped me and I fell to my knees. Because of their twisted games, my brother was no longer alive.

"Why him?" I whispered.

Zane stepped in front of me, his boots appearing in my blurry vision. "Because he had everything to lose."

***

(Coby)

Benny Tapp stared up at me from the photo.

Brogan's brother. The man who had taken care of her and her siblings after losing their parents. The man who she had looked up to like a father figure. How the hell was he in on this shit?

"Do you know anything about this?" Angel asked, stepping in front of me and tapped the photo with his finger.

"No." I looked up at him. "I don't know much about her brothers. Except for Greyson, but we all know how that story ends. This doesn't make sense. We're not here for the trafficking."

"We're never here for the trafficking, Coby," Angel said, searching another body. "It just happens that these fuckers who hold these females, find us."

"But this is different," I glanced down at Benny again. "We need to find out if he has anything to do with these bastards," I said, kicking the boot on the foot of one of the dead bodies.

"We need answers but we won't find them here," Stone said before talking into the radio. "Vice-One to base ..."

"Listen," Angel said, his voice low enough for only me to hear. "This shit is getting too close to home and it's not sitting well with me. If Benny was involved in the trafficking and the terrorist shit? It will destroy his siblings. I know Brogan can handle this on her own but she doesn't need to. The same goes for you."

"I got this," I muttered.

"Yeah, I know that," Angel cupped my nape, leaning his forehead against mine. "Remember what I told you when we first met?"

I breathed in the musky scent of sweat, tinged with a hint of fear. "You told me that I'm not an island and I don't need to stand on my own."

"We're brothers. We fight as one. We die as one."

"If Benny was in on this, it will destroy her." That was my biggest worry. I didn't care about her brothers. They could handle it but with Brogan, she was fragile. Even though she liked to think she was invincible and could handle everything life had thrown at her, this would break her.

"Well, let's make sure we find out for certain before we give her any news." Angel squeezed my nape. "Are you in this with us?"

"Yes."

"You want to bring these bastards down."

"Yes."

"You want to do this for the woman you love."

I pulled back, staring into my brother's dark eyes, my lips pulling into a wicked grin. "You have no fucking idea."

"Tell me."

"I want to rip off every inch of them and hear them beg for their lives."

"Good." Angel grunted. "Now let's get this fucking show on the road before I end up missing the birth of my baby."

CHAPTER TWENTY-SIX

Brogan

WHY DID HE leave and not take anything with him? Why spare me? Zane never gave me his name. Never told me what his sole purpose was when he came to the apartment. Was it just to fuck with my head like I had been doing to others for years? Maybe I had deserved it.

He knew I wouldn't call the police on him. What would I say?

Hello, Mr. Police Officer. This man broke into my apartment but he didn't hurt me. Oh, and I also torture people for fun.

Gripping my hair tight in my hands, I tugged and pulled.

RUDE

My phone rang, startling me from the frustrating and confusing thoughts I was having. "Hello?"

"Hi, little one," a deep smooth voice purred in my ear.

My heart stumbled over itself. "Hi, Coby."

"Did I wake you?"

"No." I squeezed the phone tight in my hand. "I miss you."

"I miss you too."

"Can we video chat?" I needed him in ways I never even knew existed.

"No. I'm not even supposed to be calling you."

"Oh. I don't want you to get in trouble."

"I won't."

I hesitated. "Is everything okay?"

"I just needed to hear your voice."

"God, I miss you." I headed into Coby's bedroom and slid onto the bed before wrapping myself around his pillow.

"Keep missing me, Brogan," he demanded. "When I get home, I'm going to show you how much I've missed you."

"Yes," I breathed. "Please show me."

"I will, baby," his voice lowered. "I'm going to show every inch of you. I'm going to show your fucking soul how much I've missed you. Your voice. Your touch. Your smiles."

My eyes burned, my throat constricting past the hard lump that had been lodged there since the moment Coby left. "And I'll show you too."

"Yes, you will, won't you?"

I laughed, wiping the tears from under my eyes that had fallen freely down my cheeks. "I love you."

"And I love you, little one." He cleared his throat. "I have to go but dream of me. Dream of me so fucking hard that I feel you."

"I will."

"Good girl."

My heart started racing. I should have told him about Zane breaking in but he had enough to deal with. I needed to go to my basement.

"Everything okay, Brogan?"

No. "Yes. I just miss you."

He paused. "I miss you too."

"Everything okay with you?" I asked, sitting up in the bed.

"Yes."

He was lying. I wasn't sure how I knew it but the way his voice lowered proved that he was hiding something. I imagined that he knew I was lying as well. And here we were, already keeping secrets from each other. I just prayed that he was trying to protect me as much as I was trying to protect him. I didn't want him to be distracted.

"I love you, little one. Always remember that."

"I love you too, and I will."

***

"Are you fucking kidding me right now?" Jay yelled, slamming her fist on the table in front of her.

Asher had done a good job at getting the club manageable enough for us to work in. None of us would live in it for a while, but no one needed to know that. I hadn't even bothered to go through the boxes of stuff that had been saved from the explosion.

"You're sitting here." Jay pointed a finger at me. "Telling me that the head of the operation that we have been trying to bring to its knees for months just randomly shows up at Coby's apartment and you're only telling us this now?"

It had been a couple days since that fucker had broken into the apartment. I had the security guard fired, finding out he had been paid off to let the guy onto the penthouse floor.

"You have a lot of shit going on," I reminded Jay, sitting back in the chair. "You don't need to worry about me."

She laughed, shaking her head. "You have got to be kidding me right now. What the hell do you think Coby would do if he found out something happened to you and I didn't do shit?"

"It's not your job to take care of me."

"You're damn right it's my job to look out for you," she screamed.

My heart jumped. I had never seen Jay react like this; no matter what we did, she was always cool and calm, never blowing up even when she should have. "Jay—"

"No." She raised a hand, stopping me. "I can't deal with this anymore."

"Whoa." I leaned forward. "Listen, I'm sorry I never said anything but I didn't want it to slip to Angel because I don't need Coby distracted. I don't need any of them distracted."

Her eyes softened. "But—"

"No. I mean it. I need Coby to come home to me. That's all I want. This will be the first thing I tell him but until then, it needs to stay between you and I."

Jay sighed, rubbing her swollen belly. "So, you didn't get his name."

"No." I shook my head, stretching my arms up and over my head. Rising to my feet, I walked to the large bay window. "I've seen him at the bookstore and had coffee with him."

"Does Coby know?"

"He doesn't." Maybe I should have felt guilty but I didn't. Coby would understand. I had a feeling the whole time about the guy and I needed to find out more about him. I just never expected him to show up at the apartment. Coby would flip his shit and get mad over the fact that I never told him but it wasn't something I could worry about either.

"Shit, Brogan," Jay cursed again. "I need this to end."

"We all do," I muttered, staring out the large window.

"Right." Jay came up beside me. "Did you find out what that bastard wanted?"

"He wanted to tell me that he had every intention of bringing Benny into the business but killed him after Benny said no."

"Brogan," Jay gasped.

I shrugged. "Whatever. It's done and over with. I can't confront Benny over it so who knows if it's fucking true or not."

"You can't be serious."

"It's what he said." I laughed. "I'm so stupid. I thought he was just a nice guy who wanted to talk about books. But I should have known better."

"It's not your fault. We've all been stressed."

"I wanted a little normalcy in my life," I whispered.

Jay wrapped an arm around my shoulders, resting her chin on top of my head. "I understand, Brogan, but unfortunately for us, things will never be normal again."

"I know." I cupped her forearm, reveling in the sisterly bond we shared. Having brothers was one thing. They protected and kept me safe but every now and again, a girl needed that female companionship.

"Coby won't be happy." Jay gave me a squeeze before releasing me.

"I'll deal with it when the time comes, but for now, it stays between us." I would make him understand why I kept it from him. And if I couldn't, it would be a fight that would be worth having as long as it kept him safe.

***

(Coby)

Shit was getting real.

Smoke billowed around me, burning the hairs in my nose.

My lungs ached, trying to breathe in the oxygen I needed to survive.

As soon as we grabbed what we needed and left the compound, someone had attacked. Shouting sounded. Voices closed in. Footsteps trampled. But what pulled me from my thoughts was hearing Dale's name.

Someone was frantic, shouting for him, but I couldn't be sure who it was.

My vision was cloudy, a ringing pierced my ears. Attempting to radio my brothers, all I got was static on the other end. "Shit."

Boots came into view, heavy hands lifted me onto my feet. "Coby." Angel shook me. "We were hit."

"Yeah." It was all I could get out as I wavered.

"Don't pass out on me now," Angel growled, giving me another shake. "I can't find Dale."

My heart jumped. Well, that woke me the fuck up. "Do we know who hit us?"

"Negative." Stone came toward us and banged his radio against his palm. "Still static."

"Keep trying." Angel rounded up Henley and Lian, indicating for them to check out the place and make sure we wouldn't get hit again.

"If something happened to Dale, I'm going to kill that fucker," Angel grumbled, leading us out of the building.

When a *pop pop* sounded, I jumped in front of Angel, pushing him behind me.

"Together," Angel snapped at me, shoving out of my grip. "We are in this together."

"You have a baby coming," I threw back at him. "Remember that."

Angel cupped the back of my neck, pulling me toward him. "Both of us have something to go home to. Don't you fucking forget *that*."

I nodded, stepping out of his embrace. "Let's find our brother."

Lian and Henley took that moment to come around the corner of the building. Wrinkles creased the corners of their eyes, dirt marred their faces. All of us were tired and sore but no matter what happened, we wouldn't leave until we found Dale.

Worry settled deep in the pit of my gut. My stomach twisted and churned over the possibility of losing my brother. My best friend. The one person who had taken me in years before when I had just joined Vice-One. We were the complete opposite in personalities but we fit and worked well together. All of us did. I didn't know Lian and Henley well but Angel trusted them and that was all I needed.

Lian nodded toward me. "You good, brother?"

"I will be when Dale is found," I said. "We need to find him."

Henley grunted. "Everyone has been taken out," he told us, his eyes shimmering. "I—"

I lifted my hand, interrupting him. And that was when I heard it again. A groan sounded close but it was far enough away that I wasn't sure if I had heard it or not. "Did you hear that?"

Angel and I looked at each other for a brief second before we made our way toward the noise.

It didn't take us long to find Dale. I wasn't sure what I expected to see but my stomach still sank to the fucking ground when I found him lying on his back.

"Fuck me," Lian grumbled, rushing to Dale's side. "He's out but alive," he said, letting out a heavy breath after checking for a pulse.

Angel and I knelt on either side of Dale and checked for injuries. He had been shot in the head but was alive.

"Shit," Angel whistled, calling in the attack.

I knew going into this line of work that our lives would be on the line but never did I think that something would happen to us. We were good at what we did. It was naïve of me to think but we had been lucky thus far.

As Dale lay unmoving in front of me, I swore that I would avenge him. I would avenge all of them. The women. The girls. The lives that were affected by this organization that had their hands in everything.

They were the epitome of evil and it was only time before we would bring them to their knees. I would praise the day that I forced them to beg for their lives.

"Don't you fucking die on me, Dale." I gripped his shoulder. "I need you. We all need you." I prayed to whoever would listen. *Keep our boy safe.* Max needed him. Whether Dale cared to admit it or not, he was about to be a father as well. And the fucker would own up to that title even if I had to force him to do so.

***

(Brogan)

Something woke me up during the night. I couldn't be sure what it was. A sound. A voice. My own body forcing me awake when really, sleep was the only thing that could get me through the tortuous wait for Coby to come home. He had been gone for weeks and it felt like even longer since I had talked to him.

The girls were antsy as shit. Jay snapping at anyone who would listen. Max was still on bed rest and more miserable than ever. Even though her and Dale weren't talking, he needed to be informed of what had happened and be there for her as best he could.

The sound, much like a bang, happened again.

I sat upright, my heart pounding hard in my ears. Pulling the covers off me, I trudged out into the hallway. No lights were on. "Hello?"

When no reply came, I turned around to head back to bed but another thud stopped me.

"Coby?" I called out. "Are you home?" I didn't know when he was getting back. Maybe he had surprised me and shown up early. "Coby?"

My stomach twisted when he didn't respond. Guess I was wrong. Disappointment settled deep within. I missed him more than I ever thought was possible. Our relationship had come on fast and hard but it fit perfectly for us. The more I missed him, the more my mind played tricks on me, letting me think he was near.

As I was about to head back into the bedroom, a figure came into view.

My breath hitched.

Coby stood at the end of the hallway, dressed casually in jeans, a white shirt and his black leather jacket. His hair had grown in some since the last time I saw him but what I noticed most, was the dark shadows casted over his face. I could only imagine that the mission hadn't gone well. Not that they ever did.

Dropping his bag on the ground beside him, he waited, staring me down with that intense heat I had grown accustomed to.

Not giving him a chance to say anything, I ran toward him and jumped in his arms. I didn't want words. I didn't need them. I wanted his touch instead.

He lifted me, crushing his mouth to mine. It was rough, needy and bordered on desperate. It had been weeks since I touched him. Since I felt him. Any part of him.

Coby ran his hands through my hair, tugging my head back and fucked my mouth with his tongue.

I moaned, scratching my nails into his thick neck.

Slamming me up against the wall, he massaged and kneaded, his fingers moving over my body. He played me like an instrument, tuning me to the point of utter destruction.

A growl escaped him, his tongue sliding in and out of my mouth, dancing along mine. Our breath mixed as one. Our touch tangled and entwined together.

I whimpered, needing him inside of me before I completely lost it.

Coby cupped my rear, pushing his waist between my hips, and rubbed his erection over my aching center.

I cried out, reaching between us and undid his belt.

His lips curled up into a smile, his hot breath leaving him in short bursts of air.

He was giving me the control. For the moment, at least.

Pulling out his straining cock, I dropped myself on him, crying out at the thick but delicious invasion.

Coby snarled, sinking his teeth into my neck and thrust his hips upward.

Another cry escaped me, my eyes brimming over with tears at the delirious pain.

My sounds only made him fuck me harder.

Grabbing my knees, he pushed them up to my chest before pulling out.

I looked between us, watching his slick cock leaving my body and thrusting into me hard. My head slammed back against the wall.

His eyes darkened, his body hard and rigid. Something was wrong and he was using me to make him feel better. Well little did he know, that I was doing the exact same thing. It was a battle of who would let go first. Who would give up their control and who would jump over that delicious edge.

Coby leaned his forehead against mine, his breathing quickening. Sliding his fingers between mine, he pulled my hands above my head.

Tightening my thighs, I held on, letting him take from me what he needed.

He grunted, thrusting hard and fast. The veins of his cock, rubbed at my center, sliding in and out until I was a trembling mess.

Once. Twice. Three times before I fell.

I screamed, the unexpected burst of pleasure hitting me right in the center. His name left my lips on a hard cry.

A wicked grin spread on his mouth before he dropped me to the ground and spun me. Pushing my head against the wall, he thrust back into my body, lifting me with each powerful move of his hips.

"Oh, god," I whispered, squeezing my eyes shut. This angle was my favorite. I could feel every inch of him. His power. His strength. The most intimate parts of our bodies fusing together as he fucked me from behind.

He pulled me upright, wrapping his arms around my body. "I've missed you," he muttered in my ear, holding me tight against him.

"Take what you need, baby," I told him, pushing back into him.

"Fuck, little one," he roared, his thrusts turning violent.

"That's it, Coby," I reassured him. "Take me."

"Shit." Cupping my throat, he bit the sensitive spot below my ear, his cock swelling deep inside me. His hips sped up, pushing me forward until he came on a hard growl. My name left his lips, his grunts and groans sliding in my ears.

I moaned, reveling in the feel of him letting go.

The warm bursts of his release coated me from within. His orgasm was so strong, he collapsed against me, dropping us to the floor.

I turned in his arms, raining soft pecks on his face and mouth, until his body reacted to my touch again.

He pushed me back, deepening the kiss until he slid back inside my body.

We never did make it to the bedroom.

***

"I guess you missed me, huh?" I smiled softly, cupping Coby's face a couple hours later. The scruff of his jaw scratched at my palm.

He leaned into it, kissing my hand.

"What happened?" I asked, touching him like he needed me to.

"So much shit, I don't even know where to start." His gaze met mine. "But I shouldn't have just fucked you. I should have talked to you and told you how much I missed you."

"You did tell me," I kissed him hard on the mouth. "You told me with your body, Coby."

He pulled me tighter against him, rubbing his face into the crook of my neck. "Dale." His shoulders tightened.

"Coby? Tell me. What happened?"

"We got hit. There was nothing I could do."

Oh, God. "Please ..." I shook my head. "I can't handle any more death."

"He's alive."

A breath left me on a whoosh. "But?"

Coby's body stiffened. "He's in a coma."

CHAPTER TWENTY-SEVEN

Brogan

THE GUILT SEEPING from Coby's pores hurt my heart and made me hold him closer. "What happened?"

"We found a bunker with girls." He shook his head like he was trying to force the nightmares from his mind. "Before we could get them out to safety, an explosion hit. The girls never had a chance."

"Oh, God, Coby," I cupped his nape. "And everyone else?"

"They're fine. Beat up but alive. Dale got hit the hardest because he was standing watch at the door. We never should have been there. We were looking for a known terrorist after taking out some of his men. None of it made sense. It shouldn't have gone down like that."

"Do they know how long he'll be in a coma for?"

"No." Coby leaned his forehead against mine. "They don't know anything. They said he's lucky to be alive. If he dies …" Coby swallowed hard.

"Oh, baby." Tears welled in my eyes. "I'm so sorry."

"There's more," he muttered, gripping my arms.

"Okay." I took a deep breath. "Tell me."

"We found Benny's picture."

"What?" I sat back. "What are you talking about?"

"We're looking into it," Coby said, running his hand down my back.

"I have to tell you something." I took a breath, bracing myself for his reaction.

"What?" he searched my face, frowning.

"That man I met at the bookstore …"

"Yeah? What about him?"

"He showed up here. It was Zane." I told him about the guy breaking in, how I had the security guard fired, and what Zane said about Benny.

"Fuck," Coby boomed, pushing me off him, and shoved to his feet. He paced back and forth before meeting my gaze. "You should have told me."

"And what would you do, Coby? You had enough shit going on. I didn't need to worry you and have you distracted."

"Well, clearly that didn't fucking help because my brother is still in the damn hospital, *fighting for his life,*" he yelled, the cords in his neck straining.

"The bastard didn't do anything," I cried, jumping to my feet. "He was fucking with my head. He told me how he and his sister wanted Benny. But I can't even confront him about it because he's fucking dead."

"Brogan." Coby's gaze softened.

"No." I pushed him. "At least Dale is alive." A sob left me, tears streaming down my cheeks and burning a path in their wake. "Benny …" I hiccupped. "I can't do this." I fell to my knees. "I feel like a part of me died with him."

Coby knelt in front of me, wrapping his arms around my trembling body. "You're strong, little one."

Throwing myself in his arms, I cried against him. So many tears fell for the man who had taken care of me for most of my life. The man who had been my role model. The man who fought for our country and lost a piece of himself because of it. "I'll kill him."

"I know, baby." Coby cupped my cheeks. "And I'll be right by your side, watching."

****

(Coby)

I knew going into the military that I would become close with the men and women I fought beside. No matter how many times our lives were on the line, it never dawned on me that we could actually die. It was naïve to think but still came as a shock when one of us became hurt or worse. Vincent Stone had lost several brothers in his career. Henley and Lian, just the same. They were rough, hard around the edges—made me look like a fucking kitten. I needed to see my brothers but for right now, I savored the feeling of Brogan holding me.

I sent up a silent prayer to whoever would listen. I believed. Sometimes. It was hard in my line of work. Seeing the shit I did, it was difficult to understand why a God so great would let this evil happen. Knowing the human race was given a freedom of choice, it still didn't bode well with me when my brother was currently fighting for his life.

"Does Max know?" Brogan asked, rising from the couch.

My chest constricted. "We told her before I came here."

Brogan's head whipped around, her eyes widening. "Really?"

I nodded.

"Oh, God. I can't imagine how she handled that information."

"I'll never get the sound of her screams out of my head," I muttered, ringing my hands together in my lap.

"We need … We need to go." Brogan slipped on her shoes. "Please. I need to be with her. You need to be with your brothers. We all need each other right now."

I nodded, following suit even though I didn't feel like being social. But Brogan was right.

"Is everyone at the hospital? Yeah, that would make sense. What if something happens to the baby? No. She's strong." Brogan's string of questions and answers forced anxiety to rush through my blood. She was losing control, and it pissed me the fuck off.

"We have to make a stop," I told her. I needed to see my old friend and get some damn answers before my little one completely fell over the deep end.

"But we need to go to the hospital," Brogan argued, placing her hands on her hips.

As hot as she was, standing there with fire in her eyes, ready to kill anyone in her path, the hospital could wait. As much as it panged me to think, Dale wasn't going anywhere and Angel would call me the moment something changed.

"Coby?"

I pulled on my jacket before pinching her chin. Placing a hard smack on her mouth, I breathed her in and landed a light swat on her ass. "I'm not happy about that fucker showing up here, breaking in, and fucking with you. But right now, we need to go see Lucas."

"Lucas?" she frowned. "That I guy a spoke to over a month ago?"

I nodded, grabbing her hand and lead her out of the apartment. I made a mental note to double check all the security and locked the door up tight. If something would have happened to Brogan, I didn't know what I would have done.

"Did you get a name?" I asked once we were in my SUV.

"If you're talking about that bastard who fucked with me…" I braced myself. "It was Zane. I knew something was off with him. I just never expected him to be … well … *him*."

I grunted. If I had it my way, the fucker would be wrapped around my knife and bleeding out at my feet.

We drove in silence, heading to Lucas's shop in a dangerous part of the city.

"I don't think I've ever been in this area before." Brogan sat forward, staring out at the dingy buildings surrounding us.

"Lucas has been here for as long as I can remember." It had been way too long since I saw the guy, and I knew for certain he was going to give me shit for it.

"Is it safe to park here?" Brogan asked, unbuckling her seatbelt.

"Are you worried?"

She scoffed. "No. This place just makes the shit I've seen look like hearts and rainbows." She smirked. "Makes me feel all warm and fuzzy inside."

I chuckled. "Yeah, Lucas will like you."

Her grin widened. "He's sick and deranged as well?" The joke left her mouth but never reached her eyes.

My stomach twisted with the knowledge that she truly believed that there was something wrong her. "You're not sick and deranged. No matter what those fucking thoughts are that travel through your head or what people tell you, you're fine."

"Yeah." She glanced out the window. "Maybe."

Leaving the safety of the SUV, I walked around to the passenger side and opened the door. "Come with me."

Brogan slid her hand in mine, letting me pull her from the vehicle.

Before we went into the tattoo shop, I gave her a soft peck on the lips, needing her to know that I was only as strong with her by my side. The words never left my mouth, though. I was a pussy, closed up, quiet as shit. Leah took that from me but she wouldn't stop me from loving this woman standing before me.

***

(Brogan)

Coby's reassuring words that I was fine and that there was nothing wrong with me helped me feel somewhat better. Benny had been the only one throughout the years to stand by me and support my dark ways. But with him gone and now Coby at my side, I knew it would get easier. It was like Coby was given to me as a saving grace. We had both done horrible things in our lives, trying to make up for our wrongs by masking them with good deeds. I did believe in religion but I believed in a higher power and I knew it was watching down over me. No matter where it was.

"He's a tattoo artist?" I asked when we approached the large shop.

"Yes." Coby placed his hand on the door. "The best." He pushed it open, the door introducing our entrance.

"It's about fucking time you show up," a deep voice growled from a large man with his back to us. He was hunched over a half-naked woman, the buzzing of his tattoo gun sounding throughout the large room.

"I told you I would," Coby said, crossing his arms under his chest.

"Ten years later?" The man grunted, placing the gun back on a tray beside him. "Sure." He sat back, taped up the tattoo and tapped the woman's butt. "All done, beautiful."

"Thanks, baby." She sat up, pulled her shirt down and kissed his cheek. "Tell that woman of yours to call me."

"I will." The man, who I could only assume was Lucas, helped her to her feet.

The woman slipped a wad of cash into his hands before coming toward us. She looked me up and down, giving me a small smile before her gaze finally landed on Coby. "I would be careful. People around here bite." She blew him a kiss and left the shop.

"A friend of yours?" Coby asked, raising an eyebrow.

The man laughed. "Come on, Coby. We both know I have no friends." He turned around.

I bit back a gasp.

Lucas wore a black eye patch, tattoos covering his thick neck and the one side of his shaved head. A black shirt clung to his torso, the sleeves rolled up to his elbows, showcasing sleeves of even more tattoos. He was dangerously beautiful.

"Are you checking him out, little one?" Coby whispered in my ear.

I smirked, turning my head to meet his mouth. "Would that make you jealous?"

He grinned, smacking me on the ass.

Lucas laughed, rubbing a hand over his shaved head. "Well, isn't this cute? Coby Porter, after all these years, a woman finally has you wrapped around her finger."

"You better fucking believe it," I said, jutting out my chin.

"Yeah?" Lucas raised an eyebrow. "And if I don't?"

"I don't care what you think," I told the large man. "I'm not fucking *you*, now am I?"

Lucas' gaze flicked between us both before he threw his head back, letting out a hard laugh. "I like her. You did good, Porter."

I grinned.

"Sounds like you did as well." Coby slid his hand to the small of my back.

Lucas' smile widened. "I sure as fuck did. Although, I still have no idea why my girl puts up with my shit." He chuckled, shaking his head. "So …" His face turned serious in a matter of seconds. "To what do I owe this unexpected honor?"

Coby stiffened beside me. "You know why we're here."

Lucas grunted. "Fine." He turned and headed to the back of the shop. "Come with me if you want to live." He laughed to himself.

I raised an eyebrow.

"He has a sick sense of humor," Coby muttered.

A dominant air slid off Lucas, thick and inviting. It made me wonder what exactly his story was and who this woman was that was able to tame him.

We followed Lucas until we reached a set of double doors.

He stopped, his gaze locking with Coby's. "As usual, if you blab shit, I'll deny everything."

Coby feigned a yawn. "Remember what happened the last time you threatened me?"

Lucas grinned. "Yeah. That was fun."

"You enjoyed it when Coby kicked your ass?" I threw at him.

"What makes you think Coby kicked my ass, little girl? It could have been the other way around."

"Because I've worked out with him, and I know how he is. He wouldn't stop until you were on the ground beneath him." I never said that I enjoyed it. I didn't need to. Coby enjoyed kicking my ass in the gym because he loved rubbing out my sore muscles after the fact.

"All right children." Coby stepped between us and clapped a hand on Lucas's shoulder. "We don't have a lot of time."

Lucas nodded but looked at me over Coby's shoulder. "I still like you even though you think your boyfriend kicked my ass."

I laughed, shaking my head.

Lucas pushed open the door, thrusting his arm out in front of him. "After you."

CHAPTER TWENTY-EIGHT

Coby

LUCAS CRANE WAS a different sort of character, but knowing that he liked Brogan filled me with all that warm and fuzzy shit. I held a lot of respect for the guy, knowing he would drop anything to help those in need.

When he let us into his office, Brogan let out a whistle.

"Holy shit," she said in awe. "This is what you work with?"

Lucas stood up straighter. "Only the best. A lot of it has been updated since meeting my girl but the old-school shit still works better than a lot of modern technology."

You would never know by looking at Lucas that he had made history with his knowledge in hacking. He did his time. Paid for his mistakes and settled down.

But when I needed him to look into someone or something, he had a work around that allowed him to research without getting caught again. He had told me that that was all thanks to his girlfriend.

Two computer screens sat on a large desk, with three hanging on the wall above them. They showed coding, numbers, shit I could never understand but I was still in awe of it.

"This is a nerd's wet dream." Brogan stepped further into the room, running her fingers along the computer desk.

"Funny." Lucas winked with his good eye. "That's what my woman said." He looked my way. "What are you wanting to know?"

"We need information." I nodded in Brogan's direction. "Her brother was shot by the head of the organization. He died after getting a blood clot unexpectedly. Zane and his sister wanted Benny but he wouldn't give in and was shot instead."

"Fuck," Lucas growled. "I'm sorry."

Brogan shrugged. "It's done. The fucker showed up at Coby's apartment when he wasn't home and broke in while I was there."

Lucas's gaze snapped to mine. "I'm surprised he's still alive to tell about it."

I smirked, rubbing my jaw. "Not for long he won't be. Between all of us, these bastards will fall to our feet and beg for their lives one way or another."

"I understand." Lucas walked toward the computer and sat in front of it. "Give me five." He cracked his knuckles, moved the mouse and the set up came to life.

"You think he can find more information on them?" Brogan asked, curling her fingers in mine.

"I know he can." I pinched her chin, tilting her head. "Have faith, little one."

"What if that faith comes back to bite me in the ass?"

I searched her face, letting out a long sigh. "No matter what happens, I'll be here for you. We'll deal with this shit together. You got me?"

She pulled from my grip, turning in my arms.

"I asked you a question," I growled in her ear.

"Yeah, and I'll give you an answer when I got one."

My dick twitched. Fuck me, her sass turned me on.

"All right, love birds," Lucas turned to us. "Names are Zane and Tina Birtch as you already know," he said more to himself. "Ah. Here's something new. Adopted by a sick fuck at the age of six. Reports say that Tina was raped and abused repeatedly by him. At the age of sixteen, she had been tried with murder." Lucas grinned. "This is where it gets good. Zane is actually the one who murdered their adoptive father but Tina took the fall thinking it would get her closer to her brother. That backfired when Zane went on trial and threw her under the bus." He pointed at the computer screen. "This is all in the reports that I've already sent to both of your emails."

"Are you kidding me right now?" Brogan looked between us both. "How the hell did you do that?"

Lucas tapped his temple. "Kidneys."

"Tell us more," I demanded, interrupting their little banter, not in the mood to ask why kidneys would have anything to do with him being smart. I swore half the time Lucas just said shit to confuse people.

"So damn grumpy," Lucas muttered, turning back to the computer. "Although Zane stabbed his sister in the back, she fell in his arms the day she was released." He pointed at the screen.

Brogan and I took a step toward the monitor.

Images of the siblings embraced in a hug stared back at us.

"How the hell did they start this organization? And why would a woman want to kidnap other women to sell them?" Brogan took the mouse from Lucas and clicked picture after picture. "This doesn't make sense."

"They're sick and twisted. Desperate times and all that shit." Lucas shrugged. "I have no fucking idea. I'm good but I can't read their minds."

Brogan huffed. "And now they're starting to kidnap men? Boys?" A string of curse words left her.

"Dude," Lucas's eyes widened. "I bet you have fun with that mouth," he told me.

I rolled my eyes but didn't respond.

"There has to be something we can do." Brogan started pacing, ignoring his comment. "And Charles Brian, is there anything on him?"

Lucas went back to his computer. "Your typical shit. They took him in. He thinks he's the powerhouse now even though clearly it's the sister."

"It's always the woman," Brogan muttered. "My brother was in the wrong place at the wrong time. Somehow I don't believe that but I obviously can't ask him about it." She stopped pacing. "We need to talk to Greyson."

****

(Brogan)

Coby let out a snarl, the deep sound rumbling from somewhere inside of him. He didn't like Greyson.

Probably never would even though Grey gave us his blessing and has left us alone. But he was there with Benny that night. I never got a chance to ask him anything about it. When my brothers got together, they tried to leave me out as much as possible. I was used to it but it still pissed me off.

"Who's Greyson?" Lucas asked, stretching his thick tattooed arms above his head.

"My stepbrother." I pulled out my phone and searched for his name until the picture of him and I popped up. My heart jumped. Letting out a sigh, I met Coby's gaze. "You fine with this?"

"I have no choice, do I?"

"Yes, you do. You could tell me that we're going to do this on our own."

He searched my face. "Call him."

The breath I had been holding left me on a whoosh.

But I knew Coby. He was challenging me. Things may have been better, Benny's death making them civil but it was still touch and go.

Leaving Lucas' office, I called Greyson, waiting in anticipation for him to answer.

"Now to what do I owe this pleasure?" Greyson purred when he answered.

I rolled my eyes. "I need you."

"Well, then," his voice lowered. "I can always accommodate that."

"Shut up. That's not what I meant."

He chuckled. "What's up, Brogie?"

I explained everything. From Zane breaking into the apartment and telling me about Benny, to us meeting up with Lucas and him giving us as much information about the siblings as possible.

"Shit."

"Yeah," I muttered. "Exactly. Listen, I need you to tell me what happened that night."

"What night?"

"Greyson, you know which night I'm referring to." I slid down the wall, landing hard on my ass, and pulled my knees up to my chest. "Please."

"I don't know what information you want."

"Yes, you do." I huffed. "Come on, Greyson."

"Brogan, there's nothing to say. We were at a bar. Benny let himself go and got shit faced. Everything after that happened so fucking fast."

"I never thought I would meet the man who killed him." I dropped my head in my hands. "He was there. Right in front of me and I didn't do anything."

"What could you have done?"

"I don't know but I could have done something," I cried.

At my outburst, Coby appeared in the hallway. "Hang up the phone."

I frowned. "I have to go. When you remember something, call me." And with that, I hung up.

"Care to tell me why you never told me how you feel?"

"I don't know what you're talking about." Denying everything seemed to run in my family.

"Try that again, little one."

My heart raced, jumping to my throat. "What do you want me to say?"

"Tell me why you told Greyson that shit instead of me. I am the one you're with, Brogan. Not him. Me." He pointed to himself.

"I didn't think of it until I was talking to him. I'm sorry. I didn't realize that it was a big deal."

"That's not the point," Coby shook his head. "I need you to come to me."

"I do," I cried.

Lucas took that moment to peek his head out into the hall. "Hey, I found something—"

"Not now," Coby boomed.

"So damn cranky." Lucas headed back into his office, slamming the door behind him.

"Tell me why," Coby demanded once we were alone again.

Crossing my arms under my chest, I tilted my head defiantly. "I don't know what you want me to say. Zane told me he killed my brother and I couldn't do anything about it. I was paralyzed with what he was telling me. Excuse me for not telling you how I felt and told my stepbrother instead."

Coby's jaw clenched, his nostrils flaring. "I've accepted that you two have fucked. I've accepted that you will always love him. But don't you fucking dare stand there and rub it in my face like I'm not supposed to be affected by it."

"Coby, I—"

"You are with *me*—" he took a step toward me. "Or did you forget that?"

"No." I shook my head. "I could never forget that."

"Then, baby, figure out whatever the fuck is going on and *be with me.*"

***

(Coby)

I was pissed. Angered the fuck out. I knew a part of it didn't make sense but knowing that Brogan and

Greyson had a history would always eat at me. I just needed to learn to control my anger before it pushed her away.

"I love you," Brogan said. "But right now, I don't need your alpha male shit. I need you to be my boyfriend and support me and just be there for me. Anything else and you can go fuck yourself." She pushed past me, heading into Lucas' office.

"Shit," I muttered, shoving a hand through my hair.

Following her, I shut the door behind me before they both turned to me.

Brogan glared my way.

God, what I wouldn't give to bend her over that desk and fuck that sass right out of her. But she was right. I was an asshole.

"Okay, so what I found out is, Tina and Zane inherited this organization or business. Whatever the fuck you want to call it. It was actually left in Tina's name but I can only assume that she wasn't able to run it by herself." Lucas clicked a couple more buttons before he continued. "The only thing I haven't been able to find is who left them this shit. A grandfather. Uncle. Their real father maybe." He shrugged. "That information is locked up tighter than a virgin."

"How do we find out where the headquarters is?" Brogan asked, crossing her arms under chest.

"That, my dear Brogan, is an excellent question. You see this dot?" Lucas asked us, pointing to the center screen of his set-up.

Brogan moved beside him, nodding.

I stepped up behind her, running my hand down her arm, and linked my fingers with hers.

She sighed, leaning into me.

I craved her touch and I was thankful she gave in.

"This is where they are." Lucas tapped some more buttons. "But there's an issue."

"What?" I grumbled. "We'll just blow the place up."

"Yeah." Lucas nodded, clapping his hands together. "Do that and see how fast you have the authorities at your fucking door."

"What the hell are you talking about?" Brogan thrust her arm out. "We have them." She turned to me. "Why didn't we call on Lucas before?"

"Yeah, Coby." Lucas sat back in his chair, crossing his arms under chest. "Why didn't you?"

I rolled my eyes. "You know why, fucker." I met Brogan's gaze. "This place is like Fort Knox."

"He's right." Lucas rapped his knuckles on top of the desk. "Nothing we can do but wait."

"What are you talking about?" Brogan looked between us both. "Are you telling me we need someone on the inside? How come we haven't sent someone in already?"

"Because it's been done." I grabbed her hands, forcing her to meet my stare. "Brogan, I understand where you're coming from."

"No." She pulled from my grip. "You don't."

"Listen to me." I gripped her shoulders, giving them a light squeeze for added reassurance. "I do. I get it. You want to avenge your brother but we have to be smart about this. Trust me. I want to go in there and make them fucking suffer for all the shit they've done. For all the pain they've caused our friends. Our family."

"I don't understand," she whispered.

"Let me see if I can help." Lucas cleared his throat. "Tina and Zane are good. They're highly respected and have their hands in everyone's pockets. They've bought their freedom. The only way they can be brought to justice is if someone bigger and more powerful comes into play."

"But you," Brogan gripped my jacket. "You're powerful."

"As much as I appreciate that sentiment—" I kissed her forehead "—I'm not as powerful as you think."

"Then what are we going to do? And what about Charles Brian? He just disappeared." Brogan pulled from my grasp.

"I haven't heard anything about him." Lucas rubbed his jaw. "He seems to be hiding. You guys must have really scared the shit out of him."

"How do you know about that?" Brogan asked, frowning.

"I know all." Lucas winked.

We were fucked.

CHAPTER TWENTY-NINE

Brogan

THE ONLY NEW pieces of information we got were the names of the people running this shit show and that Charles Brian was still hidden. Greyson was being difficult and wouldn't give me what I was looking for even though I knew there was more to that night with Benny then he was letting on.

I stared out the window, watching the few cars drive by even though it was late into the night.

"We should head to the hospital," Coby said, coming up behind me.

"Aren't visiting hours over?" I asked, not meeting his gaze.

"Yeah, but everyone is in the waiting room still according to Angel."

"Really?" I turned to him. "I'm sorry. For everything."

"I love you, Brogan." He kissed me hard on the mouth. "I understand where you're coming from but right now there's nothing more we can do."

I tried believing that but the fighter in me felt like we were giving up and pushing everything aside. There had to be something more we could do.

We said goodbye to Lucas and left the tattoo shop with Coby promising to visit more frequently.

"I'm going to go see Greyson," I told Coby. It was a last-minute decision but I knew Greyson wouldn't deny me the information I was looking for if I was standing in front of him.

"I'll go with you," Coby told me.

"Yeah," I scoffed. "Because that will go over well." I raised a hand, stopping him from doing that possessive alpha shit. "I know this is probably a bad idea. I get that. But I need you to trust me. We need to find Zane and Tina. I don't feel like being alone and Zane show up again because I don't know what I'll do the next time I see him."

"What do you want to do?" Coby asked, stepping toward me and pulled me against him.

"You know what I want to do." Talking about death and murdering someone like we were only talking about the weather was not normal.

"Tell me," he demanded, running his fingers through the hair at my nape.

I swallowed hard. "I want them both to suffer. I want to watch the life leave Zane's eyes while I gut him like a pig. I want to hear him scream. Beg. Plead for me to let him go."

"And?" Coby asked, his voice lowering.

I looked up at him. "I want Tina to suffer more. She's a woman, taking women and girls and throwing them into a life they don't deserve. She should be against this," I cried. "It doesn't make sense. None of it does."

"She clearly needs to be in control."

"I want to take that control away from her."

Coby nodded and kissed my forehead. "I know, little one."

Once we reached the SUV, Coby opened the door for me.

I realized after all this time, that I was the type of woman who needed to do everything herself. With Coby, I didn't mind if he did the small things like holding the door open for me or paying the check on our date. Even though we had never been on one.

"Brogan?" Coby leaned against the open door, staring down at me.

I sighed, stepping into the vehicle but stopped him from closing the door. Crooking my finger, I indicated for him to lean down.

He raised an eyebrow but did as I asked.

Gripping his jacket, I kissed him and gave him everything I had been feeling over the past couple of days.

"Give me your worries, little one," Coby whispered against my lips. "Put all of your pain on my shoulders and let me take care of you."

My eyes welled, burning with unshed tears. These tears would be the end of Zane and Tina. I didn't cry for anyone but they took a part of me and shoved him six feet underground.

"I'll kill them," I leaned back, cupping Coby's cheek. "I'll destroy their organization and burn it to the mother fucking ground."

His eyes darkened. "And I'll be right there beside you."

"Fuck, I love you."

He grinned. "Once this shit is done, you better show me just how much you love me."

Oh, I had planned on it. With every fiber of my being, I would unleash myself onto him and force us to fall together.

Coby kissed my forehead, my nose and then my mouth before stepping back and shutting the door closed. Walking around to the driver side, he paused, looking back at what I could only assume was Lucas' shop. He was worried and I couldn't blame him. We had spent months trying to bring this organization down and now, Zane has made an appearance. But why?

"Do you have any idea why Zane would show his face now?" I asked Coby when he sat in the driver's seat beside me.

"He's fucking with us." Coby shrugged. "I've seen shit like this before." A dark shadow passed over his face.

"Coby?" I asked, touching his arm gently.

He jumped, his head whipping around. "People like him and his sister turn me into a man who has no problem with destroying them."

I nodded, squeezing his arm. "I know. Whatever you've done in your past, it was needed."

He shook his head, rubbing the dark scruff on his jaw. "Maybe so but it doesn't mean I had to enjoy it."

I swallowed hard. He and I were in the same situation. I enjoyed bringing the evil I had met over the years to justice. Even if that meant I had to live with my guilt, so did Coby, and I would help him through that.

Coby started up the vehicle when a flash of light blinded me.

Everything next happened faster than I could have imagined.

My ears rang, my head suddenly throbbing with a brutal amount of pain. My body became heavy, my muscles no longer moving and controlling my limbs. Everything hurt and I couldn't figure out why.

Coby.

Another flash of light, a crash, and I was lifted into the air, my body slamming against the roof of the SUV. That was when I realized we had been hit. I never even got a chance to put on my seatbelt.

Trying with all the strength I could muster, I forced my arms to move. The next couple of seconds seemed to happen in slow motion. Time stopped as the SUV flipped onto its back, finally still and unmoving.

Bracing my fall, my hands flew out and my wrist snapped. I screamed. The sound of the bone breaking forced bile to burn up my throat.

My heart raced, my stomach twisting and turning as I breathed through the pain. I had been hurt before in my line of work but nothing felt like this agony.

Cradling my broken wrist against my chest, I looked up at Coby who hung from his chair. The impact had knocked him out. Blood dripped from a wound on his head and who knew how many more injuries he had.

"Coby," I said through clenched teeth. "Wake up."

Thankful for my short height, I was able to move around the SUV without getting stuck. I reached up and nudged him but his eyes still wouldn't open.

"Please wake up for me." I pushed him again, but there was no response. "Coby."

Reaching for my purse, I pulled out my cell but saw that there was no service. We were in the city. Why the hell didn't I have service? I threw my phone and reached out for Coby again but there was still no sign that he had regained consciousness.

Blinding light shone into the vehicle.

Shielding my eyes, I cowered back, not sure what was going on.

A loud bang shattered through me.

"Ah, sweet girl. You survived the crash. What a shame."

I blinked a couple of times before Zane appeared where the door used to be. "What the hell is going on?"

He tsked, shaking his head. "I had hoped you would be no more."

"It'll take a lot more than a fucking crash to end me, you sick bastard." I crawled forward when a sharp pain shot up my arm. I yelped, forgetting my wrist was broken.

Zane chuckled. "That looks like it hurts."

"Fuck you," I growled, swallowing past the tears the pain had caused.

"You see, Brogan ..." Zane leaned into the vehicle. "We could have done that. I could have given you everything you desired. I could fulfill those dark and twisted fantasies you have."

"You couldn't do shit for me."

He laughed again, his gaze landing on Coby's still form. He gripped Coby's jaw, moving his head from left to right.

Much to my surprise, Zane leaned toward him and licked up the line of blood on Coby's cheek. "Even knocked out, he's still fucking delicious." He grinned. "My sister is going to have so much fun with you," he told Coby before releasing him. "Remove him from the vehicle and leave her here to …" He waved a hand in front of him. "Actually, I don't care what she does." Zane disappeared, two large men taking his place.

"*No,*" I screamed, surging forward, and grabbed onto Coby. The pain in my wrist seared its way into my soul but I only let it give me the strength I needed. "Coby, wake up damn it," I yelled, beating my small fists against him.

He groaned.

"Yes. That's it, baby." I rose on my knees, kissing his face. "Wake up. Please wake up."

"Let go of him," Zane demanded.

"No, please. I'll do anything. Just don't take him from me. We have money." At that point the tears started flowing down my cheeks.

"Oh, dear." Zane shook his head, shoving a gun in my face. "I don't like tears. I also heard that you're supposed to be the hard-assed one of your little club." He clucked his tongue. "You don't seem so hard to me."

"I'll kill you and everyone you've ever loved," I yelled, slapping the gun out of my face.

"Oh, I like you," Zane lifted his hand, aiming the gun at Coby. "But you see, women are too common. We're overrun with females." Zane brushed a hand down Coby's cheek. "My sister wants to play with a man, and I'm willing to do anything to make her happy."

"We have money," I repeated, feeling the strength being sucked out of me as each second wore on.

"You see, little girl, so do we. We don't want your money. We want *him*."

"No," I screamed, gripping the collar of Coby's jacket.

He grunted, his eyes fluttering open. "What the fuck …" he croaked.

"Let him go, Brogan," Zane ordered. "I won't tell you again."

"I'll find you, Coby." I kissed his cheek. "I promise."

Coby's eyes became clear at my words. "What the hell is going on?" He struggled against the seat belt, wincing at whatever pain he was feeling.

A gun shot rang out, followed by a sharp pain in the side of my temple. The loud sound pierced my ear drums. My head rang. Muffled voices sounded around me but I couldn't make out what was being said.

A sudden wave of darkness washed over me, swallowing me into a blanket of bliss. I tried fighting it. I tried with everything in me to stay awake. Something was telling me to sleep. So instead of arguing, I did.

CHAPTER THIRTY

Coby

NEVER IN MY whole life had I felt a pain quite like the one searing through my blood. What made it worse was seeing the fear in Brogan's eyes as I was taken away from her. I couldn't do anything. I couldn't stop the large fuckers from carrying me to the SUV. I couldn't stop Zane from pulling the trigger. And I couldn't stop Tina from putting her hands on me.

I was down for the count. Beaten and broken. Torn from the inside much like Leah ripped me in half years before. But this was different. I didn't love her like I loved Brogan but right now, love didn't mean shit.

I had no idea if Brogan was even alive. When I heard the familiar *pop, pop*, I had struggled against my captors but it only earned me a bloodier nose and more pain.

"Oh, sweet boy," Tina straddled my lap, cupping my cheek.

I winced at the added weight on my battered legs.

She had seen the whole thing. The accident. Her brother pulling me from the vehicle. Us leaving Brogan behind.

Something told me she was still alive. Zane was the type who would pretend to shoot her just to fuck with my head.

"You're so handsome." Tina crushed her mouth to mine, slipping her tongue between my lips. "Hmm … you taste good too." She pulled back, licking the blood off her lips.

"Get off me," I grit out.

She smiled.

"Did I do good, Mistress?" Zane asked from across from us.

"Yes, baby boy." She licked her lips. "You did."

"So, what is this? You're his Mistress? You get off on this shit?" I was all for kink but not when the other person was related to me.

"He does as I ask." She gripped my chin, digging her nails into my jaw. "Not that I need to explain myself to you."

"You're sick, you know that, right?" I needed to keep them talking and find out how to bring them to the ground.

"Maybe I am," Tina shrugged, running her fingers inside the collar of my shirt. "For an older man, you sure stay nice and hard, don't you?"

I was almost thirty-five. It made me wonder just how young she liked them.

"Drive faster," she barked. "I need to play with my new toy." She turned to Zane. "Bind his hands. I don't want him hitting me."

Zane did as he was told, forcing me forward, and slipped a chain around my wrists. He bound them behind my back so it made it difficult for me to escape.

The metal dug into my skin, sending a hot shiver racing down my back. I chuckled. "Smart man."

"Isn't he pretty, Zane?" Tina clapped her hands together. "I can't wait to get home and climb him like a tree."

I scoffed. "The only thing you'll be climbing is the fucking hole of your grave."

Tina frowned.

Before I could comprehend what was about to happen, her palm landed against the side of my face but it only forced a laugh from my lips.

"You think that's funny, *do you?*" she screamed, clawing at my face.

"Tina." Zane wrapped his arms around her shoulders and pulled her off of my lap. They sat on the bench across from me while he whispered into her ear and petd her hair.

Their dominant role switched between them fast.

So, Zane was the calm one.

I kept up on my BDSM knowledge, but what they had, confused the shit out of me. "What do you want with me?" I asked, the silence between us setting my nerves on edge.

Zane and Tina looked between each other before wicked grins spread on their faces.

RUDE

My heart jumped. I wasn't one to get scared but I wasn't stupid. I realized something at that moment.

I was fucked.

***

(Brogan)

The shots banged in my ears, making my head spin. They never hit me but the sounds sure as hell pierced my ear drums. But the butt of the gun that had knocked me out had left a goose egg.

Cradling my arm against my chest, I crawled out of the upturned SUV. They took Coby from me to only God knew where. I would find them, and I would destroy them. The girly part of me wanted to cry but with rage on my side, I embraced that darkness that Coby had taught me was okay to have, and pushed forward.

Being in the shitty part of the city, no one was around to make sure I was okay. They minded their own business, not wanting to deal with the cops or have their faces seen. I understood because it wasn't like I would have talked to anyone anyway.

Pushing myself to my feet, my knees buckled. My body was stiff, my muscles tight like I had just spent hours working out. Everything ached and throbbed but it wouldn't stop me from finding Coby.

I needed a phone.

Walking as quickly as I could, I made my way back to Lucas's shop. Thankful his business was still open, I pushed the door open.

"Lucas?" I called out, my voice cracking. Clearing my throat, I tried again. "Lucas."

"Hey, Brogan," he said, coming from the back of the shop. "I thought you guys were—holy shit." His eyes widened. "What the hell happened?"

My legs took that moment to collapse under my weight. I fell to my knees, breathing through the nausea that had surfaced suddenly.

"Shit." Lucas knelt in front of me, rubbing a hand over my back in small circles. "Where's Coby? Brogan, tell me what happened."

"We got hit," I breathed, swallowing through the bile that was burning my throat. "Zane and Tina." I shook my head. "I need a phone." I pushed out of his grasp and jumped to my feet, wavering slightly. Grabbing hold of the counter, I took deep cleansing breaths.

"Brogan," Lucas barked. "Tell me where Coby is."

I met his gaze, tears burning my eyes. "They took him."

"*Fuck*," Lucas bellowed, punching his fist into the wall. "Brogan—" he turned to me, his eyes shining "—we need to get him back."

I nodded and took a deep breath. "I need to make a call."

*****

(Coby)

Being dominant for most of my adult life, I never claimed the title officially but it was how I practiced. Now I was chained to a wall, my arms held above my head, the metal biting into my wrists like tiny sharp teeth. I prayed to whoever would listen that Brogan would forgive me for whatever was about to happen.

I was chained to a cross but it wasn't fancy like a St. Andrew's Cross. No. This one was meant to torture. To remind the victim who was in control. But no matter what happened, these sick fucks would never get my mind.

"He doesn't want to break," Tina pouted, pacing back and forth in front of me. "What would your little girlfriend do if she found out?"

"She's dead, remember?" I growled, fighting against my restraints. Pain shot through every inch of me. I didn't know how much damage the accident had caused but I couldn't move my legs. Not good. Not good at fucking all.

"Poor, baby." Tina's lips pursed. She ran a hand through her dark hair before pulling it back into a pony tail. "I think I'm going to fuck you first."

"I'd rather die than have my dick inside of you," I said through gritted teeth.

She raised an eyebrow. "Who said anything about you being inside of me, baby boy?" She winked. "I'm the only one who does the fucking around here."

Well that took a turn I wasn't expecting. When I didn't respond, she barked out a laugh.

"I bet that tight ass is a virgin too." She moaned and walked to a large vanity sitting by the far wall. "You see, there is only one man who I'll let fuck me and even then, I control every move."

"Both of you are disturbed."

"Maybe," she shrugged. Tina pulled out a large strap on that had a fake dick attached to it. It flopped around with each step she took as she walked back toward me.

"What if you're related?" I asked, pulling away from her as best I could with the restraints that were holding me.

"Doesn't matter. I love Zane and he's the only one who has been there for me. And who ever said that it's him I've been fucking?" Tina grabbed hold of my jaw, digging her nails into my cheeks. "Enough about us. Ever been fucked before, Coby? Ever lose control to the greatest pleasure of all?" Her hand roamed down my bare chest, her gaze moving even lower before popping back up to my face. "I bet that little whore loves it when you throw her around. Tell me, Coby. Does she submit like I can?"

I let out a growl, pulling against the chains around my wrists. "Let me go."

"Why?" she frowned. "We've only just begun." She gave my cheek a gentle slap before lowering to her knees. "Move him to the floor," she yelled.

A large man standing by the door, grabbed hold of a lever on the wall and started cranking until I was lying flat on the ground.

Tina leaned over my waist, licking her lips.

My eyes widened.

Throwing my head back, I stared up at the ceiling, ignoring everything around me. Thinking about Brogan, I tried with everything in me to force my body from reacting.

"I'm so fucking sorry," I whispered, my words floating into the air. This wasn't my fault. I knew that but I didn't do anything to stop it. Not that I could with the chains wrapped around my ankles and wrists. My thoughts battled it out.

You want this.

It's not your fault.

You can't settle for one woman.
Brogan knows you love her.
Leah ruined you for others.
There's nothing you can do.

It went on. And on. For minutes. Hours. I couldn't be sure. Tina forced me to succumb to her madness.

Her hands wrapped around me. Her lips caressed every inch.

But I held back. I fell into myself and imagined Brogan was with me, telling me that it would be okay. That I would make it through this. What if she was truly dead? What if Zane shot her? I yelled out a curse, embracing the new rage coursing through me. My hips bucked, knocking Tina back on her ass.

She grinned, wiping her mouth. "I like it dirty, baby boy." And then she was on me. Her nails scratched into my skin, poking and pushing into my previous wounds and made them worse.

I winced but I refused to give her any sounds that she was hurting me.

"I'm going to scar you up, Coby so when you go home, she'll see me all over you. I'll be inside you. In your head. You think you're so strong. Just wait." She licked up the side of my face. "I'm going to fuck your mind and you're going to enjoy every moment of it."

CHAPTER THIRTY-ONE

Brogan

I PACED BACK and forth.

Voices sounded around me but all I could focus on was Coby. I knew he was alive. I couldn't quite explain how I knew but I felt him. I just prayed he could sense that I was alive and not give up. *God, please don't let him give up.*

It had been at least an hour and a half since the accident but it felt like a lifetime. The longer Coby was missing, the greater of a chance he had at not surviving. But I didn't even know where to begin when it came to looking for him.

"Let me do up your leg."

I paused in my pacing, staring up at Greyson.

He pointed to my thigh.

I followed his gaze, frowning at the large gash in my hip. I was numb to the pain. Even when I forced my fingers to run over the torn flesh, I still couldn't feel anything.

Greyson pulled out a stool at the kitchen island, patting the seat.

I did as I was told, letting him stitch me up.

"You'll need to get your wrist looked at," he said, his voice monotone.

I nodded.

"Boss," the VP to Hell's Harlem stepped into the kitchen. "You good?"

Grey closed up the medical aid kit and leaned against the island. "I'll be better once we find Coby."

The vice president nodded once before whistling to the rest of the crew.

In a matter of seconds I was surrounded by men. Large men. So big in fact they sucked the air right out of the room. But they were brothers.

Hell's Harlem had come for me when I called Greyson, telling him I needed him.

Lucas stood off to the side. He adjusted his eye patch and continued texting on his phone.

"Tell her I'm sorry," I told him.

The chatter silenced, all eyes focusing on me.

Lucas met my gaze. "You have nothing to be sorry about."

"I'm bringing you," I took a breath. "All of you into a shit storm."

"Baby girl," one of the newest members to Hell's Harlem, clapped a hand on my shoulder. His face was scarred and although he looked mean, his eyes were gentle. "You are Greyson's stepsister. We also hold high respect for you and your club. It's not often that women can handle this world. We are one and we stick together."

Resounding grunts aired through the room before Greyson's voice boomed straight to my heart.

"We have to get him back because I refuse to watch Brogan lose another part of herself at the hands of those bastards," Grey squeezed my good hand. "Now, Lucas. Tell us what you know."

Lucas grinned, sliding his phone into his back pocket. "Well …" He placed a tablet in the center of the table.

My eyes widened as the blue prints stared up at me. "Is this …"

"It's their compound," he tapped the screen, enlarging the screen so we could see every square foot of it. "We have no way of knowing if this is where Coby is. These bastards own several places."

"He could be anywhere," I mumbled.

Grey squeezed my shoulder.

"Right. I checked the GPS on Coby's phone and nothing. I'll keep checking but all I can suggest is splitting up and some of you go to the compound and the rest of you hold back." Lucas rapped his knuckles against the wooden surface of the table. "Although, if it were me, I'd blow every last one of those buildings down until I found him."

"We have to do something."

"Can't have our little sister upset."

"I'll kill them."

My eyes burned at everyone chiming in their thoughts and concerns. For me. For Coby. For all of us. Every woman, young and old. And now men. No one was safe.

"Did you call Vice-One?" Greyson asked.

I swallowed hard, looking down at my hands and pretended not to hear him.

"Brogan," Grey barked. "Answer me. I don't need those assholes shitting on my step for keeping this from them."

"No," I sighed. "I haven't told them."

"*Fuck*," Greyson boomed. "You realize they will find out, right?"

"Yes," I rose to my feet. "I know that but I refuse to put them in danger again. Look at what they've been through already. I would never forgive myself if something else happened to them."

"They won't care about that," Greyson shook his head, letting out a long whistle. "Girl, you are in for it. I hope you're prepared."

I stood up straighter. "Yes. I am. They can hate me forever. My sisters can hate me. As long as they are alive, that's all I care about."

"Who's this Vice-One?" one of the club members asked.

"Navy SEALs and mean as fuck," Greyson muttered. "Especially when shit involves their own."

I let out a heavy sigh, cupping Greyson's hand. "I'm sorry for bringing you in on this but right now, I need you."

"Brox and Blake are going to kill me if something happens to you," he muttered, grabbing hold of my hand.

"They'll get over it. Right now, I need you to look at me as a partner and not your stepsister." I paused. "Please."

Greyson let out a string of curses before pulling me into his arms. "I'm blaming you."

"That's fine." I hugged him back.

"Brogan," Lucas said over the chatter. "Can I talk to you?"

I nodded, released Greyson and followed Lucas into his office.

Lucas closed the door before leaning against it. He crossed his arms under his chest, staring at me.

"What?" I asked, the stare down sending my nerves on edge.

"You need to know that whatever you walk in on, is not Coby's fault."

"I know that."

"Do you? Because I don't think you understand what these people are capable of. I've hacked into the records. I know what the victims look like after they're disposed of."

"Coby isn't dead." I refused to believe it until I saw his cold lifeless body myself.

"I don't think he is and that's not what I'm referring to." Lucas rubbed the back of his neck. "Tina could have done things to him. Actually, I'd bet my fucking life on it that she already has."

I swallowed hard, my heart picking up speed.

"You need to be aware that they might have fucked."

A whimper escaped me at the thought of her touching him. Of him enjoying it and giving her everything she craved. "No."

"Brogan, I'm not trying to upset you." Lucas took a step toward me. "But I can tell you from experience; it's not easy saying no."

"What if I walk in and see him touching her like he touches me?" I whispered, slumping hard on the chair.

Lucas knelt in front of me and grabbed my good hand. "I don't know you that well. Hell, I hardly know you at all but I know you love him. I can see it. I also know that you trust him to do whatever it takes to survive."

"Yes," I nodded. "I need him to remain strong."

"Exactly. So, I'm just warning you that you might not like what you see or what you find out later."

"I'll kill her. If I find out that she forced him to fuck her, I'll rip off every inch that touched him and skin her alive."

Lucas chuckled. "Yup. I can definitely see why he loves you." His face became serious in a matter of seconds. "Don't leave him. Whatever you do. He's going to need you after all of this."

That was if we could even find him. No. I shook my head, ridding myself of those thoughts. Coby was alive. I could feel it. But common sense told me that it was a possibility.

"All right, fuckers," Lucas clapped his hands together. "On average, missing people have seventy-two hours before they're killed so we need to hurry the fuck up and find Coby."

****

(Coby)

I was drowning within myself. The light Brogan had given me over the past couple of months was snuffed out and replaced with the evil and despair of my captors. Between Tina and Zane, I couldn't be sure who was worse. As they both took turns with me, the pain and abuse mixed as one.

My eyes would flutter open every so often as I looked up to the ceiling and prayed for someone to come find me. This was my lowest breaking point.

Even after everything I had been through in my life, nothing came close to this. I was a man. Strong and dominant but even that power held little to no value when I was chained to a wall.

Time wore on. I couldn't be sure how many hours or even days it had been since Zane dragged me from my SUV. A part of me wished they would just kill me and get it over with.

A heavy slap landed on my cheek, forcing my eyes to pop open.

My gaze landed on Tina's soulless gaze.

She smiled, licking her full lips. "You're not so strong, are you? All of you dominant men think you can control every aspect of your life. Well guess what, baby boy? I'm going to break you of that. You will submit and you will fall apart for me. You will like that too, won't you?"

"Fuck you," I said through gritted teeth.

"Aww," she pouted, wrapping her fingers around my cock. "We've done that already, sweet boy. You didn't seem to like it very much when I rode you. But guess what?" She licked up the side of my face, while tugging and pulling at my dick. "I don't care. You can't hold that orgasm in forever. No matter how much training you've had."

"It's called Tantra you bitch. I'll hold it in for the rest of my fucking life." I knew it wasn't possible but there would be no way I would give her that satisfaction of knowing that eventually, she would have all of me. I was human. I could only control my body as best I could before Tina got what she wanted.

"I wonder what will happen when Brogan finds out." Her eyes twinkled. "I would love to be there for that conversation."

RUDE

"Fuck," I shouted, pulling against my restraints all the while laughter sounded around me. My body was used. Stabbed. Broken to the point, I had no strength left to fight. I prayed with everything in me that Brogan or someone found me. And soon. Because I knew it was only a matter of time before Tina owned me completely.

CHAPTER THIRTY-TWO

Brogan

WE HAD ONLY an inkling of an idea where Coby was being held. It had been twenty-four hours since we started searching. And I feared that it would be another day or two before we would actually find him.

Tina and Zane had compounds all over the country but everything in me said that they weren't even the ones in charge. I wasn't sure why I felt this way. It seemed to me like they were only interested in the sex trafficking. Not the drugs. Weapons. Or even terrorism. They wanted control of the human nature. I wasn't even sure where Charles and his brother fit into that mix.

Hell's Harlem called in back up, instructing the other clubs to split up and head to the other compounds in the city. Coby couldn't have been far.

Even though his GPS indicated he was in one spot, once we got there, we found the building had been vacated for months.

I was getting frustrated. Tired. And worried as fuck.

We had reached three more compounds before I finally snapped.

"We're doing something wrong," I screamed, pushing Greyson. "Why can't we find him?" I knew my emotions were getting the best of me and it wasn't the way to go into this, but there was nothing I could do to control them. After Lucas' warning, my mind reeled with possible images of what Tina was doing to Coby. She could be touching him. Hurting him. Or worse. As selfish as it was, if I found out he was forced to fuck her, I wasn't sure what I would do. I had never been cheated on and even though Coby wouldn't have a choice in the matter, that small part of myself would blame him.

"Brogan," Greyson gripped my shoulders, giving me a gentle shake. "You need to calm down. Right now. This won't do you any good and your emotions running rampant will only get you killed. All of the shit that Coby is going through will be for fucking nothing if you're dead."

I let out a hard scream, shoving out of his grip. "Don't you think I know that?"

"Well than use your head," Greyson shot back. "Focus and help us find him but don't you dare just charge into building after building without making sure it's clear first. Do you understand me?"

My jaw clenched as I stared my stepbrother down but after a couple beats, I gave in. "Yeah. I understand."

But what I didn't understand was that we hadn't seen anyone. We had been to a couple buildings already and they were all vacant. I called Lucas.

"Yeah," he grunted after the first ring.

"It's me. Have you heard of Tina and Zane having empty buildings? Maybe as a ruse?" I started pacing back and forth. "We haven't found anything or anyone."

"Shit. Let me check."

I could hear him clicking away on his computer. As soon as I was about to ask if he had found anything, he let out a string of curses that made even me blush. "Something wrong?"

Greyson looked my way, raising an eyebrow while the other guys surrounded us.

"Put me on speaker," Lucas demanded.

"Done." I laid the phone in my palm. "Go ahead, Lucas."

"These fucks enjoy messing with your head. They buy buildings, have people go in and out of them so it looks like people are there but when the FBI show up, fucking nothing."

"So, Coby could be anywhere." I let out a breath. "How many compounds left in the city?"

"I'm guessing maybe ten," Lucas cursed again. "I'm sorry, Brogan."

My eyes burned but I wouldn't let this new revelation stop me. "Whatever. We'll find him. We have to. Even if it's … even if he doesn't make it. I won't stop until I have his body in my arms."

Greyson cupped my shoulder, giving it a light squeeze. "We won't stop until we make that happen. But Coby is strong. If anyone can make it through this, it's him."

I wished I could believe that. Coby *was* strong. He was the only reason I was able to get through the death of Benny.

But any human being, no matter how strong they were, had a weakness. And mine was Coby. It would always be Coby.

****

(Coby)

"Coby, Coby, Coby," Tina pursed her lips. "Remember what I told you would happen to that pretty little thing of yours if you didn't give me what I want?"

I breathed out through gritted teeth. New pain sliced into my side. Slow. Deep. It burned its way into my soul, searing onto my skin like a hot knife. "You touch her and I'll ..."

"You'll what, Coby?" Tina pushed the blade further into my side.

I yelled out. Not wanting to give her any satisfaction, I tried keeping it in but I couldn't take it anymore. The more she tortured, the more I broke.

"You can't do anything chained to my wall, baby boy?" she kissed my cheek. "But wait. Now you're on my floor. I love this new toy, Zane made me." Her lips brushed over the shell of my ear. "And why would you want to leave? We've been through so much already." Pulling the knife free from my body, she ran her tongue up the blade. "Mmm ... every part of you tastes so fucking good."

My stomach churned.

Part of me felt like less of a man because I couldn't fight this woman off me. It didn't make sense. I knew that. It wasn't like there was anything I could do. Two men stood at the entrance to the make shift dungeon. Zane was always around, watching and waiting to make his own move. Whenever Tina barked an order, he jumped to her demands. I was royally fucked.

"Just kill me already," I told her.

"Now what would be the fun in that?"

"Zane already shot Brogan. How do I know she's not dead already?"

"Oh, she isn't dead. He didn't even shoot her," she whispered, patting my cheek. "But I will order for him to grab her if you don't give me what I need."

"I don't have a choice anyway."

"You always have a choice."

"No," I yelled. "I never had a choice. You forced me you fucking whore." Having a pistol to my head, knowing the magazine was loaded because Zane had shot me with it, forced me into a submission I never wanted.

"It's all about choices." She laughed. "You could have chosen to say no and I would have just killed you." She shrugged. "Do you really love life that much that you would cheat on your girlfriend to live?"

"I need to go back to her," I whispered, my body slumping in defeat.

She clucked her tongue. "Well then, I guess you'll just have to pay the consequences, now won't you? Think Brogan will stay with you? Think I won't leave you? No matter what happens, Coby," she gripped my chin, forcing me to look into her dark eyes. "I will always be with you. Every time you close your eyes, you will see me. You will feel my pussy for the rest of your fucking life. You will taste my desire on your tongue. Think your precious little Brogan can erase that?"

"You bet your fucking life she can."

A hard fist landed against the side of my head.

Spots danced in my vision, forcing me into a darkness that I suddenly craved. A vision of Brogan appeared out of nowhere. She was smiling, blowing me kisses. She was like an angel. She motioned for me to go to her and I did.

***

(Brogan)

"Tell me where the *fuck* they are?" I yelled, digging my nails into the cheeks of the bastard lying beneath me.

He chuckled, blood gurgling out of his mouth. "I'm not telling you shit."

Sticking my finger into the gunshot wound in his shoulder, I pushed until he was writhing beneath me. "Tell me. Where are Zane and Tina holding Coby Porter?"

He cried out, sweat coating his brow. "Fuck you."

Grabbing the blade from the back of my pants, I dug it into his throat, forcing his head back. "Tell me or I'll gut you like a fucking pig."

"Go ahead. It won't be any worse than what they'll do to me."

"Come on, Brogan." Greyson came toward me, careful not to come any closer. "The fucker isn't breaking."

I glanced back down at the victim beneath me. I grinned. "I hope you remember me when you burn in fucking hell." Sliding the knife along his throat, blood spurted my hand.

He croaked and groaned, gasping for breath.

I sat back, wiping the blade on my pants and watched the life leave his eyes. "Serves you right, fucker." I shoved off him and stopped, staring around the entry way to another compound we had raided. Only this time, there were people there. But there was still no sign of Coby.

"We'll find him," Greyson told me, gripping my shoulders. "I promise you."

I nodded; unable to form any words for fear that I would burst into tears. I didn't need emotions right now. They only got in the way.

"I will kill every person I see until I find him," I turned toward Greyson. "Do you still love me now?" I stormed off, not waiting for his reply, knowing it would be a *yes*.

Grabbing the hem of my shirt, I lifted it and wiped the sweat and blood off my face. I stepped over body after body until I made my way out into the cool night air. I could feel eyes on me, burning into my skin but I didn't give them the reprieve of meeting their concerned stares. I was losing the control I tried so hard to keep. As each minute passed with Coby missing, I could feel it being sucked right out of me. My body hurt, my muscles aching with each step I took but it only pushed me forward. I was driven mad with the need to find him and avenge his suffering.

"Brogan," Greyson called from behind me. "Wait up."

"No." I hopped on my bike. God, it had been so long since I had ridden her, I almost forgot how she felt between my legs. Greyson had one of his guys go get her for me which I had been thankful for. I hated waiting around for the cleanup. I wanted to go in. Kill. And move on to the next compound until I found Coby.

"Brogan," Grey snapped.

I whipped my head around.

"Lucas found him." He handed me his cell.

I held it up to my ear, waiting with bated breath.

"Brogan," Lucas answered from the other end.

"Tell me."

"I was finally able to hack into one of the compounds security systems and saw a van pull up just over twenty-four hours ago. They dragged a body from the vehicle. I couldn't tell who it was but I know it was a man. Their camera system sucks balls."

"Lucas," I barked. "Focus."

"You and Coby are perfect for each other," he grumbled.

I rolled my eyes. "Please tell me something."

"I can't be sure but I think it's Coby."

The world spun around me, all the air leaving my lungs on a whoosh. "Where?"

"I already gave Greyson the address. Listen, Brogan ..."

"Yeah?"

"Avenge him. Kill every mother fucker you have to but bring our boy home."

"I will," I breathed. "I will."

CHAPTER THIRTY-THREE

Coby

MY BODY WAS lifted into the air and chained back against the wall. A sharp pain stabbed me in the shoulder and I knew without a doubt that it had been dislocated. The injuries from the accident only became worse as Tina and Zane tortured me. I couldn't walk. I couldn't stand. I could no longer fight them off me. When I didn't move, Zane pushed me, forcing me to do things I never would have done even in my darkest of days.

A hard slap to my cheek rang through my ears. "Wake up," Tina demanded. "I don't need you dying on me." She lifted a glass to my mouth, pouring a cold liquid between my lips.

The water slid down my parched throat until I gagged and choked.

"Good thing you're not gay," she shook her head. "You would suck at deep throating."

"He can learn," Zane grabbed my jaw. "I could teach him to take it all in. Couldn't I?"

"Fuck you," I whispered.

"I'm sorry," he turned his head, leaning his ear toward me. "I didn't hear you."

"Fuck you," I said a little louder that time.

"I've tried but my sister isn't done with you yet," he slapped his hand against my cheek. "Just wait until I'm ready for you. You think *she's* mean?" A cold laugh escaped his lips. Releasing me, he turned to his sister. "Don't kill him before I have a chance to taste his flesh."

Tina giggled before glancing back at me. "He's so funny." And with that, she spun on her heel and followed him out the door.

I was alone. Finally.

Taking a deep breath, I pulled myself up, wincing and breathing through the new onslaught of pain. Although my one eye was swollen shut, I was still able to take in my surroundings. I had been right. I was locked away in a dungeon. The only items were the cross I was attached to and the dresser near the far wall.

But I didn't see anything I could use as leverage to break myself free from these chains. For the first time in my life, I needed help and there was no one around to ask.

Please, God, save me from this hell.

I prayed, pleaded, begged for my life but my words left my lips and disappeared into the silence of the room. All the shit I had been forced to endure was unforgivable. And I knew without a doubt that even though it wasn't my fault, Brogan could possibly leave me. That revelation alone was worse than the torture I had experienced. I would throw myself at the mercy of Tina and Zane if it meant Brogan would stay with me.

***

(Brogan)

It had been two days since I saw Coby last. Since I felt him in my arms and his hot breath on my lips. I prayed with everything in me that he was still alive.

Once Lucas gave us the information on where Coby could possibly be, I hightailed it out of there and drove as fast as my bike would allow. The drive seemed to go on forever, the closer I got to the location, the further I fell into myself. I had killed several men already in the past couple of days. It wasn't something I was proud of, taking another life and all, but these men were monsters. Vile human beings who worked for an organization that stripped the innocence from anyone they could get their hands on.

Greyson and his club followed behind me, their headlights shining in my side mirrors. The other club he had called on, drove in front of me, leading the pack to keep me safe. If anyone would be hit unexpectedly, it would be them.

I wasn't sure why these men were doing this for me. I didn't even know how to ask. But I appreciated it more than they would ever realize.

Glancing at the GPS on my bike, the red dot flashed, indicating that the building was a mile ahead. This was it. It was time to save Coby and get the fuck out of dodge. He just better be there or I wasn't sure what I would do.

We slowed down, turning onto a long narrow driveway before stopping a couple yards from the building. This one wasn't like the rest. It was a mansion, not a rundown building like the others.

"Brogan—" Greyson came up beside me "—be smart about this."

"He has to be in there." I shut my bike off and slid off of it before pushing the kick stand down with my foot. "I can feel him, Grey." I didn't know how but something nudged at my heart. I knew once I found him, it would never be the same. I could only imagine what Tina and Zane had done to him during these past two days.

Taking a breath, I pulled what little strength I had left from deep within and took a couple steps toward the large house.

Greyson barked demands from behind me but all I could focus on was with each step, I was getting closer to finding Coby.

Gunshots sounded around me as security finally caught us sneaking around in the yard. My knife and pistol stayed at my back until I was ready. The next lives I would take would belong to Zane and Tina. Especially her.

"This fucking place is loaded with security," one of Greyson's men grumbled, shoving the end of his rifle into a security guard's mouth. He pulled the trigger, the man's head exploding into pieces of brain matter around him.

"That means he has to be here," I said. "It only makes sense."

"Go on ahead," Grey told me. "We got your back."

I nodded, took a deep cleansing breath and made my way up the large set of stairs leading into the front of the house.

Pushing open the double set of doors, I let out a sigh of relief at finding the hallway empty.

"Look for Zane," Greyson demanded. "The rest of you, come with me."

Grey's orders gave me piece of mind so I took them as my cue and made my way down the hall. Peering into room after room, I couldn't see anything out of the ordinary. It was like any other house. But I bet if the walls could talk, they would tell a tale about the souls who died here.

Once I reached the end of the hallway, I came across another door. This one led into a cold damp basement.

Looking back over my shoulder, I saw Greyson and some of his club members coming my way. I indicated for them to follow me and made my way down the stairs. When I stepped foot onto the last step, a wave of nausea took over. A putrid scent wafted into my nose forcing the tiny hairs on my body to stand on end.

Breathing past it, I walked up to the only door I saw and pushed it open.

Nothing could ever prepare me for what I saw next when I walked into that room. Coby was chained to a wall, his arms and legs spread apart like the shape of an X.

He was naked. Bloody. Beaten.

Forcing myself forward on shaky legs, I ran to him while the others continued getting rid of the security.

Greyson stood guard at the door, shutting it slightly to give us some privacy.

"Coby," I sobbed, touching him gently. But no matter where my hands grazed, his skin was purple and bruised. Bloody. Sliced up. What the hell did Tina do to him? "Coby, wake up, baby." I kissed him on the mouth, the metallic taste of blood coating my lips.

And then I smelled *her*. Tina. Her scent was all over him. Her floral perfume. Her pleasure. My stomach churned, bile rising to my throat but it only drove that rage deeper inside of me.

He stirred, his one good eye fluttering open while the other remained swollen shut. "Brogan," he groaned out. "You're alive."

"Shhh … don't talk." I tried getting the chains off him but they were wrapped around his wrists so damn tight, they dug into his skin. "I can't get these off you."

He struggled against them, trying to no doubt escape what was done to him.

"Coby, please stop. You're going to hurt yourself more." I shouted for Greyson. "I need your help."

He came into the room, his gaze darkening when they landed on Coby's broken form but he didn't say anything.

Thankful for the crowbar Greyson liked to use, I watched as he tore it into the wall.

As soon as the chains broke free from the wall, Coby collapsed against me.

We fell to the ground.

"We need to get him to a hospital," I pleaded with Grey. "And tell your guys to get out of here."

He nodded.

"Thank you," I whispered, holding Coby against me.

"Anything for you, Brogan." Greyson turned on his heel, barking orders at his men to clean up as best they could and get the hell out of there.

I would take the fall first for my stepbrother before I saw him go to jail. It was the least I could do when he helped me.

Coby stirred against me.

"Shh … you're safe. We'll get you to a hospital." I was strong but I wouldn't be able to carry him on my own.

He lifted his head, his brows narrowing in the center. "You're bloody."

I smiled. "Yeah. It was a little harder to get to you than I would have liked."

"I'm sorry," he whispered, his big body shaking.

"Don't," I said, my voice firm. "You're safe. That's all I care about. We can deal with the other shit later."

"I love you," he leaned his forehead against mine. "Everything I did was so I could get back to you."

Tears streamed down my cheeks, my chest aching with each breath. I couldn't form any words at his confession. All I could do was kiss him. I cared what happened. Of course I did. I was human. Yes, I was beyond infuriated over what Tina did. She would get hers and I would be the one to watch the life leave her eyes.

Greyson stepped into the room, followed by the rest of his club. "The place is cleaned up."

"What are they still doing here then?" I frowned. "You need to leave," I said, looking at each of the men.

"Not going to happen," Greyson clapped a hand on the newest member's shoulder. "Give her your hoodie."

The prospect who I had come to know as Twitch, did as he was told and handed me the warm fabric. It was bloody but I knew that Coby wouldn't care.

I tied it around his waist. "You guys can't stay. The cops will be here in no time." They all had records and time they never did because they ran or didn't get caught.

"We don't care," Greyson knelt beside us, wrapping his hand around Coby's bicep. "This is going to hurt but we need to move him. Who knows how long it will take for the cops to show up."

"Where is she?" I asked, helping him with lifting Coby to his feet.

"Don't worry about her." Greyson hooked an arm around Coby's middle, careful not to hurt him further.

"I asked you a question."

Coby grunted, leaning his weight on me.

I let out a heavy sigh. "Greyson, tell me where she is."

"She's gone all right?" Greyson snapped. "I have no idea where the fuck she is."

He was lying. Tina couldn't have just disappeared.

"Go find Zane," I demanded. I needed some sort of reprieve when it came to these two. If I couldn't get rid of Tina, I'd go after her damn brother.

"We're looking for him," Grey mumbled, helping me walk Coby up the stairs before heading back down into the basement to assist his men in cleaning up the mess.

As soon as Coby and I stepped onto the main floor, my eyes widened.

Tina stood a couple feet away, her gaze roaming over the bodies cluttering the floor. She looked our way, a small smile splaying on her face. "I see you found him."

Much to my surprise, Coby pulled me closer to his side and grabbed my pistol from the back of my pants. Lifting his arm, he aimed it at her.

Tina frowned. "You going to shoot me after what I did for you?"

"You didn't do shit for me," Coby growled, cocking the gun.

"Aww," Tina pouted. "But I did. I made you feel good. Better than this little whore could ever do."

Coby shouted and pulled the trigger.

The shot rang in my ears, forcing me to stumble against him.

Tina clasped her side, blood pooling between her fingers. Her eyes were wide, bright and shining with fear. Instead of cursing him out, she headed down another hallway, disappearing from our sight.

"Fuck," Coby lifted himself off me, his broken body wavering on his feet.

Getting him as quickly to the van as possible, I helped him into the back of the vehicle.

I cupped Coby's cheek, kissing him gently on his split lips. "I love you, Coby. More than I can ever tell you. I *will* avenge you."

His eyes fluttered open, darkening with sorrow and understanding. "Finish her, little one. Rip out her fucking soul."

The fact that he understood where I was coming from and my need for vengeance, made me fall in love with him even more.

Coby was all alpha male but he also knew when he had to take a step back. We were equals in this relationship. Neither of us more dominant than the other. We took turns and switched roles when necessary.

I kissed him one last time before walking away. I felt Tina's presence in the building. She may have had control of these men, but she hadn't met me yet. And I would praise the look on her face when I held her beating heart in my hands.

CHAPTER THIRTY-FOUR

Coby

BROKEN AND DEFEATED.

I never thought I would end up this way. Maybe I deserved it for all the shit I had done. Although it had been my job, the lives I had taken would surely haunt me for the rest of my life. Even if they *were* evil incarnate. But no one was like Tina. Her touch would forever be seared in my soul. Her viciousness would be burned on my skin. I hated her. Everything she was. She couldn't be human. No person in the right mind would even consider doing what she had done. To these girls. To *me*.

I could still feel her claws digging into my skin. Her teeth sinking into a part of me that belonged to Brogan. I thought of my little one the whole time, but it wasn't enough. It would never be enough. I would spend the rest of my life, apologizing for what I had done. I had no choice if I wanted to survive.

"Coby."

Opening my good eye, I found Greyson standing in the open doors of the van.

"Whatever happened wasn't your fault," he told me.

I grunted. "I should have fought harder." *I should have done something.*

"These people are evil. You had to do what you could to live."

Tears burned my eyes. *Fuck.* I wasn't an emotional man but knowing what I did to get back to Brogan tore at me. "She made me do things."

"I know," Greyson's voice softened. "Listen, I love Brogan. I always will. But she loves *you*. She doesn't blame you."

"How do you know that?" I tried sitting up on the blanket I was laying on but my broken body wouldn't allow it.

"Trust me," he rubbed the back of his neck. "I know when she's pissed. She trusts you. She knows you didn't want to do anything you did."

"I can still feel her on me," I muttered, my voice cracking. "I can feel her claws in my skin. Her mouth … her body." I shook my head, gripping my hair. "I didn't want to do anything. I didn't want to … let go."

"Shit, man." Greyson crawled into the back of the van, ordering his men to stand watch and if they saw Brogan, to let him know. He closed the doors behind him before sitting beside me. "I need to know. Did you fuck her?"

I searched his face. "I … had no choice."

Greyson raised an eyebrow.

"I know what it sounds like. Tina told me she wouldn't let any man fuck her except for one person. I don't know who that is. I can only assume it's her brother she's talking about. But I had no fucking choice when I was strapped to that board and lying on the fucking floor for her to do whatever the hell she wanted."

"That's some sick shit right there."

I nodded. "But she ..." I swallowed hard, feeling vulnerable and small like a little boy.

"Did she fuck you?"

When I didn't say anything, Greyson let out a string of curses.

But no matter how hard she tried, I never gave her my orgasm. After years of practice, I had learned to control my releases so I could focus on pleasing the women I had been with. Brogan was the only female to make me come fast and hard. All my pleasure belonged to her and her only.

I chuckled, remembering the look on Tina's face when I told her that.

"What's so funny?" Grey frowned.

"I told Tina she would have to kill me first before I would ever shoot my load for her. Her expression was fucking priceless." And it earned me a knife in the side and her teeth in my dick. I let out a heavy sigh. Once I was fully healed, I needed to give Brogan all of me. Every inch. I needed her to erase this torture from my mind and replace it with her sweetness.

Until then, I would scald my skin with hot water, washing away the evil and the scent of depravity.

****

RUDE

(Brogan)

"I see you've found me. Again." Tina pursed her ruby red lips, reapplying gloss all the while holding her wounded side. "Came here to finish the job? I'm surprised your boyfriend missed. I hear he's good at what he does." She glanced at the blood soaking through the fabric of her red dress. "Clearly he's not *that* good."

I leaned against the door, shutting it closed behind me and locked it. It didn't take me long to search her out. "I want answers." I knew Coby would tell me everything that had happened. As much as I didn't want to hear it, I needed to know so I could help him heal.

Tina clucked her tongue. "You want to know what I did to your boyfriend."

"Yes," I said even though it wasn't a question. "Did you fuck him?"

Her lips turned into a smile. "You know, it's funny. I brought out the strap on but changed my mind." She moaned. "He did taste good though."

My body buzzed, images of her on her knees with her lips wrapped around his cock soared into my mind.

"But he wouldn't come," she pouted. "As much as I sucked him off, he wouldn't let go for me. As long as I rode him, he wouldn't come inside me." She licked her lips. "He did react to me though. A man can never have only one woman."

A breath left me on a whoosh at that revelation.

"No matter how hard I tried." She shrugged. "Ask me more. You know you want to."

"He fucked you."

"Only because I made him," she pointed at me. "He loves you."

"You made him touch you," I repeated, shaking my head. I knew it happened. I wasn't stupid but hearing the words made me want to throw up.

"No. I made him *fuck* me. Big difference. Only his dick touched me and what a delicious moment it was. Or moments I should say." She giggled. "I can still taste him on my tongue you know. His salty pre-cum. So fucking divine."

I took a step toward her. "He wouldn't."

"Oh, little girl," Tina rose to her full height. "Don't be upset. You should be proud. You taught him well. The multiple orgasms he gave me will be something I'll never forget."

I screamed, charging for her. "You fucking whore. I'll kill you for what you did to him."

A maniacal laugh escaped her.

Forcing her to the ground, I wrapped my hands around her throat but it only caused her to laugh harder. "I hope you die thinking of me," I growled.

She choked, the smile still on her face.

Suddenly, I was on my back with her on top of me.

Tina grabbed my hands, forcing my arms above my head and knelt between my legs. "You see," she leaned down to my ear. "I like it rough." She pushed her hips into mine. "I would have so much fun turning you into my pet." She licked up the side of my face. "When you kissed him, did you taste my come on his lips?"

I whimpered, squeezing my eyes shut before I pushed her back. "You can tell me whatever you want," I grit out. "I don't give a shit but whatever you say, it won't make me think any less of him."

"Really? Is that a challenge?" She sat back, holding my wrists.

I cried out as a sharp pain shot straight up the length of my arm.

Her grin widened. "What if I told you that I can still feel him inside of me? Full and thick. Throbbing. Every pulsing vein. He was so damn hard. I could have had him explode inside of me but you all showed up."

My stomach tumbled. "So, you raped him. Did it get you off?"

"Yes," she licked her full mouth. "Several times. Especially when he fought me. My brother had to hold him down. Too bad he didn't get a taste before you guys stormed in. Zane would have loved to get a feel of his tight ass."

I cried out, taking that as my strength and forced her off me. "I will end you."

"Then do it already," she screamed, staring up at me from the ground. "Kill me."

"Tell me why the hell you did it."

"Don't you know already?"

"Know what?" I shook my head, attempting to grasp this whole situation before I completely lost it.

"He begged me. He told me he would do anything as long as I left you out of it. That man loves you but fucked me to keep you safe. How does that make you feel, Brogan?"

Numb. Completely and utterly numb.

CHAPTER THIRTY-FIVE

Brogan

I FELT LOST.

Tina's words floated around me, jabbing me every so often with their taunting.

Coby fucked her.

He didn't have a choice. I got that. But it still made question everything I knew about us.

When I smelled her on him, I already knew just how far she had gone with him but it still didn't make me feel any better when the confession left her lips.

Tina stared into my eyes, her mouth moving over words I couldn't hear.

Her slender fingers wrapped around my throat. "I'm going to enjoy watching the life leave your body," she whispered in my ear. Her mouth grazed the length of my jaw before reaching my mouth. Crushing her lips to mine, her fingers tightened.

A gasp escaped me as her tongue invaded my mouth while the air was forced from my lungs.

"Hmm …" she moaned. "You taste just as good as he does. I wish I could have you both together but alas, that can't happen. You've seen too much. You forced my brother to disappear."

"I'll find him," I croaked, digging my nails into her hands. "And I'll kill him."

"Maybe so," she fisted my hair in her hand, pulling my head back. "Fight me, Brogan. I like it."

I screamed, shoving my body against her but the weight of the past couple of days took its toll on me.

Tina laughed. "Maybe I should see what has him so addicted to you," she purred, inching her hand up under my shirt.

"Fuck you," I pushed against her, forcing the strength from within and had her beneath me in a matter of seconds. "I'm going to destroy you," I wrapped my hands around her throat, gasping in fresh bursts of air.

Her eyes widened, popping out of her head. She struggled beneath me, digging and clawing at my hands and arms.

"You've messed with the wrong woman," I snarled. "And I don't share. At all. Whatever you think you got from Coby will be nothing compared to what *I'm* going to give you."

Her screams slid over my skin, heating me from the inside out.

Taking all my frustration, anger, every emotion I had felt over the past couple of months, on her body and mind. She may have fucked my boyfriend but I was going to fuck her soul.

Sliding my blade into the gunshot wound Coby had given her, our wrath melted together.

Tina pleaded for her life, breaking down into that shy timid girl hidden by the barriers of hate.

"Did you listen to Coby when he begged?" I pulled the blade out of her side and pushed it against her throat. "Did you listen to him when he told you to get off him? When he pleaded for you not to fuck him?"

"He wanted it," she croaked out. "He wanted everything I had to give him."

"Yeah? And how about you?" I placed a hard peck on her mouth. "Do you want everything I have to give you?"

Tears welled in her eyes, rolling down her cheeks while she gulped and gasped for air. "He loved the feeling of my pussy."

"But he's a man," I tapped the blade against her cheek. "They can't handle only one pussy. Isn't that what you said?"

"I was enough for him," she pushed her face against the blade, a drop of crimson liquid erupting from the small cut on her cheek.

"You were never enough." Not wanting to hear anymore, I slid the knife in a quick move over her throat.

She sputtered, blood bubbling from her lips while what little soul she had left, faded from her eyes.

Rising to my feet, I wiped the blade off on my shirt and stuck it in the back pocket of my pants. Although she was gone and she paid for what she did to Coby, I didn't feel better. Relief pushed on my shoulders that she would no longer be an issue but Zane was still missing. Charles was nowhere to be found and Coby and I had a lot of shit to deal with.

But for now, I would take reprieve in the fact that Tina Birtch was dead.

I avenged Coby and now I needed to confront him over the new revelations that had been revealed to me.

The battle we dealt with on a day to day basis had officially turned into a full-blown war.

CHAPTER THIRTY-SIX

Brogan

ONCE I LEFT the compound, I approached Coby.

Greyson sat with him in the back of the van while the other men stood around the van.

Coby and I locked eyes.

He looked away, his body shuddering under my stare.

Greyson took that as his cue and left the vehicle. He instructed his club to leave but other than that, I didn't hear any more of what was being said.

Once I crawled into the van and shut me in with Coby, the weight of the night came down hard on my shoulders.

"You know," Coby said, his voice thick.

"I know." I met his gaze that time. As much as he needed me, as much as I wanted to crawl into his arms and stay there forever, I couldn't.

"Brogan," he shook his head and sat up straighter, wincing at the sudden movement. "I'm sorry."

"I know," I whispered, ringing my hands together in my lap.

"I don't know what else I can say but I'll show you for the rest of my fucking life how sorry I am."

My vision blurred. "Tell me it didn't mean anything. Tell me you didn't enjoy it. Tell me you saved that part of yourself for me. Tell me … tell me you love me."

"Fuck, baby." He took a deep breath, averting my gaze. "It didn't mean shit." That time, he looked at *me*. "I could never enjoy someone else. Every part of me belongs to you and only you. I love you. I worship the ground you fucking walk on. I am yours. I am so damn sorry."

A sob escaped me but I still couldn't go to him. *Fuck*. "I see you with her." I looked at him through my tears. "I love you with my every breath but … she took you from me and replaced my touch with hers."

"No," he shouted, slamming his fist on the floor of the van. "Your touch is embedded in my skin. Don't you ever fucking forget that."

"You fucked her, Coby," I cried, my body wracking with bone crushing sobs.

"She would have killed me or worse."

"Nothing is worse than that."

"Yes, there is." His breath hitched. "She threatened your life. It was me or you. I chose myself. She told me what she would do to you. She would force me to watch. She … fuck … I should have just let her kill me because the pain I'm feeling right now over you blaming me, is worse than death."

"I don't blame you," I whispered. "I'm sorry."

"Why are *you* sorry?" He reached for me. "Can I touch you?"

I threw myself in his arms, needing his touch more than ever.

"I'm sorry, little one," he whispered in the crook of my neck, hugging me as tight as he could with his damaged body. "I'm so fucking sorry."

"It's not your fault. None of this is. I'm sorry for what she did to you. I'm sorry you were the victim in all of this." I cupped his cheeks, kissing all over his face. "I'm not mad at you. I could never be mad at you. You did nothing wrong, baby."

"I still feel guilty."

"Don't." Digging my nails in his hair, I pulled his head back and crushed my mouth to his.

He grunted.

I didn't care that he was in pain. I didn't care that he was beaten down or that pieces of him were broken. That dark sadistic side of me needed to remind him who he belonged to. That he was mine and I was his. It was a battle in my head because I knew it wasn't right. I should let him rest. But I couldn't. So I did the only thing I knew how. I kissed him harder.

Shoving my tongue in his mouth, I sucked and pulled, nipping and sinking my teeth into his skin until a growl escaped him. "You're mine," I whispered against his mouth. A possessive cry left me and I forced him back.

His good eye became dark, the pupil dilating. "Hit me, Brogan."

He didn't have to tell me twice. But instead of hitting him, my fist connected with the wall of the van before I could stop myself. The sound reverberated through the van, bouncing off the walls before slamming into my heart. The pain was nothing like I had felt before. It was agony and pleasure all at once, blending together in a delicious heat.

"I'm so fucking mad," I cried, tears burning down my cheeks.

Coby pulled me against him. "Show me how mad you are. Hit me. *Beat* me. But don't ever stop loving me."

"I could never stop loving you. I hate *her*. I hate what she's done to you. But I could never be mad at you over this. It's not your fault." My cries for what was done to him, hardened, giving me what little strength I had left.

Coby wrapped his arms around me, pulling my body against him and covered my mouth with his. His tongue forced its way between my lips, stroking hard against mine.

Shoving him back, I straddled his lap and pushed my lower body onto his.

He winced, his face twisting with pain but his cock jumped.

I was momentarily surprised that he was still able to react to my touch with how beaten up he was. It proved to me right then, that no matter what, we would always be together as one.

"You will forget her," I told him. "Everything she did to you, I will replace with my touch. You're mine, Coby. Only mine."

"I am," he snarled against my mouth.

"I don't care that you're in pain." I sat back just enough so I could slide my pants down one leg. "I don't care that you're broken."

He watched my every movement, nodding after each sentence that left my mouth.

"I killed her." I cupped his jaw, dropping my body onto his.

He shouted, trembling beneath me.

Digging my fingers into the hair at his nape, I held his head and watched his eyes all the while fucking him hard. It was sick and disturbing. The blood on our bodies mixing as one while the scent of our pleasure wafted into my nose. I no longer cared about anything else and embraced that darkness inside of me that I had spent my whole life running from.

Coby was *mine*.

"I'm the only woman you come for," I told him, taking what I needed from his body.

"Yes," he leaned his forehead against mine, his hot breath brushing over my face. "Take me, Brogan. Fuck me how you want."

His words gave me the strength to move forward. To move on.

My hips circled against him.

His cock lengthened, filling me to the point stars danced in my vision.

But this wasn't about sex.

Tina had taken Coby from me and used him for her own twisted pleasure. She raped him and forced him to fuck her.

"Don't shut me out, Brogan," he growled. "Fuck me. Yell at me. Give me your wrath. I'll even take your fucking hatred. As long as you love me, I'll take everything you have to give me but don't close up on me."

"I don't hate you," my voice softened. "I could never hate you. It's not your fault. Not your fault at all."

"I love you," he whispered, thrusting his hips upwards.

"This is mine," I rode him hard. "This is all *mine*."

"Yes," he shouted, the chords in his neck straining. "Yours. So fucking yours, it hurts."

His breathing quickened, his body hardening even more under my rough touch.

"You're going to come for me, Coby. Give me the orgasm you refused to give her."

Suddenly his hand was in my hair, tugging my head back. His jaw was tight, his eye dark to the point of black.

I released him, waiting. For what I wasn't sure. The air of dominance surrounded us. It was a battle that neither of us could win. I wanted to dominate him for fucking her and he wanted to dominate me because it was in his nature. And I knew this battle wouldn't end. I was just waiting for it to turn into a full out war.

✳✳✳

(Coby)

For the first time in my life, I needed give my power and control to someone else. The desire to have Brogan take everything she needed from me, forced me into a submissive state.

Fisting her shirt in my hand, I pulled her against me and slid her body back down the length of my cock.

When she had first touched me, my body reacted to hers. Her look of surprise showed she wasn't

322

expecting it. But little did she know, I could be on my fucking death bed and I would still become hard as a rock for her.

Digging my fingers into her hips, I guided her up and down my length.

Brogan's breath caught but she remained silent as she rode me hard.

I craved her wrath. Sex didn't solve anything but right now, it was all we had.

"Make me come, little one," I said, leaning my forehead against hers.

She whimpered, her body tightening around mine.

"I love you," I whispered.

"And I love you."

Wrapping my arms around her, I held her as tight as I could while I thrust my body into hers. It wasn't enough. It would never be enough. I wanted to bathe in her scent, forgetting everything that had happened and just be one.

CHAPTER THIRTY-SEVEN

Coby

"BONES ARE SET. Wounds are cleaned and bandaged." The doctor listed off item after item, like he was reminding himself on what he needed to do to fix me up. He had set me up with a therapist as well, ordering me to see one after I had healed physically. If only my mental state could be fixed just as easy.

"Coby," the doctor barked.

I nodded but didn't say anything. All I could do was focus on the woman standing a foot away from me.

Brogan leaned against the wall, her arms crossed under her chest, watching me. She was probably waiting for me to break and if I did, I knew she would be there to pick up the pieces.

What had happened in the van was dark and dangerous. I could still hear our cries of anguish and pleasure as they mixed together.

Greyson had driven us to the hospital, staying with us until the doctor could get me in.

I could never repay him or his club for what they had done. I owed them for what they did for Brogan and helping me to safety. Although it wasn't in time and shit still happened, I was alive. But a part of me wished I wasn't. The guilt had set in, eating and twisting at my stomach. I had no reason to feel this way, Brogan was right, but I still couldn't stop it.

Once the doctor told me to get some rest, he left.

For the first time in three days, I was alone with Brogan.

The weight of everything that had happened finally settled on my shoulders. It knocked the breath out of me.

Brogan slid onto the bed beside me. "I love you," she whispered. "We'll get through this. I will do everything I can to help you heal."

"I don't deserve you," I said, my voice cracking.

"You're stuck with me, Coby," she kissed my lips. "For as long as you'll have me."

"Forever," I admitted. "I want you forever."

Her breath caught. "Then you'll have me. Always."

***

(Brogan)

Only time could heal the wounds created by those monsters.

Coby held me against him, petting his hand over my head and whispered over and over how much he loved me. Every so often, his battered body would shudder, like he was trying to shake off the memories of the past two days. The forty-eight hours that he had been missing.

His hand reached beneath my shirt, curling around my side. His tense body relaxed a little at touching my skin.

I looked up at him. "We'll be okay, Coby. *You* will be okay. You're strong. You're the strongest man I know. Look at what you've been through already."

His eyes shone. Kissing my shoulder, he squeezed me tight. "How's your wrist?"

I huffed at the change in subject. "Hurts like a bitch but luckily it was a clean break," I mumbled, lifting my arm that now had a cast on it. "But it won't stop me from losing myself in you."

He cleared his throat. "We'll lose ourselves together."

"Promise?"

"I promise."

"Good," I shivered. "Because I need you right now. No Vice-One. No King's Harlots. I need just you and me. For days. Weeks. Months. The rest of our lives. I don't give a shit. Please give that to me."

He nodded. "You have my fucking word."

"Where the *fuck* are they?"

Coby and I looked at each other at the sound of Angel's deep voice booming from the hallway. It had sounded like a tank was rolling on through the building. After Greyson had called them once we arrived to the hospital, I knew they would show up. I had just hoped it wouldn't have been so soon. Coby needed rest. Time. He didn't need the badgering of his brothers asking questions.

"I got this," I told Coby, kissing him hard on the mouth.

"Are you sure?"

"Yes." I rose from the bed. "I'm not in the mood to put up with anyone's shit. Your brothers are no exception." Not waiting for a response from him, I headed out into the hall and shut the door behind me.

Angel was talking to reception when he looked my way.

Asher whispered something in his ear but it seemed to die off in the air as Angel glared at me.

His jaw clenched, his face turning a deep shade of red.

Stone clapped a hand on Asher's shoulder, nodding my way.

"I don't even know what to say to you right now."

I jumped, spinning around and saw Jay standing a few feet away from me with Meeka and Creena on either side of her.

"Why didn't you come to us?" Jay continued. "We could have helped you."

"By doing what, Jay?" My question was laced with malice but at that point, I didn't care. "You couldn't have done shit. I needed to do it on my own."

"You could have been killed," Jay cried.

"Well I wasn't." She was right though. My emotions had led me to Coby. Nothing else.

"Out of everyone, I never thought it would be you that would betray us," Jay muttered, her voice cracking.

"I'm sorry." I rubbed the back of my neck, my muscles twitching at the added movement. "I am. But I couldn't have you there with me. It would kill me if something happened to you. I've already lost Benny. I can't ..." I forced the intensity of the night back, not needing it to break me down again. It could wait. When Coby and I were alone.

"Why didn't you call us?" Angel bit out. "You don't think we could have helped?"

"Listen." I turned on him. "I didn't call you because of what happened to Dale. You're about to be a father, Angel. Maybe it was selfish of me to do this on my own but I'd rather you all hate me then be the reason for your deaths. Or worse." I knew eventually they would want to know what happened. I wasn't sure if I would ever be able to tell my sisters or if Coby could ever tell his brothers. They were too close to us.

"Fuck," Angel shook his head. "I want to stay pissed but I understand."

"We all do," Asher added. "With what happened to Dale, I get it."

"Exactly. I *am* sorry," I told them. "But I had to go with my gut. So, I called Greyson and his club. I knew they could handle anything and … well …"

"Not get too fucked up over it?" Stone added, leaning against the wall across from me.

"Yeah," I muttered.

"How is he doing?" Angel asked.

"Physically? He has a broken arm and a couple broken ribs from the accident. Bruises and cuts as well. The stab wounds are from … are from being tortured. He was shot but that was dealt with." I swallowed hard. "Mentally …"

"Fuck me," Angel snarled.

Jay stepped into his side, wrapping her arms around his middle.

"I don't know if he'll ever be able to talk about what happened," I added quickly before I closed up completely. "But he's alive."

"Be there for him," Stone said to me. "That's all he'll need to get through this."

I nodded, my throat burning.

"If you need us," Meeka placed a hand on my shoulder. "We will be there."

"I …" Tears streamed down my face. "I've done horrible things."

"We'll talk in a couple of days," Angel said. "Right now, let's see him and then go visit Dale." He glanced my way. "We will need to know what went down. Not the full details if neither of you can handle that but we need to know if things will still be an issue."

Meaning, if we took out Tina and Zane or not.

I nodded. "Coby needs you guys but please don't ask questions." I wasn't sure if I could handle them.

I pushed open the door. "Coby? The guys are here to see you."

Coby pushed himself up higher in bed. "Hey," he greeted his brothers. "How's Dale doing?"

After the guys entered the room, I shut the door behind them, giving them the privacy they needed.

"Brogan, there's something we should tell you." Jay looked at Meeka and Creena.

"What is it?" I frowned, my heart thumping at the possibility of being given more bad news.

Meeka took a breath. "Max lost the baby."

CHAPTER THIRTY-EIGHT

Coby

MY BROTHERS STOOD around me. All of them except for Dale. I made a mental note to go visit him before I left the hospital. "Any news?"

"None," Angel muttered, slumping down in the metal chair beside my bed.

Asher did the same on the other side of me while Stone leaned against the wall a few feet away. I realized he did that often. Maybe since he was new in Vice-One, he felt like he didn't belong quite yet. I didn't agree. He was there and that's all I wanted.

"How are you doing?" Stone asked, nodding toward me.

"I …" Memories from the past two days threatened to take hold of my mind. "A lot of shit went down."

"You were gone for two days," Asher said. "I imagine you don't want to talk about it but know that we are here for you, brother."

I swallowed hard, nodding.

"Something happened though," Angel pressed. "Brogan's different."

And she would be for a long time. I had to earn her trust back. "We have a lot of stuff to work through. It will be hard. Tina and Zane put a wedge between us. But please don't ask what happened. Whenever Brogan is ready to talk about it, we can discuss it then but until that happens, it stays between her and I."

"We understand." Angel rubbed the back of his neck.

"I want to kill them for what they did," Asher mumbled.

He didn't have to worry about that. "We'll talk about that later but know that Tina will no longer be an issue."

"You'll have to tell us how Brogan took her out," Stone rubbed his jaw. "That woman of yours is strong as fuck."

She was. He was right about that.

"Coby needs his rest," Angel rose to his full height and clapped a hand on my shoulder. "Take care of yourself, brother."

I nodded. It was the only thing I could do for fear of completely losing it like a little pussy.

"Get better. I need a workout partner." Asher winked.

"We need you back in the field," Stone's gaze darkened. "But you need to take care of you and that woman of yours first."

"I will," I mumbled. "Thank you."

Adjusting myself in the bed, I tried everything to get comfortable but the mattress was hard as shit and Brogan wasn't with me. Letting out a frustrated sigh, I pinched the bridge of my nose.

"Coby."

My gaze snapped up, finding Angel still in the room.

He came over to the bed and sat on the mattress. "I know Dale is your best friend and you talking is like pulling fucking teeth but I need some reassurance that you're okay."

I searched his face, waiting.

"Listen," Angel rubbed the back of his neck which I had come to know was his signature move whenever he was nervous. "You're going to make me fucking ask, aren't you?"

"That depends on what you want to know."

"Fuck," he muttered. "What happened?"

"What didn't happen? I had no choice but to do things that I didn't want to do so Brogan would be safe. Even her life had never been threatened; there was nothing I could do if I wanted to live."

"Shit, man."

"Exactly." I paused. "Have you ever done something thinking it was the right thing to do only to regret it later?"

"We all have, Coby," Angel shifted his weight on the edge of the bed. "It's a part of life."

"Life." I scoffed, rolling my eyes. "Yeah."

"How did Tina and Zane put a wedge between you two?"

I didn't want to answer that but I did anyway. "I fucked Tina."

***

(Brogan)

"Oh God," I slid down the wall, landing hard on the floor. "I ... she ..." My chest constricted, taking my words away.

"We tried calling you," Jay explained. "But I now know why you didn't answer your phone."

"I'm sorry I wasn't there for her. For all of you." I dropped my head in my hands. "I'm sorry."

"We understand," Meeka sat beside me. "Max lost the baby two days ago. The doctor said it was due to stress."

"I knew she hadn't been feeling well but I had no idea that something was actually wrong." My heart ached for my sister. "How is she doing?"

"She's ..." Jay let out a sigh. "Not good. She buried the baby but she wouldn't let any of us go with her."

My eyes widened. "She buried the baby on her own?"

"Yes," Jay's chin quivered. "She's still staying with us but she won't leave her room. I'm worried about her." Jay placed her hand on her bump. "I try hiding my belly as best I can but it's getting harder and harder."

"Shit," I leaned my head back against the wall. "We take one step forward and a million back."

"No fucking kidding," Creena grumbled.

"Max is strong. She *will* get through this." Jay sat on the other side of me, grabbing my hand. "All of us need to stick together right now. No more secrets. We have to be there for each other and for Max."

"I understand," I leaned my head against her shoulder and lifted my broken wrist. "What I've experienced in the past couple of days is nothing compared to what Max must be going through right now."

"Don't compare your pain to hers," Creena said. "We all handle our shit differently. I don't know what happened between you and Coby but I can see it in your eyes that you're hurting."

"I ..." I swallowed past the hard lump in my throat. "Tina and Zane started going after males. It's why Zane killed Benny because Benny wouldn't agree to it. Zane needed to get his sister a new toy. I'm still not sure why Greyson was there when Benny was shot. He won't tell me shit." Bile rose to my throat at the memories of the night before. "Coby and I went to see his contact and when we left, we got hit. And ... and ..."

Jay squeezed my hand.

"Tina tried everything to destroy us. I'm worried for Coby. She fucking broke him." A sob escaped me as fresh tears welled in my eyes. This emotional shit was starting to grate on my nerves.

"Oh God," Meeka clasped a hand to her mouth. "He didn't."

"He had no choice," I cried. "It was either that or they would come find me or kill *him*. Zane already found me once. I love Coby. I love him with everything that I am but this won't be easy for him to get past."

"Shit." Jay let out a low whistle. "I can't ... wow."

Creena shook her head. "I can't wait to find out what you did to her."

***

(Coby)

"Shit," Angel paced back and forth. "You have got to be fucking kidding me right now. And Brogan knows all of this?"

"Yes." I had told Angel everything. A part of me felt a little better over letting it all out but it still wasn't enough.

"I …" Angel shook his head. "I know nothing I say will make any of this better but I have a shit ton of respect for you right now, my brother."

"You do?" I asked, raising an eye brow. "How?"

"Coby, you saved Brogan's life. Yes, this will be hard for you to get past but in the short months I've known her, she's a reasonable woman. I've seen her work. I understand the whole kill or be killed shit."

"You're not judging me?" I asked, my voice thick.

"Fuck no," Angel sat back on the bed. "As much as it would have killed me, I probably would have done the same thing. It wasn't like you had a choice."

"I had no strength to fight but I did what I could. It wasn't enough though."

Angel let out a heavy sigh. "I want you to take as much time as you need. I'm recommending a medical leave."

"Okay," I whispered, not having the strength to argue.

"Let me go get your woman," Angel rose from the bed and paused for a beat before pulling me into a hug. "I love you, man."

RUDE

I hugged him back. "I love you too."

CHAPTER THIRTY-NINE

Brogan

COBY WAS FINALLY coming home from the hospital today. It had only been a couple of days but it felt like a year when I wanted the solidarity of having him all to myself. I needed his hands on me, the reassurance that we would always be together even after everything that has happened. I needed *him*. And I needed to show him that I wouldn't leave. Ever.

Both of us almost laughed when the doctor told us not to have sex until Coby's wounds had healed. Too late for that. My mind took me back to our dangerous moment in the van.

"Brogan," Coby whispered, brushing his nose into the crook of my neck.

I squeezed his knee, impatiently waiting for the cab driver to drive us through the city and back to Coby's place.

"I need your warmth," Coby muttered, licking his tongue up my ear.

I needed him too. More than he could ever know or understand.

He was still healing from his injuries so I knew it would give me the power to dominate and have control over him. This battle wouldn't last. I got that. But right now, he knew I needed his submission.

"Tell me you need me." His hand inched beneath the hem of my shirt, his rough calloused fingers grazing over my skin. "Tell me you can't wait to have me inside you."

A shiver rippled down my spine but I still didn't give him the words he asked for.

"Please, Brogan," he pleaded, brushing his fingers up my torso to my breast. Running his thumb over the puckered peak, he pinched it.

A soft gasp escaped me, heat curling low in my belly.

"Tell me," he demanded, his voice taking on that tone that I had come to love over the past couple of months.

Turning toward him, I licked my tongue along his bottom lip. "No."

His eyes burned into mine at my defiance.

The cab pulled to a stop in front of Coby's apartment building.

I paid the driver and helped Coby out of the vehicle. He was stiff and walking slow but the doctor had said that he was on the mend. *If* he took it easy. Well right now, neither of us wanted easy.

It was sick and twisted but I knew that Coby wanted to feel the pain and anger that bitch had caused me. I knew it had never been his intention but knowing that he had been inside another woman, forced this new darkness to come to light.

Once we reached the elevator, Coby pulled me back against him. His hand remained up my shirt, his lips moving ever so gently over my neck and just below my ear.

Pushing against him, I reached behind me and cupped his erection over his pants.

His breath hitched, the hot air caressing the side of my face. "Use me, little one."

Oh, I would. I would take everything I had needed from him. This would be the first time for us since the van. A part of me was nervous that nothing would ever be the same but I knew with time, we would get past this hurdle that life had thrown our way.

"I will, Coby," I whispered. "I will use every inch of you."

"Fuck, yes." His fingers pinched my nipple, igniting a soft cry to leave my lips.

His cock grew beneath my touch. *I caused that. I* made him feel good. No one else. *Me.* He was *mine.* Every inch of him was mine. This possessive need to claim him as such took control.

When the elevator came to a stop, I grabbed his hand and pulled him out into the hall.

With his hands still on me and my fingers wrapped around his clothing covered cock, we stumbled down the hall until we reached the doors to his apartment.

I unlocked the door and pushed him inside, kicking the door closed behind me.

His eyes were black, so damn dark, his pupils were no longer there.

Stripping out of my clothes, I tossed them aside and waited.

He did the same, standing naked and so fucking hard, my mouth watered. But then I saw them. Cuts. Scratches. Bruises. Deep wounds that had been stitched up. Tina's mark. Well fuck her. I was going to replace her touch with mine.

"Sit on the couch," I demanded, my voice firm.

He did as I said, his cock jumping under my command.

Under normal circumstances, I would have liked that he enjoyed being told what to do. But this wasn't normal. Was it?

Kneeling in front of him, I wrapped my fingers around the base of his cock. Knowing *she* had done the same made my stomach twist. I pulled at his dick, tugging and squeezing until his hips bucked under my touch.

"Fuck, Brogan," he groaned, beads of sweat coating his brow.

Wrapping my lips around the tip, I swallowed him whole. When he reached the back of my throat, I breathed through my nose and sucked him hard and rough.

"Shit." His fingers brushed into my hair, urging me deeper.

I gagged around him, releasing him with a pop. Licking my swollen lips, I kissed and licked up his torso. Every cut. Every scratch. The pain would be replaced by me.

Once I reached his mouth, I straddled his lap and dropped my body onto his cock. Circling my hips back and forth, I rode him fast.

His fingers dug into the cheeks of my ass, encouraging me to move harder.

My hips slammed against him, my pussy tightening around his length.

When he didn't say anything and only watched me, I rode him even faster.

"Fuck," he leaned his forehead against mine, his hot breath fanning my face. "Baby, fuck me faster."

I smiled, licking along the seam of his mouth before delving between his lips.

He growled, cupping my nape and deepened the kiss. "Take me."

"I am," I whispered against his mouth. "I'm taking all of you."

"Yes," he lifted me and laid me back on the couch with me beneath him. "I love you, Brogan."

"Fuck," I cried out when he thrust forward. "I love you too." Tears welled in my eyes. "I love you so damn much."

"Yes," he growled. "Don't you fucking stop loving me." His hips sped up, his cock thrusting violently into my body.

I trembled, shaking beneath him and wrapped my arms around his back. My nails dug into his skin, scratching down his muscles until they cupped his ass. Lifting my hips, I took him as deep as possible forcing us both to shout out.

"Come for me, little one. Come all over my dick. Claim me, baby." His teeth sunk into my neck, his fingers curling between mine. We linked hands, holding each other as we proved our love to each other.

"Come inside me, Coby."

"I will," he brushed my hair off my forehead. "I'm going to come all over you."

"Yes." I moaned, meeting him thrust for thrust. "Come, baby. Come fucking hard."

He snarled, pushing forward until his body shook. He reached between us, pinching my clit.

I screamed, my body shattering around him.

With a final thrust, my name left his lips on a hard roar as he coated me with his release.

I sighed, wrapping my body around him and held him tight against me.

"I will never deserve you," he petted his hand over my hair before pinching my chin to meet his mouth. "But I will spend my every breath until the very last one, proving how much I love you."

Turning on my side, I brushed the back of my hand down his cheek. "I know." I took a breath. "God, I know that." I sat up, rubbing my hands up and down my arms. "I'm sorry," I whispered, looking down at him.

"What are *you* sorry for?" he asked, pulling me back into his arms.

"I'm … I wish I could bring her back so I could end her all over again. I don't want you to judge me," I muttered, swallowing past the hard lump in my throat. Confessing my true feelings lifted some of the added weight that had fallen on my shoulders but with anything, time was the only thing that could truly help us.

Coby pinched my chin, forcing me to look up at him. "I could never judge you. You saved me, baby." He kissed my nose. "I would have done the exact same thing if the situation was reversed. But I need you to do whatever you need to do to make yourself feel better. Just don't stop loving me."

"Never," my eyes welled. "I could never stop loving you."

"Good," he muttered, his voice cracking. "I'll never forgive myself for what I've done."

Wrapping my arms around his neck, I breathed him in. His scent. His desire. Everything that made up Coby Porter.

His body became tense, shaking against me. "I'm sorry," he mumbled, laying us back down on the couch.

Coby lifted his head, staring down at me with nothing but love. He swallowed hard. "I … fuck …" his eyes shone, glossing over with unshed tears.

Our emotions took hold of us as we lay wrapped in each other's arms.

He kissed me repeatedly, pouring all his love into his touches until they would forever be burned on my skin.

When his mouth came down hard on mine, he forced new breath into my lungs.

We had spent the rest of the night like that. Falling asleep only to wake up and take our pain and undying want out on each other. Neither of us complained, even when we were sore and exhausted. I never thought it would happen, especially what we had been through recently, but I fell in love with him a little more. He understood that I had needed time. And I understood that when he woke up during the night from his nightmares that he would use me until he passed out again.

For the next couple of days, we would only get out of bed to eat and shower. We didn't see anyone. We didn't talk to anyone. We had each other. It was a start to our healing. It would take time. It would take a shit ton of time but I loved Coby with every fiber of my being. Until then, we would grow and love as one. No one could take that away from us.

EPILOGUE

Coby

A month later

"WHY HAVE YOU come to see me?"

Brogan squeezed my hand in reassurance, nodding for me to answer the doctor's question.

"I was ordered by the hospital to see a therapist but I felt it wasn't enough. I've heard that you're good at what you do and you don't take any shit." I shrugged. "It's what I need … what we both need right now."

Dr. Santos sat back in his chair, placing his notepad on the table beside him. "You're military."

"Yes, a Navy SEAL."

"So, with the stress of your career and what happened, you felt it was due time to see a psychologist."

"Yes," I nodded, pulling Brogan tighter into my side.

The doctor caught that movement and pointed in our direction. "From the information the hospital gave me, this has affected both of you."

"That's right," Brogan answered. "But the hospital only knows what they saw. We didn't give them every detail."

"I understand," Dr. Santos tented his fingers. "You remind me of another couple I know."

"We do?" I frowned. "You only just met us."

"Doesn't matter," Dr. Santos shook his head. "I can see it. You went through shit," he pointed at me. "And you are getting the brunt of it," he told Brogan.

"Something like that," she muttered, holding my arm in her lap.

"I'm happy to help you both work through this but I will warn you, I'm honest and I won't hold back. I also need to know everything."

I nodded. "I understand."

"Are you willing to work with us?" Brogan asked, chewing her bottom lip.

Dr. Santos smiled, his dark eyes shimmering with warmth. "I am."

***

"Do you like him?" Brogan asked later that evening.

I pulled her against me, running the cloth over her shoulders, her torso and into the water. I reached between her legs, rubbing the fabric back and forth over her center. "I do."

She shivered, cupping my knee. "Do you think he'll be good for us?"

Focusing on that sweet part of her that still tingled on my tongue, I cupped her throat. "Yes," I answered and nibbled the soft spot under her ear.

She moaned, cupping my hand between her legs and guided me. "Do you ..." her breath hitched. "*Fuck.*"

I chuckled, let go of the cloth and covered her hand with mine. "I think he'll help us move past this," I said, my voice low and pushed her finger inside of her body.

Brogan whimpered, her hips moving back and forth against her hand. "There are some things he won't help us with though."

"I know, baby," I kissed her fully on the mouth. "I know."

I spent the rest of the night making love to her body. And I would spend the rest of my life showing her just how much I was in love with *her.*

Time was the true master in this situation and only with it, could we move on.

Tina was dead and Zane had disappeared like the coward he was. Although they weren't around, they left a dark spot on my soul. Because of them, I would never forgive myself. But they did show me just how much I loved this woman and what I was willing to do to keep her safe.

Leah may have been my first love, my wife, the mother of my unborn baby.

But Brogan was the air in my lungs, the life in my veins.

She was the beginning to my end.

We shared the same darkness and for the first time in our lives, we didn't run from it. We ran towards it.

RUDE

THE END

Grab Numb (King's Harlots, #5):
https://www.aboutjmwalker.com/numb

ABOUT

J.M. Walker is an Amazon bestselling author who also hit USA Today with Wanted: An Outlaw Anthology. She loves all things books, pigs and lip gloss. She is happily married to the man who inspires all of her Heroes and continues to make her weak in the knees every single day.

"Above all, be the HEROINE of your own life..." ~ Nora Ephron

Website: http://www.aboutjmwalker.com/
Facebook: https://www.facebook.com/jm.walker.author
Reader Group: https://www.facebook.com/groups/JMsJems/
Twitter: https://twitter.com/jmwlkr
Instagram: https://www.instagram.com/jmwlkr/
Goodreads: https://www.goodreads.com/author/show/5132169.J_M_Walker
BookBub: https://www.bookbub.com/authors/j-m-walker
Amazon: https://tinyurl.com/y7dpjkud
Newsletter: https://tinyurl.com/ya9hycak

Want more? Head on over to my website for my

complete backlist!

https://www.aboutjmwalker.com/books